MOMMY, MAY I?

by

A.K. ALEXANDER

CHAPTER ONE

1968

Before . . .

THAT LAST NIGHT was so cold that Richard could see his own breath. Even the Beatles, his favorite group, belting out "Yellow Submarine" from the other room couldn't warm him or make him feel better. The next few hours would be miserable no matter which record his mother decided to play. Hail barreled down outside, sounding like pellets from his BB gun hitting the roof. The constant drip from a leak in the ceiling hit the bucket his mother had set in the corner of his room, certain to be filled long before morning. He pulled the cape of his Superman pajamas tighter around himself as he listened to his mother read to him.

His light flickered inside the cramped room of the two-bedroom house, illuminating worn wallpaper and the young boy's pale face. His stomach twisted into a knot so tight he thought it might burst open and release the snakes he imagined lived inside him. Then they would slither into the next room and bite his mother's visitor to death.

When her visitors stayed over, Richard would bury his head under his pillow, trying to drown out the noises that came from the other room. Sometimes, when he heard the front door close behind his mother as she'd leave for a date, he would lie awake waiting to hear the click of the lock opening again, and her heels on the linoleum. The stupid babysitter would always sneak her boyfriend into the house and tell Richard to keep his trap shut. Then she'd laugh and say, "As if it really matters to your mom that I have a guy here."

"'But he never knew that it really was his own bunny, come back to look at the child who had first helped him to be real,'" Elizabeth Shelton read to her son. She closed *The Velveteen Rabbit* and patted Richard on the head.

"I love that story, Mom."

"I know you do, honey."

Beer on his mother's breath mixed with the jasmine incense she'd lit in the other room in attempt to rid the house of its mildew smell made him pull his covers up tighter around his face.

The eleven-year-old boy loved when she read to him, when he could pretend they were like every other family. It was their nightly ritual. On many nights, some man—young, old, fat, or skinny—waited for her in the family room, along with the stupid babysitter.

"Do you have to go out tonight?"

Elizabeth Shelton kissed her son on the cheek, her lips soft. "I'm sorry, baby, you know I do. I wish I didn't have to, but you're gonna need new clothes for school when it starts next week. You'll be in the sixth grade, and we can't have you looking scrappy."

Richard also knew that Mom liked to buy him the best clothes, and she usually bought a few expensive things for herself when they went into Portland. She liked buying clothes, shoes, and cosmetics much better than she liked fixing leaky roofs. She claimed that the money she earned was one of the perks of her trade, which, she explained to Richard, was being like a friend or kind of a nurse to people who were lonely. Men. Richard knew the truth. Everyone knew the truth.

"But, Mom, I want you to stay home."

"If I didn't have such wonderful friends, then we wouldn't have food on the table. They're kind enough to give us money and gifts, so please try to understand."

A tear rolled down Richard's face. He didn't understand. He wanted his mother to be like everyone else's mother. The kids in school called her a whore. Even so, he loved her fiercely. He'd do anything for her, and had been suspended more than once for fighting with the older kids who taunted him about her.

"Oh baby, no, don't cry." She wiped away the tear. "Tell you what, I won't go out tomorrow night. I'll cancel the date, and we'll go to town and see a movie."

"Really?"

"You bet." His mother hugged him. "How's my lipstick look?"

"Perfect."

Elizabeth Shelton had a thing about her scarlet lipstick, always drawing the line around her mouth and filling it in just so. It was worth the effort; she always had beautiful lips. Richard loved them.

"Thank you, precious. Now remember, tomorrow it's just you and me."

She hugged him again, her body warm. He watched her leave his room. Her laughter from the other room echoed in his ears as he tried to fall asleep. He hated that men could make her laugh like that.

Had his father made her laugh? His father? Richard's mother said that his father had been Mills Florence, the great cosmetics guru of the fifties. But Mills never had the opportunity to know about Richard. As his mother explained to him, their affair was brief, but they were very much in love. She'd met him on a vacation in Hollywood where she'd gone to try out her acting abilities. She'd wound up pregnant instead. By the time she planned to tell Mills, he'd been killed in a car accident.

There was no proof that he was Mills Florence's son, and therefore, he wasn't heir to the fortune his father's company had produced. His mother never achieved her dreams, but made an existence for them the only way she knew how—with her looks and personality.

Richard was the outcast amongst his peers—the bastard son of a whore. No one ever believed that Mills Florence was his father, and so Richard learned not to repeat it. He knew, however, that he was not a bastard.

The next day Richard didn't disturb her. He'd figured out early on that she was always tired in the morning. She usually didn't rise before noon.

They lived in a small town in Oregon, right outside of Eugene. When it wasn't raining, Richard liked to explore. This morning he walked along a dirt road lacing its way against the Cascades, playing kick the can and whistling. Buzz saws rang out in the distance followed by the rumble of falling timber as it hit the ground. It had rained earlier that morning and the dampness hung in the air. Richard was happy that tonight he'd be alone with his mother.

A truck full of kids passed him, then stopped about a hundred yards up. Richard watched as they jumped out. He knew he was in trouble.

"Hey, look, it's whore boy," they yelled. "How's that whore mama of yours?"

Anger rose inside Richard at the words, like the giant Grizzly known to stalk the woods. But there were too many of them to take on, and basic instinct urged him to run. He sprinted through the pines, their taunts filling his head.

"Bastard boy, where are you?"

Richard kept going, but they were impossible to outrun. The boys surrounded him. There were about eight of them, all at least fourteen. They closed in on him. He tried not to cry, tried to break through them as his heart pounded hard against his chest. Trapped, he could hear his own breathing and wanted to scream, *Leave me alone!* His legs grew weak, and the trees swirled into one big blur.

The gang closed in. "I'd like to fuck your mama, she's pretty sweet."

"Nah," another one said. "I'd just make her suck me. Who knows what she's got crawling inside her."

Richard covered his ears. He hated what they were saying,

hated them. His skin burned. His mother was beautiful and good. They were evil. If only he was bigger...

When the largest kid hit him first, Richard went down and curled into a ball. They kicked him hard all over while cursing and spitting on him. One blow to his head almost caused him to lose consciousness. As the beating, angry words, and sound of his own heart pounding against his chest blended into one, a loud gunshot rang out disturbing the attack, and the boys rapidly dispersed.

"Get on outta' here!" someone yelled. Richard felt strong hands lift him up. "You're a mess, boy." A lumberjack, one of his mother's friends, dusted him off. "You okay?"

Richard nodded. "I think so." He was still dizzy.

"Well, you got a few cuts and bruises, and that gash on your head looks like it hurts pretty bad. Why don't I give you a ride home?"

Richard replied, "That's all right." He was afraid the man might want to come inside and see his mom.

"Hmmm, well, okay then. But them kids might come back for you."

"A ride halfway home might be okay," Richard said.

The lumberjack respected that, and dropped him off down the road from his house. He washed up with a hose outside, not wanting his mother to see him this way. She should be up by now. He prayed she hadn't been crying this morning. She did that a lot. He wished he could make things better for her.

He opened the front screen, then stopped for a moment and listened. The house was silent. Normally, she would be in the kitchen making her coffee and his lunch right about now.

"Mom?"

She didn't answer. He peered inside the kitchen. The coffee canister was still in the pantry—untouched. The shower wasn't on. Richard went on back to her bedroom, where her door was shut.

He knocked. "Mom?" Still no reply. His stomach started hurting. His mouth went dry. He was afraid he'd find her in bed with a man, but he had to find out why she didn't answer.

He opened the door a crack, then wider.

"Mom!" he screamed. His mother lay there on the bed, sheets stained with blood. She was not breathing, and when he pulled back the sheets he could see the gaping wound caused by a gunshot. He grabbed the phone on the nightstand, his hands shaking as he tried to dial the number to the police station. He was crying hysterically by the time a voice on the other end answered. He could barely get the words out as his voice quivered with emotion, "My mom, my mom's been shot."

In minutes the police arrived. Several had been friends of his mother's. All the men liked Elizabeth.

The chief of police took off his hat as he walked into the bedroom, bowing his head. "What a shame," he said. "She was such a pretty thing, too. A sweet lady, and she loved you very much." He patted Richard on the head, but Richard had no reply as fresh tears filled his eyes.

It didn't take but a matter of hours to make an arrest. In a fit of rage, Trudy Walker, the wife of one of Elizabeth's customers, had decided enough was enough upon reading a love letter that she found tucked inside her husband's jacket pocket. Trudy had known about Mr. Walker's visits with Elizabeth for some time, but when she discovered that he had real feelings for her, she became enraged. She'd taken her husband's revolver, gone to Elizabeth's house that morning, broken in, and shot her. She'd actually even confessed when the police had gone to question Mr. Walker.

"Yeah, I killed that husband-stealing whore. She was nothing but a disease-spreading slut. And, I'm not sorry for it," she said to the police as they arrested her.

Even though his mother's killer was behind bars, nothing could pacify Richard. Hatred brewed deep in his heart. He spent the night at the police chief's house, sobbing and waiting for morning, when the aunt and uncle he'd never met would arrive from Redding, California, to take him home to live with them.

CHAPTER TWO

Present day . . .

HELENA SHEA CRADLED the tiny infant in her arms, understanding now what she'd missed for years. She twirled a tendril of his silken hair between her fingers. Looking at him at that moment, it was hard to believe that his entry into the world had been less than desirable. "He looks wonderful, Rachel."

The baby stretched, opening his mouth, blinking his eyes.

"It's all because of you. If you hadn't helped when I was using, who knows where Jeremy and I'd be. You know, I'm just sorry I didn't quit sooner. Then maybe he wouldn't have had to stay in the hospital for so long." Tears rolled down Rachel's face. She had celebrated her eighteenth birthday and the homecoming of her son three days earlier. He'd been hospitalized for two months with an addiction to crack cocaine, caused by his mother's drug use while pregnant. The doctors and nurses who'd worked on him were dedicated to healing him, as was Helena Shea who continued to be an angel to both of them.

"No, Rachel, it was because of your own willpower and love for your son. Now, you have to learn to love yourself."

"That's easier said than done."

Helena set the baby down in his bassinet. She put her arms around the petite girl. Rachel was now very pretty with coffee colored skin and a face resembling a young Lena Horne. The scabs that only a few months ago ran along her arms had faded into scars and her face had cleared from the acne caused from the drugs. She hadn't gained more than fifteen pounds during her pregnancy, and Helena was constantly bringing her food in hopes of keeping her healthy.

"Remember, that's your past, and right there lies your future," Helena said gesturing to the baby who'd fallen back asleep.

"I know, but it's still hard."

"Yes it is. And, that's why you've got me, the staff here, and the new friends that you've made."

"You're right." Rachel smiled and tucked a piece of loose hair back into the braid Helena had plaited for her. "Speaking of new friends and the staff, how are things coming for Shea House? You know, Lindsay gave me thirty days notice to move, since I turned eighteen and I've been sober for six months," Rachel said. Lindsay Covner ran the Sober Living House for teens.

"I actually spoke with her the other day about you and the move. I assured her that it's not going to be a problem as far as Shea House being ready. The plumbers are supposed to finish up this week, and then, once we've passed the final inspection, you and your little guy can start moving in. We've been told by the city that it might be as early as next week, but I'm betting it'll be more towards the end of the month. Anyway, no worries. It'll be ready by the time you need to be out of here."

"Good. I can't wait. I love it here, you know. But I like the idea of a new place with more girls my age, and being able to focus on getting a job and such. I'm really excited, Helena. Girls like me don't get much in the way of second chances."

"You deserve it. Well look, I hate to go, but I've got a meeting to get to, and it appears that Mr. Jeremy here wants to rest. Maybe you should get some sleep, too."

"I need to study for that diploma."

"That's true. But you also need to keep up your rest. Balance is key."

"You're our angel, Miss Helena. You are certainly our angel."

"No, you two are mine," Helena said, shutting the door to Rachel's dorm room.

Smiling, Helena walked down the hall, confident that in a few weeks the adult residential center she'd funded and designed for addicted mothers would be ready. Many of the teens here would be fed into that center, to continue their recovery program and adapt to the responsibilities of parenthood. She finally felt like she'd done something right in her life, because it felt like the entire world knew nearly everything that she'd ever done wrong, thanks to her bad choices and a few unscrupulous people. This was her own second chance, and maybe her own child would be able to find it in her heart to forgive her if she did this right.

Despite the light sprinkle falling, Helena decided to walk to the community center where her AA meeting was held. It was less than a mile away, and she'd always liked the rain. It, too, reminded her of new beginnings and that things never stay the same.

On her way, she passed a newsstand. A familiar face on the front of *Weekly Entrepreneur* caught her eye. There he was— Patrick. Her stomach sank as it always did when she saw his face. At least his being on the front cover had nothing to do with her or anything that had happened between them. And, thank God, it was a business magazine, leading her to believe that they wouldn't mention Frankie in the article. To ease her mind, she went ahead and bought it. Flipping through it quickly, she saw a small blurb about her daughter that read, "Frances Kiley appears to be doing well after moving from Los Angeles to Santa Barbara last year with her father. According to Mr. Kiley, she sees Helena Shea often, and the two are forming a relationship after the bitter scandal that rocked the family."

"Even a damn business magazine has to get a blurb in there. Unbelievable." Helena took a deep breath, wondering if it would ever really be over. Reporters, gossip, "friends" looking for tidbits of information had taught Helena a thing or two, and she'd become a woman who'd learned to be cautious of the world around her. But after glancing through the magazine, her mind began filling with kaleidoscopes of taunting memories. She didn't even see the headlights approaching until the van slammed to a stop only inches away.

Stumbling backwards, Helena jumped back, nearly tripping over herself, the magazine flying out of her hands. Blood rushed through her ears—she wanted to scream, but fear and the stench of burning rubber clogged her throat. The headlights of the van switched off, but there was no other movement. What the hell was this guy doing? A few seconds passed, and she couldn't get her legs to move. They were like cement and Jello all at the same time. And damn if her heart wasn't going to come right out through her chest. There was an unreal quality about the situation. Wasn't this guy going to get out and apologize? The only visible sign of life from inside the van was the glow of a cigarette. Somewhere in the distance a horn honked. Then a powerful fear began to crawl over Helena's skin like a rash.

She fought to compose herself and bring her stomach back up from her gut, as the driver continued the bizarre standoff. Her heart raced faster. The driver revved the engine, blasted the horn, and flashed the high beams on her. She protected her eyes from the blinding light.

Not so long ago, she would've flipped the finger at him, but not now. Fear coursed through her, and running at this point seemed a good option. The only option.

Helena bounded across the street and through the front door of a Denny's. Several patrons turned to look. She ducked into the restroom not wanting to be recognized. The strong odor of ammonia made her dizzy.

She splashed her face with cool water. Her cell phone rang. The number came up as unknown. *God, not now.* Still trembling, she answered.

"Ms. Shea?"

Goosebumps crawled across her flesh. The voice on the other end sounded muffled, mechanical, demonic. "Yes?"

"You really should be more careful when you cross the street."

Helena slumped against the wall. "Who is this?"

"The important question is, who are you? I am the one you will never forget. I know how this began and how it will end. As they say, revenge is sweet, Ms. Shea."

"Who the hell is this?"

"Your worst nightmare, come to life. By the time I'm finished with you, you'll wish you were never born." His voice rose an octave. "You're such a stupid bi . . ."

Helena flipped shut the phone. It took a lot to shake her, but this scum had achieved it. She steadied herself against the sink, feeling nauseous. She was startled by her reflection in the mirror. The green eyes that helped make her famous were wide-eyed with fright. She wiped sweat from her face, smearing her make-up.

A woman walked in, smelling of body odor and beer. Helena glanced up. The lady asked, "Aren't you . . ." She snapped her fingers, then pointed at her, " . . . that model?"

"No."

"Sure you are. I've seen you on the cover of *The Scene*. You got a drinking problem and gave up your kid when you was what, seventeen? That ain't right. You sure don't look so pretty right now. Been on a bender? Why'd you dye your hair brown? You look better as a blonde, except them roots you had."

Helena walked out. Instead of following old patterns and finding the nearest bar, she opted for the safety of her home. Shaken, she took a cab back to the Sober Living House where her Suburban was parked. Once behind the wheel, she broke all speed limits to get to her comforting sanctuary. Trying to urge more speed from the huge vehicle, she found it was no match for the Mercedes she'd recently traded in for the older, bigger car. She'd done so with the knowledge that she'd be transporting new moms and babies around before long.

Who had called her? Who'd tried to run her over? The paparazzi were crazy enough. Everyone knew that. Maybe there was nothing new about Britney or Angelina and Brad. Maybe they were back to dig up more dirt on her. Nothing like making her look crazy to sell a few magazines, which is exactly what would happen if she called the police. Word would get out, and before long every trashbloid around would have the story, and God knew that was the last thing she wanted.

Locking the doors of her Malibu beach cottage behind her, Helena breathed easier. Ella, her Siberian Husky, greeted her with several yaps.

"Well, Ms. Fitzgerald, did you miss me?" The overgrown puppy jumped up to lick her face, almost making her forget the evening's frightening events. She was glad she'd bought the dog after announcing her sobriety to the world. Ella eased the loneliness at home that could come with a sober lifestyle. No more friendships with a bottle.

"Okay, give me a sec, and I'll take you for a walk. Let me check the messages real quick." Helena went into the kitchen and replayed the answering machine. There was a message from Tim. Maybe Frankie had called, but decided not to leave a message. Teenagers were like that.

"Call me when you get home from the meeting, lovey. I want to hear how it went. I'm so proud of you." Tim sneezed before hanging up.

Tim was Helena's friend and assistant. He had a cold, preventing him from attending the meeting. Should she tell him that she hadn't made it either? She knew she had to; if she didn't, someone else would. Besides, the backbone to the AA program was honesty.

While changing from her street clothes, the anonymous caller's threat again echoed through her mind. Would a paparazzo go *that* far to get a story? Weren't they tired of her yet? Whoever it was had really tried to scare the shit out of her. Was he caller and driver, one and the same? Why hadn't she looked at the plates?

Comfortable and dry in a pair of sweats, she lay back against her pillow, softly scented with lavender, and dialed Tim's number. He answered on the first ring.

"You sitting on top of that thing or what?" she asked.

"Funny. I haven't been out of bed for three days now, and you hit me with a smart-ass remark. Hey, what time is it?"

"Around 8:45."

"Aren't you home a bit early? What's the deal, Ms. Shea? Didn't you go? Tell me you didn't blow it off because you were over rocking babies again at the center. I can understand your need there, lovey, but you've also got to continue working your own program."

Helena reached for her cigarettes on the nightstand and lit up before telling Tim about the evening. Then the story came out in one breath.

"Oh my God! Shouldn't you call the police?"

"Come on, Tim, and have my face spread across all the rags for everyone to have another shot at me? I can see it now: *Drunk model swears she's being stalked!* I can't do it. I don't need that kind of publicity now, or ever again. Shea House will be opening soon, and I'm sure there'll be little quips here and there about my past, but I want to make this about the moms and their kids and showing them that there is a better life out there. I've already put my family and friends through enough, especially Frankie."

"No, dear, Leeza put y'all through that. That little hussy didn't need to show your dirty laundry to the world."

"If she hadn't, someone else would've." Helena stubbed out the cigarette, reminding herself that she was trying to quit.

"Go to the cops."

"I can't."

"Do you want me to come over?"

"You've got the flu."

"Are you afraid of my big bad germies?"

"Really, I'm okay. And, yes you know I'm a big germaphobe. I don't need a babysitter, and I certainly don't need the flu. It's probably just some weirdo with my picture posted in his room, or a wannabe paparazzo. You know those freaks. I'm going to put it out of my mind and not worry about it."

"Good Lord, someone nearly runs you over and has your private cell phone number, and you're not going to worry? Sounds a little worse than a lovesick puppy with a hard-on over your picture. You're not being practical."

"I'll be all right."

"Always the tough cookie. Always gotta play it like everything is a-okay. What about the liquid factor? Not thinking of falling off the wagon, are you?"

"Well, I wouldn't mind a shot of tequila right now. But I won't."

"Jeez, maybe I really should be with you."

"No! I'm tired and achy. I want to lay low."

"Obstinate child, that's what you are! Promise you'll call if you reach that shaky point where the demons are telling you "just one" is all right. I wish you'd call the police, or at the very least, let me come by. I've taken enough Sudafed to clear out the nasal passages of everyone in this godforsaken city. I'll come over for some decaf, and we can watch the late show. Come on," he pleaded.

"I've got Ella. You stay in bed. I'll call if there's a problem."

"Oh yeah, Ella, the guard dog who'd show the guy where the good stuff is as long as he'd give her a doggy bone. If you had to have a dog, I wish you'd gotten a Doberman."

"Don't go knocking my puppy. She comes from great show lines."

"Helluva lot of wonderful that'll do you with some stalker dude around."

"I doubt anyone's stalking me. This stuff happens all the time to people in my line of work." Helena knew she was trying to convince herself as much as Tim.

"Then why did you call me? I mean, if you're not bothered?"

"I'm bothered, but maybe the best thing to do is just to be careful and start carrying some Mace. Besides, I took that self-defense class. And I called to hear your voice, not because I'm scared." She picked up a throw pillow next to her and fiddled with the tassels.

"Tsk, tsk, you're such a poor liar. You're scared, but I'm getting nowhere with you, so *please* call me first thing in the morning. I worry about you. I'll try to make it in tomorrow."

"Good."

Helena hung up the phone. Tim always made her feel better. His flamboyance and energy could lift her spirits. He understood the deal. He'd been in recovery for five years himself after losing his lover to AIDS. He was a loyal friend and her personal assistant at *Shea Models*, the agency she'd started barely after she turned twenty-five. That was when she'd discovered that fourteen-year-olds on the covers of magazines sold more *Vogues* than she did.

She may have felt better about not drinking, but the idea of a stalker still haunted her. Maybe she should go to the cops. But any more malicious gossip to hit the papers could prevent Shea House from receiving the continued funding that it needed. Plus, it might drive another wedge between her and Frankie. That business article had it right when it reported that Frankie and Helena had been visiting more often. They were making real progress. Her daughter was her number one priority.

Helena looked over at Ella and said, "Want that walk now, girl?" The dog bounced up and twirled in circles for her mistress. "Okay, okay." Helena zipped up her jacket as she opened the door. She shivered as the cool night breezed through her anyway. She breathed in the salty ocean air, apprehensive about taking the walk, but knowing that her poor dog deserved their nightly ritual. It made her feel better to see lights on in several of the beach houses along the Pacific Coast Highway.

As she and Ella approached their turnaround point, the dog became rigid and alert, the ruff of her neck bristling. "What's wrong, girl?" The dog whined, glancing back at her. Helena had never seen this behavior in Ella, and it flooded her already edgy nerves with adrenaline. Ella growled while lunging forward, pulling on her leash. Helena couldn't see anything, but decided to turn around instead of walking the extra quarter mile to their usual turnaround point.

"Come on, puppy, let's go." Helena tugged on the leash. The dog reluctantly followed her.

Helena broke into a jog, and they made it home in minutes. As she took her shoes off, she laughed. "We're paranoid," she said to the dog, thinking about the caller and angered that he'd frightened her so badly. "You're a silly dog, and I've got an overactive imagination." Ella wagged her tail.

Once they were back inside the cottage, Helena double-checked all the doors and windows. She noticed that the curtain rod in her living room was askew, and half the drapes on the oceanfront window drooped. Part of the pull cord was missing. Ella must've gotten a hold of the drapes, as she had once before. Nothing else was missing or out of place, and everything had been locked.

Helena rechecked the house, this time carrying a carving knife as she opened closets and peered inside the bathroom. When she thought she saw movement behind the shower curtain, she raised the knife, tore open the curtain and saw that the washcloth had gotten soaked and fallen off the rack.

"Jesus, I feel like Norman Bates," she said aloud. She laid the knife on the back of the toilet, her hands shaking. When she finally settled down enough, she finished checking the house. No signs that anyone had been inside. She decided she simply hadn't noticed the damage to the drapes before.

Helena collapsed on her bed, and Ella curled up next to her. She patted the puppy's head. "Normally, I'd say get your butt off, 'cuz you need a bath and you sure got some stinky breath. Besides, you were obviously naughty when I had my back turned. But tonight, either I'm going crazy, or the bogeyman is after me." She laughed aloud hearing how stupid that sounded.

CHAPTER THREE

IN THE BACK issue of *Vogue* spread out on her bed, Frances Kiley, nicknamed Frankie, studied the photograph of her mother's face. Bono singing about a beautiful day boomed through the stereo speakers. Frankie's fingers traced the outline of the picture thinking about all the times she'd admired Helena, not knowing the famous model was her real mother.

The photo was taken three years ago, before Helena had retired from modeling and started her own agency. Their resemblance was huge—both had green eyes, raven hair, and skin as pale as a geisha girl's.

She choked back her sobs. She had known that this woman was her mother for over a year, but Frankie still couldn't figure out how she felt about such startling news. At first, she'd been furious that her parents had lied to her and that Helena had abandoned her. Then that rage turned to sadness mixed with love for a woman she was just getting to know. Shrinks, her father, Helena, even people whose business it wasn't, told her, "Don't worry. It will all sort itself out." *Yeah, right.*

Life had thrown her some curves during the past year. At least her dad had enough sense to move them out of LA away from the jet set, who talked trash about others because their own lives were so mundane.

But the media maggots—Frankie's name for the ever-present paparazzi—followed them no matter where they went. To her, the media were people paid to dig up good gossip, lay a few poisoned eggs, spread garbage around, and *voila*—deliver the kind of sensationalism craved by bored, overweight, undersexed, Hollywood-worshipping wannabes. Everywhere she'd gone in the last year, the media maggots were always in her face, popping flashbulbs and begging for any morsel of dirt they could use. Her family's scandal had been headlined in detail, and in most instances, fabricated for every gullible moron to accept as gospel.

True, there were many things Frankie had finally come to understand. She remembered when she was much younger, having shown the woman she'd always *thought* was her mother a picture of Helena in a magazine. Frankie had wanted to get her hair cut like the woman in the photograph. Leeza had smacked her across the face, taken the magazine, and burned it. This made perfect sense now, but there had been several nights she'd cried herself to sleep, wondering why her mother didn't love her.

When she was twelve, watching *The Exorcist* at a friend's house, she wondered if she might be possessed. Why else wouldn't a mother love her only child? She'd dreamed that her head would twist around and she'd vomit green slime, like Linda Blair did in the movie.

A knock at the door caused her to wipe the tears away. "Frankie?"

"Yeah, Dad?"

He cracked the door and peered in. "You want to turn that down?" She reached across her bed and flipped off her stereo. "How was your day?"

"Fine." She closed the magazine and reached for Stuart, the stuffed puppy-doll he'd given her one Christmas long ago. He was soft as down, smelling like Spaghettios, Frankie's favorite as a little girl. At least Stuart remained her faithful companion.

"Can I come in?"

She shrugged. "I guess."

Patrick Kiley sat down at the edge of his daughter's bed. "Did you talk to Helena today?"

"I called, but she must've been out."

"Did you leave a message?" She shook her head. "Honey," he said, scooting closer to where she sat, Indian-style, hunched over Stuart. "I thought we all agreed that you'd start making a real effort. I know she wants to see you this weekend."

"I did call. But I hate answering machines."

"Since when? I hear you leave messages for your friends all the time. Don't you want to go see her?"

Frankie flipped her hair back behind her shoulders. "Actually, I *do* want to see her."

"Good. I think that's *good*." Her dad was a bit too emphatic for Frankie not to notice.

"I called her Mom the other day."

Her dad grimaced, which he quickly forced into a smile. "Really?" He touched the ends of her hair and sighed. "Terrific. Look, kiddo, I know all the secrecy and confusion has hurt you, and that was the last thing we wanted to do."

Frankie tossed Stuart aside. "But it does hurt. You've lied to me since I was a baby. And you let Mom, Leeza—whatever she was—treat me like crap. You were too busy to notice how mean she was. I never understood why." She pulled her knees up underneath her chin. "God, Dad, she'd spank me or scream at me if she didn't like something I'd said or done. I never knew what would set her off."

Her dad looked as if she'd slapped him. They'd had this same discussion several times before, and Frankie hated guilting him like this. She was aware that it had become a manipulation.

"I'm sorry, honey. She'll never hurt you again. If I could change what happened, I would. I thought Leeza would get over my affair with your mother and love you because you were an innocent child. But she won't ever hurt you again."

"Are you kidding? She didn't have to do what she did. You have no idea what it's like to go to school and hear kids call me 'the drama queen.' It really sucked."

"That's why I moved us up here to the ranch," he said. They'd moved to their new place in Santa Barbara soon after the story broke, hoping that getting out of Los Angeles would help heal the wounds.

Frankie studied her father for a moment. He was so old-guy handsome, like Robert Redford in "The Horse Whisperer"—one of her favorite movies of all time. Because she loved her dad so much, she'd never reveal *how* rotten Leeza had really been to her. Frankie wanted to be a part of a family and always had. The only stability she'd had growing up was from her dad and her nannies.

"Helena would call me if she wanted to." Frankie hugged her knees tighter.

"Giving you up wasn't her fault. I convinced her, and so did Leeza, that you would be better off with us. She didn't want to give you up. It broke her heart. But she was very young, and I was married to Leeza. Helena's modeling career was beginning to take off, and we persuaded her that it would be best for everyone. Now, I know that separating you and your mom was wrong. Leeza lied to me about loving you. She didn't want a scandal, and she didn't want another woman to have me, even if that meant pretending to accept you."

"Scandal? *She's* the one who's told everyone!"

"She was paid a lot of money for those stories. I guess that years of anger and a chance to finally get even with me and your mom was what spurred her on."

"Why is she still so mad after so many years? Is it because you still love Helena?" Frankie held her breath, waiting for the answer. As hurt, frustrated, and confused as she was, she hoped her dad did still love her mom. Frankie wouldn't give up on being part of a family.

Her dad patted her knee and stood up. "You're an incurable romantic, my girl. But I think it's time we both got some sleep."

Stepping outside her room, he paused and without turning to face her, said, "I'm glad you'll be spending more time with your mom. It's hard on me, because of everything I've put you through. I don't want to see you hurt any more." Frankie could've sworn he was crying. "You have a right to explore a relationship

together. I pray she can be the mother to you that Leeza wasn't."
He shut the door behind him.

Frankie cuddled Stuart and said, "Know what, Stu? I hope
so, too. But how can you be someone's mother after so many
years?" She held the stuffed animal out in front of her. In her best
Robert Stack voice, she said, "And that, my friend, is another
unsolved mystery."

CHAPTER FOUR

ONCE AGAIN, FBI Agent Tyler Savoy found himself working around the clock, struggling against what he'd come to regard as evil. He'd seen more than his share of violent acts during his career, some that put slasher movies to shame. Even though he'd witnessed brutally slain corpses and dealt with the bizarre minds of those who'd raped, stolen, and plundered—being an agent with CASKU—The Child Abduction and Serial Killer Unit of the FBI—was his life. Now that Susie was gone, his work was his only focus.

The face Nick Yamimoto had been reconstructing for Tyler was taking shape and was beginning to appear human. The transformation was remarkable, from the skull that detectives had found in a shallow grave out in the Mojave Desert, to what Tyler could now see had at one time been that of a young woman.

Nick's office was filled with many other clay formations, as well as sketches of victims and of possible predators. The small, brightly lit office smelled of acrylics and clay, combined with the stink of formaldehyde from several jarred human organs.

Tyler stared at what was taking shape from the clay Nick had been expertly molding. The victim was young—twenty tops. Tyler thought this one might have died at the hands of someone she knew. Not unusual—a majority of murder victims met their deaths that way.

Tyler's intuitive gift—or curse, depending on how one looked at it—was what had led him into this line of work, combined with his own sense of personal loss. It enabled him to tune in to some of the country's sickest minds. Before Susan had been murdered, he'd never guessed he possessed this so-called gift.

But from the moment Susan was killed, he *knew*. Tyler suddenly discovered within himself an innate ability to tune into the evil lurking within the minds of the sick and twisted and almost *feel* the pain that they caused. He actually thought he sensed the final electrifying slice that had eviscerated his wife. However, he convinced himself that he was a profiler through study rather than gift of spirit. Even though the moment he had begun to have unexplainable hunches and detailed visions and feelings somehow coincided with the day his wife was murdered.

Susan had been at home, in her bath. She'd been four months pregnant on the day that the demon saw fit to disembowel her, slaughtering their baby and leaving his wife to bleed to death.

Tyler had had a bad feeling all day about leaving her, but he was needed in the city on an ongoing investigation involving a large drug ring that was also responsible for several murders.

At that time, he'd been a homicide detective. But after her murder, he knew his destiny was to track down the hunters of this world. He'd specifically chosen the serial killer unit. For him, it was more than avenging his wife's death and that of their unborn child.

It took nine months and three days to find her killer. Tyler had tried to worm his way into the investigation, but it was difficult as he was a family member. But he'd bellowed enough to make the detectives pay attention and was finally allowed to review everything they'd done to find Susie's killer.

It was a tip from an unknown source that had led the police to Samuel Paul Nelson. They'd staked out a woman's house where they thought Nelson might be headed. Sure enough, he was there and very nearly succeeded in murdering his fifth victim, but they had arrived in time to save her and arrest Nelson. Forensics discovered a DNA match with Nelson's blood found under Susan's fingernails. Samuel Paul Nelson was now on death row in California, awaiting lethal injection.

Tyler realized why this current Jane Doe case had him so focused. This asshole reminded him of Nelson. They both had an overpowering need to dominate their victims. Nelson, however, had never been acquainted with the vics; he chose women who fit his profile, then convinced himself that they should belong to him. He followed them for days, until he finally decided to kill them.

Nelson believed that he had a harem waiting for him in the afterworld consisting of those he'd sent there, including Susan. But this new killer knew the young woman he'd strangled to death. Tyler was convinced of that, and *that* was where the killers differed.

"So what do you think?" Nick asked.

The scientist was tops in forensic reconstruction, a genius of a man. Tyler liked and respected Nick.

"I think he knew her, and she isn't his first. Or his last."

Nick listened, his eyes darkening. "What makes you say that?"

"A feeling. And that she was found in the desert. It fits a particular profile. One we have to consider."

"But wouldn't a desert burial suggest this perp was a transient? Or could your vic have been on the move, too? A hitchhiker turns down his sexual advances, pisses our perp off, and he loses it?"

"Maybe," said Tyler, setting the clay back down on the laboratory table. "But, like I said, I've got a feeling he's a pro with an agenda. How much longer until you can get me full features?"

"Four, five days, if I work my ass off."

"Do it. I'll make sure old Uncle Sam kicks in overtime."

"Yeah, right! Then I'm taking a break. I need a smoke and some coffee."

"No problem."

"Want to join me?"

"Thanks anyway, but I've got some other things to take care of. Call me when she's ready."

"Sure thing." Nick stepped outside while Tyler sifted through sketches.

Looking down at possible identifications of the young woman, Tyler was forced back in time by a frightening feeling—the same sensation he'd had when Susan was murdered. Some woman out there, possibly on this very night, was about to meet her maker. Tyler's nightmare was that he couldn't pinpoint who or where. He wasn't into this asshole's head yet, but like a reel of film, the images had already begun.

Tyler divined through profiling, and his gut told him that the killer felt his motives justified his actions. He was Tyler's latest nightmare—one that would consume him until he saw it to the end.

CHAPTER FIVE

June 1970

Before . . .

"'VILLAIN!' I SHRIEKED, 'Dissemble no more! I admit the deed!—tear up the planks! Here, here!—It is the beating of his hideous heart!'" Uncle James emphasized each word as he read *The Tell-Tale Heart* to Richard for the second time that evening. Richard applauded, and his uncle bowed.

"I don't know why you have to read that garbage to the boy," Aunt Valerie shouted from the other room.

Uncle James winked at him. "He likes it, Mother."

"Well, then he's as nuts as you are. I can tell you this much, the Lord don't like that filthy stuff. He's condemning your souls to hell, right now."

"So be it," whispered Richard's uncle.

"You should be reading Bible verses to him." Uncle Richard winked at Richard in a conspiratorial kind of way.

Aunt Valerie rarely referred to Richard by his name, always "him" or "he," but if she really wanted to anger Richard, she'd call him Ricky. He found that insulting. Richard also knew that later, when his uncle wasn't around, his aunt would make him pay for sharing this time with his uncle. She believed that sparing the rod spoiled the child. But Richard didn't care. It was worth it to spend time with Uncle James.

"Let's take a walk, son."

"Sure." Richard knew that his uncle wanted to escape his aunt's preaching, too.

"We're going for a walk, dear."

They grabbed their coats and walked into the late night. As much as Richard loved his uncle, he hated his aunt. Not only for the beatings and mean words, but also for the way she treated his uncle. Aunt Valerie ruled their home.

"I know she's a horrible woman, Richard. And I know sometimes she's awful hard on you. But we've been married for so long now."

"So? Why don't you leave her? You don't need her."

"I can't."

"Why?"

Uncle James put his arm around Richard as they walked next to the man-made pond Uncle James had built on his five-acre ranch. He sighed and said, "Sometimes people know things about one another, things that they don't want others to know."

The crickets and night bugs reminded Richard of a symphony his mother had taken him to long ago in Portland. The mountain air smelled of pine. "What could be so bad that you'd have to stay with her? What terrible thing could she possibly know about you? I can't believe you'd ever do anything wrong."

"Let's just say it is, and leave it at that. We all make mistakes." Uncle James rolled and lit a cigarette. He let Richard have a drag off it.

Richard couldn't imagine his uncle having any secret so horrible that he was forced to remain married to the thing back at the house. Uncle James couldn't hurt a fly. Heck, when he found spiders inside the house, he carefully removed them and set them out in the yard. He was also conscientious about his work: Making the bodies he worked on look peaceful and happy in death and soothing the families of the dead.

"I'd like to work with you this summer," Richard said. It had been two summers since his mother died, and he felt ready to see another dead person again. In fact, the idea captivated him.

"You sure about that? Funeral homes can be sad, dark places at times."

"I'm sure. I want to learn the business. You never seem sad or dark."

"Of course I am. Why do you think we read from Edgar Allan Poe every night? I'm as macabre as the old horror master himself," James replied, chuckling.

Richard wasn't quite sure what he meant, but he laughed along anyway. Uncle James's laughter was infectious, like his mother's had been.

"Do you believe in God, Uncle James? I mean, Aunt Valerie's always reading from the Bible and telling you that you're going to hell. What's that all about?"

"She's pretty devout, that one. But I kinda got my own beliefs. You sort of have to when you're in my business."

"Tell me."

"I think we all got a place inside that we think of as Heaven. We see it, feel it, and it's nice. That's what happens to us when we go. We finally get to that place and stay there."

"Hmmm. That sounds good. But what about God?"

"Well, I don't know too much about Him. But I'm sure He exists somewhere. I just like the peaceful Heaven idea, where we go where we want."

"Me too. I'm not sure I believe in God."

"Why's that?"

"He took my mom away from me."

"That's hard stuff."

"I miss her." He sighed. "How come you never visited us?"

"You know your aunt runs the show around here, and your mother really never wanted us to. Valerie was awfully jealous of your mom, and Elizabeth felt it was best if we all kept our distance. I wanted to visit you, though. I thought about you two a lot. When I didn't have the wife looking over my shoulder, I'd send your mom some money from time to time."

"I wish you could've visited," Richard said, hating his aunt even more for keeping his mother's only brother away. Richard understood that his aunt was jealous, because she had let him know exactly what she'd thought of his mother.

"Me too, son. Me, too." Uncle James flicked the cigarette away. "Anyhow, you want to come to work for me, huh?"

"Yes, sir."

"All right," he said, stopping and putting his hands on his lower back stretching. "Expect to rise and shine with the sun in the morning and get to work."

"Really? Oh wow! Thanks, Uncle James. Thank you so much. And I'll do a good job for you, I promise."

"I'm sure you will."

They headed back toward the house, Richard filled with excitement about working at his uncle's funeral home.
****

Richard enjoyed working with his uncle as much as he thought he would. He was learning a lot and not stuck at home with his aunt who, given the chance, would send him to the basement to think about the evil he'd done. It was like being set free from a dismal prison with her as the warden.

Two weeks had passed since coming to work with Uncle James, and Richard knew that he was a good apprentice. He strolled through the front room where all the caskets were on display, pretending he was the funeral director.

"Mahogany," Richard sang out, "this one is pure mahogany. And notice the silk lining. It's a hundred percent silk." Richard ran his hand across the soft, fine material as a tingle shimmied down his back. He was practicing for the mourners. "And this one is a good buy. That's solid pine." He knocked on it with his knuckles.

"Richard?" Uncle James walked into the room. Richard jumped, startled and embarrassed. "I'm glad you're learning all about the caskets." Uncle James smiled. "It's a huge part of our business. But today I'd like to teach you something new: We'll be embalming an elderly woman brought in last night. Come on, son. Follow me." Richard followed his uncle into the embalming station. "Put this on." Uncle James handed him a facemask.

As Uncle James flipped on the lights, Richard's nose stung in a wonderful way from the formaldehyde. Each nerve in his body came alive, enthusiastic over what his uncle was about to teach him. The room was only large enough to hold a table and the necessary tools for the embalming process.

"Now, this here is the pump we use to regulate the pressure and flow of mixed water and embalming fluid into the remains," Uncle James said.

Richard looked at the pump, but his eyes kept wandering to the white sheet covering the body. He'd seen a few dead people in the past couple of weeks; today he'd actually touch one. Something about that made his stomach stir, but not like he was nauseated.

"Okay, now in case we've got a problem and the formaldehyde becomes a contaminant, you'll need to get under that shower over there," Uncle James said pointing to a nozzle against the far end of the wall. "That'll only happen if I don't measure my chemicals just so, but it could burn your skin something fierce. So it is always vital to be prepared and cautious."

Richard glanced at the anatomy posters. He'd have to study them. Though he hated school, he learned fast. The stigma of being different had stuck to him like insects on a fly strip, and he hadn't made friends any easier in this town than he had in Oregon.

Uncle James looked up at the clock on the wall. "Well, let's get started. We've got a busy morning ahead, and I'd like to get the embalming finished before lunch, so we can come back this afternoon to dress her and apply the makeup."

"Yes, sir." The word *makeup* stirred something deep within Richard, remembering the way his mother always applied her lipstick so flawlessly. He hoped that Uncle James would let him do the lips.

Uncle James removed the sheet. "Hi, Ruth," James said stroking back the gray hair from the woman's pale face that was etched with the lines of time.

"Did you know her?"

"No. I know her name, and that her family loved her dearly. I like us to get acquainted a bit before I start invading her body. It's only proper and polite."

"Do you think she can see us?" Richard looked heavenward.

"I don't know, but if she can, then she knows we're gonna be as gentle as possible." James then covered her head with what looked like a swimmer's cap. He and Richard wore gloves and lab coats. "This is a fairly simple process, son. We use the body's own circulatory system," he said. "We use formaldehyde because blood is drained during the process, and the fluid contains dyes to give a pink color to the skin."

Richard smelled an offensive odor coming from Ruth. Uncle James took a bottle of disinfectant off the shelf and wet a sponge. He poured some of it into another sponge, handing it to Richard.

Uncle James pulled the sheet back only to her waist. Her small, shriveled breasts were exposed. Richard shrunk back. His mother's breasts certainly didn't look like these.

"It's all right. She won't bite." Uncle James sponged her down. Richard followed his lead, and soon the cleanser's strong fumes replaced Ruth's putrid stench. Touching her body was strange. She was so very cold.

"It is important that this procedure be done with care," Uncle James began, sounding like a professor. "If one does this step carefully, the next can be done smoothly. If the body isn't disinfected, then the embalming procedure will not work. It also prevents the spread of germs."

When Uncle James pulled the sheet completely off, Richard tried hard not to look at the woman's private parts, but couldn't help it as he watched his uncle cleanse the area. Richard wondered what it was like to touch that private place without the sponge, and then tried to erase that thought from his mind.

Once they'd finished cleaning Ruth, Uncle James placed embalming fluid and water inside the pump. "It usually takes about four gallons to finish the job." Uncle James carefully measured his liquids, and then hooked Ruth up to an IV.

Richard watched in awe as his uncle inserted the needle,

fascinated by the whole procedure.

"We usually use the femoral or carotid artery for this. That way it goes into the heart and the circulatory system pushes it out, replacing the blood. I like to use the jugular. You okay? You've hardly said a word."

"I'm fine. Listening, that's all."

"A good student, that's what you are, Richard. A good student."

"Yep."

"Okay, now, see those tools over there?"

"Uh huh."

"Hand the first two over."

Richard handed him the scissors-like instruments. "What are these for?"

"We use these to remove any blood clots and to open the veins where the embalming fluid can't get through."

"Oh." Richard's tone had become hushed while watching his uncle work.

"Okay, now switch on the pump, please." Richard did. "We have to be very careful during this part. Improper embalming will make the cosmetology process impossible. God knows when I started I had a few messes. Let me tell you, son, there were some families not too happy at what I'd done to their kin. But patience is as important with the dead as with the living. If you treat this old gal here on the table as kindly as we treated her husband who came to us, then we usually have success on all accounts."

The sound of the pump along with the ebb and flow of fluids being drained and replaced was as rhythmical as rushing waters. Richard stared at the body while the fluids filled her, distorting her emaciated form into odd shapes, almost like a balloon being blown up. He liked the way it looked. He wanted to open her eyes to see if they were bugging out. God, his uncle was great.

"Never rush the work, because I can't tell you how it easy it can be to swell the face, and if that happens it's impossible to fix." Uncle James applied the steady pressure. "The frequent drainage of the fluids is crucial."

Richard watched, sweat forming on his brow. He wished he were the one injecting and draining the fluids!

After the process was finished, Uncle James took off his gloves and washed his hands in a corner sink, then pulled on a new set of gloves.

"We're not done?"

"Oh, no. We still have to do the cavity embalming."

Richard was pleased. He smiled as he stared at Ruth, whose body was now full of chemicals.

Uncle James went to the shelf again and took down a bag of powder, which he mixed with water. "Some out there swear by kitty litter, but something tells me that most of our departed friends here wouldn't be too pleased with cat litter inside their thoracic cavity."

"No." Richard shook his head vehemently.

"This is necessary when the chest is sunken, and Ruth's is a bit. So we'll give her some help." Uncle James stuck a tube down her mouth and filled it with the material, which he then pumped into her. Richard stared as her chest expanded.

"Next, we re-aspirate the lungs, cork the windpipe, and then the anal vent, which we open if we notice any bloating from the build up of gas."

"Like a fart?"

"Richard!"

"Sorry."

"Yes, like a fart." They both laughed. "Okay Ruth, we'll let you rest, while we grab a bite. I'd ask you to come, but..." Uncle James wasn't the least bit condescending or sarcastic; however, Richard couldn't help giggling.

They washed up and headed to the deli across the street. Janie Keaton was there with some friends. Richard glanced over, but tried not to pay any attention. He thought that Janie Keaton was the prettiest girl in school. She smiled at him while he bit into his ham sandwich.

"I think she likes you," Uncle James whispered.

"Nah, no one likes me," Richard replied, while chewing his

sandwich and shaking his head.

"I don't believe that. You're a good-looking boy, son. Remind me of your mother with your big brown eyes and blonde hair, and those dimples, well, those would woo a gal anytime."

Richard shook his head and smiled sheepishly. Maybe his uncle was right. He was a really smart man, with a good sense about people. It would make his day, week—no, *year*—if Janie Keaton liked him. If she liked him, then everyone else would too.

As Janie and her friends left the deli, she passed by their booth. "Hi, Richard. How's your summer going?"

Richard had no idea Janie Keaton even knew his name. He'd never imagined she knew he was alive. God, this was the best day of his life. "Good."

"Yeah, what you up to?"

"I'm working with my uncle."

Janie took a step back and looked at Uncle James. "At the funeral home?"

Richard hung his head. "Yes."

"Ooh creepy, but sort of cool, like in a freaky way, you know."

Richard looked up. "Yeah, it is."

"Wow. Okay, well maybe I'll see you around again. Have a good summer."

"You too."

Uncle James patted his hand and said, "Good going. She's awfully pretty. I told you so. She's got her eye on you. You handled that one just right."

"Thanks." Richard watched Janie Keaton walk away, her long hair, the color of sunshine on wheat in the late afternoon sun, swung from her ponytail, made him feel funny, but a good funny. He hoped that he would see Janie around again and be able to look in those blue-sky eyes.

After lunch, Uncle James taught Richard the art of applying makeup to the deceased. His favorite part was when they sewed Ruth's lips together then applied a thin layer of wax across them before putting on her lipstick.

Richard's thoughts kept wandering back to Janie Keaton. When Uncle James had to take a phone call, Richard escaped to the bathroom where his mind floated from Ruth's exposed genitals to Janie. He touched himself thinking of what it would be like to do all the things to Janie that they'd done to Ruth today. He felt weird but wonderful, as his body grew warm and tingled all over.

As he pleasured himself, he wondered what color he'd paint Janie Keaton's lips if she were lying on the table.

CHAPTER SIX

FRANKIE DOVE FOR the phone, hoping it was someone wanting to hang out. She doubted her luck could be that good. Her best pals were on cheer squad and at practice, and another was grounded for sneaking out with cutie pie Dean Ryan the other night. No, most likely it was probably Dad making sure she was doing her chemistry homework. College was less than two years away, something he repeatedly stressed. His major rule was homework before play, and though she resented it, she figured it had some merit.

"Frances?"

"Leeza?" she whispered. Frankie hadn't heard her voice in over a year. But it couldn't be mistaken, with a little-girl pitch and the slight southern lilt Frankie knew she'd tried hard to get rid of.

"That's right, it's me. How are you, darling?"

"What do you want?"

"Well, honey, I wanted to say how sorry I am about everything. I've thought a lot about it lately, and I feel real bad. You were always a pretty good kid, and I suppose I didn't treat you so well. I'm really sorry about that."

"Next, you'll tell me you've gone all Jerry Falwell on me and found Jesus. If I remember right, your interests run more along the lines of Jerry Springer." Frankie picked at her fingernails. "Looking for forgiveness, are you? If that's it, Leeza, you're calling the wrong girl. I actually used to pray at night that you'd go away and I'd find out you weren't really my mother. Thank God that prayer came true."

"Oh dear, I see you haven't lost your sense of humor."

Frankie stopped picking at her nails, a knot wrenched tight in her gut. "No, Ma'am, I haven't. That's how I got through all your abuse."

"Now, Frances, there's no need for so much spite. I called to tell you that I am sorry—truly. I hope someday you'll accept that, and maybe realize that I really do love you."

"Love isn't in your vocabulary. I don't know what you're up to this time, but I don't really care. You can't hurt me anymore." Frankie slammed down the phone, then snatched it up again and threw it against the wall. She put on her Fuel CD, and as the music blared from her speakers, she collapsed on her bed and began to cry.

Before long a fitful sleep took hold, and she dreamed she was walking along a cliff, her dad beside her. They talked about her not having a mother, how that must feel to Frankie, how sad it was. Up ahead, a figure emerged through the fog. As the being came closer, she saw that it was Helena. Frankie looked up at her dad who smiled. When Frankie didn't understand who this woman was, her dad told her that it was her mother.

She ran toward Helena, but her mother slipped at the cliff's edge. Frankie ran faster, her dad right behind her. They had to save her, to keep her from falling to the rocks below. Helena was too far away. They didn't make it in time.

Horrified, Frankie watched as Helena fell. She'd only just found her, but she was lost again. Now she would never know how it felt to have a mother.

When she woke, the tears dried on her face, Frankie picked up the phone and called Helena. She didn't want her real life to emulate the dream in any way. It was time to reach out and give her mother a chance.

CHAPTER SEVEN

"HEY, HOT STUFF, want a cup of latte?" Tim said, as he bounded into Helena's office. Helena smiled at his enthusiasm, which he had plenty of for just about everything, from caffe lattes to his latest conquest—whose attributes he loved telling Helena down to the last detail. Although there were times when these details made her uncomfortable, she tried not to let on. Tim was a good friend, and she never wanted to hurt his feelings.

He set the coffee down on top of the glass table Helena used as her desk and planted himself in a cushy leather chair opposite her. He smelled of lemongrass soap and clove cigarettes. Tim's attire was Banana Republic to a tee, from the khakis to the maroon, cable knit turtleneck. Pretty boy handsome, Tim looked as if he'd walked out of the pages of GQ.

His wide-eyed expression told her that he wasn't going anywhere until she confided in him. "Okay sugar, what's cooking in that wee head of yours?"

"It's nothing," she said.

"That's it, lie, lie, lie. We addicts are all the same. You might lose the addiction, but never the lying."

"You're a pain in the ass. I liked you better when you were flat on your back." She breathed in her coffee, the perfect wake up call, strong and sweet.

"Yeah, well now I've got a clean bill of health. So do tell. I'm always ready for some good dish. No more phone calls, I hope.

Or anymore freaky incidents?"

Helena sighed, knowing she couldn't escape his third degree. "No, that was the only one, and I think I know who might've been behind it."

"Really?"

"I've thought long and hard and there's really only one logical answer—Leeza."

"No!" He waved his hands in an exaggerated gesture. "What makes you say that?" Tim leaned in, his elbows on her desk, his chin resting in his palms, squinting his dark eyes—the captivated audience.

"I don't know why I didn't think of it before. It makes sense. Leeza would do anything to see me fail with my daughter just out of plain old spite. It's obvious she never loved Frankie, so I don't know why she doesn't let it go. I can't imagine being consumed with so much hatred she would waste her time on me. But she clearly is, and it all connected for me yesterday when she pulled another stunt."

"God! That bitch. What did Miss Tell-All do this time?"

"Helena slammed her fists on the desk. She called Frankie yesterday!"

"No. Where does she get her gall? What the hell did she want?"

"Frankie called me yesterday afternoon all upset about Leeza calling her and telling her that she loves her and wants her forgiveness, blah, blah, blah. The poor kid was beside herself." Tim rolled his eyes. "Can you believe her? Telling my daughter that she loves her. Are you ready for that? After all the crap she's thrown at us, she has the audacity to tell Frankie that she loves her. That woman couldn't love anyone."

"No kidding. She hasn't gotten over her first love affair." Helena raised her eyebrows. "By which I mean herself, dear."

"You're right about that," she laughed.

"So what did the kid say?"

"She told the woman to leave her alone, then hung up on her." Helena nodded in satisfaction and smiled as she sipped her coffee.

"Like mother, like daughter. When do I get to meet this kid, anyway?"

"Hopefully on Saturday you'll get your chance. She's great. I'm trying to convince her to come to the meeting, since it's my anniversary. I thought maybe we could grab a bite, too. I'd love to make a day of it with her and take her over to Shea House and the Sober Living House. I want her to meet some of the girls."

"Oh." Tim clapped. "That sounds delightful. Plan it! But about this thing with the ex-step mommy, why are you so worried about her phone call? It sounds like the kid handled the Wicked Witch just fine. And the fact that she called you and clued you in is also another positive in your court." He leaned back in the chair, crossing his legs.

"Maybe so, but it still disturbs Frankie. Her therapy gets setback every time someone brings up this scandal. Frankie feels betrayed by everyone she's loved. She truly doesn't know who she can trust and who really loves her. Last week, she called me "Mom" for the first time. We've really been getting closer, and I don't want anything to ruin that. But after Leeza's meddling phone call, I don't know what'll happen. I also have to wonder what Leeza is up to. It's not innocent, you know. Like I told you the other night, I don't need any more ugly press." Helena reached for her pack of cigarettes on the desk, then set them back without taking one out. "If Leeza starts mixing it up, Frankie might end up hating me all over again. She might change her mind about wanting a relationship with me. She's still coping with the fact that I gave her to Patrick and Leeza when she was a baby. She thinks that I never wanted her, which isn't true. She knows Leeza never wanted her. I wish Dad were still alive; he knew what she meant to me. He knew how much it hurt to give her up."

Helena picked up the silver frame with her dad's photograph inside. It was one of him fishing down at the lake they went to every summer when she was a kid. She was seven in that picture. Her mother had already passed on from an undetected case of ovarian cancer.

"You're truly sounding ridiculous now. It's nothing fifteen years of therapy won't cure." He laughed at his own joke.

Helena frowned. She knew Tim was joking, but the reality was that Frankie would need a lot of counseling. Frankie was strong, and Helena hoped, through her love along with Patrick's, that her daughter would heal in time. However, she wasn't going to kid herself. She knew how long it took to heal deep, emotional wounds.

"Helena, you're wonderful, and anyone would be lucky to have you for a mother. Look how far you've come. Look at the way the girls at the center look up to you. My God, you're like the Virgin Mother herself over there."

"Hardly, and the fact is that Frankie really is my daughter, and she certainly doesn't see me that way." Helena choked back her tears, reaching for her coffee again.

"Don't let this little incident set you back. Take charge." Helena nodded. She knew exactly what he meant. "Now, what you ought to do is go see your daughter. Do some damage control. Don't assume the worst. Take the train up today after work. I'll go by and feed the pup while you're away. I'm sure the kids at the center will understand if you can't make it over for an afternoon. They've got plenty of support there. You know that."

She nodded. "Thank you."

"For what?"

"The best advice in town."

"No shit! Stop paying that shrink so much and give me a raise instead. I do a much better job."

"I'll talk to personnel about that," she said with a wink. They both knew that personnel consisted of Tim, a payroll manager, a handful of scouts, and herself.

"Ha! Funny. Well, I'd love to stay and chat all day about your dysfunctional life, but I have to call the studio to make sure the girls got there. And the cattle are already out there, waiting to be called in."

"Oh, God! I dread the first Wednesday of every month." It was the day they held their monthly open call for fresh faces. It also typically became the longest day of the month, with hundreds of young men and women waiting to be seen, hoping for their big break.

"I know, lovey. The go-sees you get to look over are tons of fun. But maybe you'll find a good one today. There's a nice-looking young man cooling his heels out there. He may not be your type, but *I* wouldn't mind having coffee with him."

"Yeah, well, remember who loved you first, baby. Listen. Will you weed them down to thirty? You know what I'm looking for. I'm checking out early, taking your advice about that damage control."

"Now you're using that noggin. I'll pick the best prospects and send the rest packing. Do you want me to take care of Ella for the night?"

"I'll go home first and feed her, and I've got to run by Shea House and meet with the plumber. Besides, I also need to ask Patrick if it's convenient for me to go up there today. If it is, I'll drive up, then come back after dinner." She sat twirling her pen between her fingers.

"Sounds like a mighty late night. I don't think you should be driving back in the wee hours." He stuck his hands on his hips.

He reminded her of a mother hen. "Always the worrier. I'll be fine. I don't want to be intrusive, so I won't stay late. Remember, Frankie is supposed to come down to LA this Friday anyway."

"Be careful driving."

"I will." Helena watched Tim leave, shutting the door behind him. He'd been a godsend after her assistant Brianne had left so abruptly while Helena was at The Betty Ford Center. It bothered her for a long time that Brianne had never contacted her. But Helena had spiraled out of control during that time and been pretty horrible to everyone around her just before she'd checked herself into rehab. It was a miracle that she'd been able to pull her business back together. If not for Tim, she couldn't have done it.

Focused on the business at hand, Helena finished quicker than she'd expected. However, before she went home she decided to make one stop first—one she wasn't eager to make, but felt was

necessary.
****

Helena pushed the buzzer six or seven times before she heard high heels clatter against marble.

"Guess it's the maid's day off," she muttered as the front door opened. Leeza Kiley stood there in all her steely, redheaded glory, an ironic smile flickering across her face.

"Greetings, neighbor," Leeza snorted. Once the divorce was final and she'd sold the house she'd shared with Patrick for so many years, she moved to this house, only a mile or so from Helena.

Leeza shook her head and tsk tsked while giving Helena the once-over. "So what's your story? If you have a bone to pick, why didn't you do that, oh, say, a year ago, when the celebrity story of the century broke?"

"Wasn't worth my time."

Leeza swung open the door. "Okay, what's worth your time now then?" she asked, raising her perfectly waxed, eyebrows into a curious arch.

"My daughter."

"Ah, I see. You two must be getting pretty tight. That's great, but I really don't have time for chitchat, much less a reunion with the woman who stole everything from me. How am I cramping your style this time?"

"It's not about me, Leeza."

"It never is. You can steal a woman's husband before you're even eighteen like a jail bait Lolita, have his baby, toss her aside, go on to become queen of the world, make a million bucks, fall flat on your alcoholic ass, and then become Joan of Arc by coming clean about your past and starting some center for crack whores with kids. No, Helena, it is certainly never about you."

Helena considered walking away, knowing that the conversation was already out of hand. But this was about her child, the one she'd betrayed in so many ways. After all these years, she could finally protect her and owed her that much. "Wow, that was quick. You must have been practicing in front of the mirror! But

I have to tell you, you're paying way too much for those acting lessons. Might want to get a new coach. You haven't changed a bit. Still playing the same aggrieved innocent."

"Insults will get you nowhere."

Helena closed her eyes, sighed, and collected herself before opening them again. "Fine, I didn't come here to take a trip down your inaccurate perception of memory lane. I came here to talk about Frankie."

"I never meant to hurt her." Leeza picked up a large cat that smelled like baby powder who had nonchalantly been rubbing itself against Leeza's fake-baked legs.

"Patrick and I can take the heat, but she's only a kid."

"Look, I love Frances as much as you do. Don't forget I raised her." She cradled the cat like a baby, kissing it on the nose.

"No, Mary Poppins did that."

"Well, who do you think she called Mommy?" Leeza tickled the purring cat under his chin.

"Only to be scolded and told to call you by name, except when Patrick was around."

"She said that?"

"Spare me the drama." Helena's face burned.

"At least I didn't abandon her." Leeza's grin made her look very much like the Batman's rival, Joker.

Helena stepped back as if punched in the stomach. If she didn't control herself, she'd smack this woman hard, this manipulator who'd begged her sixteen years ago to give Frankie to her and Patrick, telling her it was the best thing for all of them. "I did not abandon my child. I gave her to you and Patrick believing that she would be loved and raised by a family that wanted her. But all you wanted was Patrick's money. That was why he turned to someone else in the first place, to someone who could love him for who he really is."

The cat struggled free from Leeza's arms. Helena ached to choke the life out of Leeza. "I want you to leave Frankie alone. It's that simple. Don't call her. Don't write her. And don't even consider pulling another one of your bullshit stunts." Leeza looked stunned. "Yeah, I'm not the dumb-ass you think I am. I know you had someone try to run me down, then the crank-call. That was pleasant. Very clever of you."

"You're a whack job, always were. I have no idea what you're talking about. And if I want to call Frances up and have a chat, that's exactly what I'll do."

"I'm not playing here, lady. Stay the hell out of our lives, or you will regret it!" Helena stormed off and headed for the Suburban parked on the side of the Pacific Coast Highway.

Leeza yelled, "Is that a threat?!" No answer. "You're nuts! You've done too many drugs and fried the rest of your already half-baked brain. And you know what? That *did* sound like a threat to me. I'll bet there's a reporter or two who'd love to hear about this. Think I'll give Claire Travers a call, Miss High and Mighty. Remember her?!" she screamed. "She wrote nice stories about you, didn't she? Leave your family alone? You should've left my fucking husband alone, you whore!"

Helena slammed the truck's door and revved the engine. "Get over it, for God's sakes. It was sixteen years ago, you bitter bitch," she muttered.

As she squealed out onto the highway, Helena knew that she'd made a grave mistake. Leeza was probably on the phone this very minute, once again seeking some type of twisted revenge.

CHAPTER EIGHT

CLAIRE TRAVERS LOVED a good story as much as the other sob sisters who wrote for the tabloids, but she had to admit that Leeza Kiley was becoming a bore. The woman shrieked at her for a good five minutes before Claire could get a word in.

"Okay, calm down, Leeza." Claire switched the phone to the other ear. "Let me get this straight, Helena Shea came to your place and said some nasty things to you?"

"Nasty? Nasty? Yeah, you could say that! I wanted to kill the slut. Who does she thinks she is?"

Claire put her hand over her free ear. The buzzing inside the newsroom made it hard to hear. "Leeza, do you mind if we meet up tonight? I've got a deadline."

"You're not putting me on the back burner, are you, Claire?"

"Of course not. How about seven at Kate Mandolin's Restaurant?"

"I'll be there."

Claire hung up and rubbed her temples. She cringed as the resulting breeze of her co-worker Fred's sour stomach wafted her way. "Jesus Fred, did you eat Mexican again? Man, I got one word for you. Beano."

"Funny, Claire," Fred replied from the other side of the cubicle.

She leaned back in her chair, the springs creaking. God, what would it be like to have a real chair, in a real office, where people had real manners?

Tossing her pencil onto her desk, Claire pondered her next move. If she printed every tidbit Leeza called her about, she'd have a two-thousand-page novel.

But today's tidbit was fairly interesting typical Hollywood diva stuff, with Helena Shea threatening Leeza. And then there was the fact that Helena was opening that new drug center for pregnant women and new moms. This could put a twist on things. But that really wasn't cool. Here she was trying to do a good thing. Could it only be Leeza trying to stir things up? Highly likely.

The story wasn't even lukewarm now. New scandals popped up everyday. People were bored with the Shea/Kiley feud. Claire picked her pencil back up and ran her fingers along it. Someone was listening to Howard Stern on the radio blabber about boobs.

"Oh honey, yours are great. You don't need a boob job. Does she, Robin?"

"I'm not looking," Robin Quivers replied.

"Sex sells," Claire muttered. That reason alone justified her being entertained by Hollywood's latest queen of flamboyance. Hell, if the scoop about Helena didn't pan out, Leeza herself was good for an exposé. Rumor had it—and Claire was sure Leeza would confirm it—that the new divorcée had agreed to do a spread in *Playboy*. That would spin a few people out of control, and knowing Leeza, that's exactly what she had in mind. She loved pushing people's buttons, especially if those buttons belonged to her ex and his ex-lover. And all Claire had to do was get the scoop while it was juicy, write it down, make it flow, and it would be printed in thousands of papers around the country.

Claire picked up last week's copy of *The Scene*. She loved newspapers—the visual of the black ink against the white background. This paper *was* trash, but it paid the bills.

Claire held the paper to her nose, breathing it in. It no longer had that fresh ink and paper aroma she adored. It was now as stale as yesterday's news. Was the Helena Shea scandal just as stale? She knew that people loved a real-life soap opera. Maybe Claire could light a fire under her fading serial.

CHAPTER NINE

August 1970

Before . . .

THE SUMMER FLEW by for Richard, and his uncle surprised him towards the end of it by taking him into San Francisco for his thirteenth birthday, only an hour's drive from their small town of Dobson.

Uncle James took him to the marina where they shopped, ate fresh fish, and visited the Ghirardelli chocolate factory. Uncle James let Richard buy whatever he wanted.

At home, Richard hid his chocolates under the bed for fear that Aunt Valerie would trash them. She wasn't happy about their escapades and really let Uncle James have it.

"That's no place for the boy!" she'd yelled.

For the first time, Uncle James had stood up to her. "It's a special birthday for him," he'd said in a low voice, "and he deserves to go. He's helped me all summer at work. It's not like he has any friends to invite over."

"That's because he's weird. I see the way he is. I know. And I don't care what you say 'bout him, no amount of prayer will save him. He's evil, being born out of that whore. He's got tainted blood."

"Don't talk about Elizabeth like that."

She'd stormed out of the room. It struck Richard as odd, but made him ecstatic, that a simple retort with the mention of his mother's name could send her away. Uncle James had tossed Richard his jacket and said it was time to go.

Richard took the box of candy from under his bed now. He ate one a day. He was getting low on them, because a week had already passed by since their trip. He popped one with a caramel center into his mouth. It was the best thing he'd ever tasted with all its rich, gooey sweetness.

Life wasn't so bad in Dobson. He enjoyed working for his Uncle James, but he hated listening to his aunt rave on about how they were all sinners and had to repent. Richard wanted to tell her to shove it up her fat ass. Life would be a heck of a lot better if she'd take a hike.

One evening after supper, Uncle James went to shower, which he never did at night. He was always too tired to do much of anything after work. Richard watched Aunt Valerie pour herself a glass of sherry. Her hands trembled, and she had trouble putting the stopper back into the decanter.

She sat back down in her rocker across from Richard as he watched television. Old witch! She only allowed him to watch an hour a night. Tonight that suited him fine, because he was going to meet with Janie Keaton again. He had friends. Well, he had one friend anyway.

"So, how was work?" Aunt Valerie asked.

"Fine." Richard tried not to look at her ugly, scowling face. Why was she interested in his day?

"Must've got a new one in today, huh Ricky?"

He cringed. Why did she have to call him that? "A new what?"

"Don't act stupid. A body. A dead woman. A corpse." She took a long swig of the sherry, and a little dribbled down her chin.

He turned to glare at her, filled with contempt at her tone and the mere fact she would even speak to him. "Yeah, so?"

"Must be a young woman?"

Richard looked back at the TV, desperately trying to tune her out.

"Ricky, I asked you a question."

"What? Yeah, I guess she was pretty young. Maybe thirty something."

"How'd she die?"

"Why do you care?"

"Ricky." She shook a finger at him. "Don't speak to me in that tone. You know what the good Lord says about respecting your elders. Now by the grace of God, for your sake, we've been designated to raise you. God knows, with that whore for your mother, you didn't stand a chance. You really should be more grateful. I've got a right mind to get the rod, teach you a lesson or two."

Richard started to sweat. He was thankful she had the gout and wouldn't get up to beat him. She hadn't hit him in quite some time. He'd recently had a growth spurt and now sensed that she was a bit frightened of him. He liked that. In a low voice that sounded close to a growl he replied, "Please do not refer to my mother like that." He stood up, feeling heat in his face, his jaw clenched.

He considered shutting her up. There were many ways he could do that. He thought about it quite a bit. His favorite fantasy was simply to take a sharp kitchen knife and slice her open and let her bleed to death—she'd watch as her blood and guts oozed all over her stupid, perfectly cleaned house. Richard would enjoy doing that to Aunt Valerie, and there'd be no way to preserve her. They'd have to cremate her. Aunt Valerie brought this hatred on herself the way she treated him and spoke of his mother.

"Oh, *sorry*." Her sarcasm didn't go undetected. "I know how much you loved your dear, departed mommy. Forgive me. You're exactly like your uncle. I'm surprised you're not showering, getting ready for a night out on the town."

Richard clenched his fists, blood rushed through him. Did she know that he was meeting Janie tonight? Was that why she was acting so strange? And why had she said that about his uncle? He never went out at night.

"She must be a special one. I haven't seen him like this since before you came. It's been awhile. I thought maybe he'd gotten past it."

Richard's mind raced. Her insinuations about his uncle fascinated him, but he refused to give her satisfaction by showing any interest. Besides, Uncle James was way too straight-laced to do anything nutty. He felt his face flush.

He looked back at the clock, almost eight. His aunt would be in bed by nine, but with his uncle going out, it might present a problem. His stomach jumped around making him anxious.

He and Janie had agreed to keep their meetings secret. They always waited until their families were asleep before sneaking out, not too difficult for either of them.

"My parents are drunk by eight," she'd said one summer day when he'd found her crying down by the river—alone and very upset. Her dad had beaten her mom that morning for not having his breakfast ready. Janie had run out of the house. Richard had sat next to her and they'd skipped stones across the river, marking the start of their summer friendship.

"Excuse me Ricky, but I was speaking to you."

"Yes."

"The woman who was brought in today. How'd she die? It couldn't have been a car wreck, or at least not one that ruined her face." Spittle flew as she spoke, and Richard sank into the couch, wishing he could disappear.

"Uncle James said something about drugs. I think she must've overdosed."

"Ah. Okay, well she must be something special all right!" Aunt Valerie slowly got up from her chair and waddled away, bumping against one wall and then the other as she headed down the hall to her room. "Turn off that TV!" she hollered back at him.

Thankful she'd gone to bed, Richard's only concern was meeting Janie without anyone finding out. Not even his uncle could know. It wasn't that Uncle James would be angry; Janie insisted on it.

Uncle James came into the family room dressed in a coat and

tie, his dark hair slicked back. Richard had never seen him so dressed up. "Wow, where you going?"

"Oh, there's a funeral director's convention up north."

He was glad, because now he wouldn't have to worry about sneaking in and out.

"What are you smiling at?"

"Nothing. I'm happy you're getting out of here that's all. You deserve some time off."

"I'd love to take you, but with school starting so soon and as early as we rise around here, you need your rest."

"Hey, no problem. Probably just a bunch of stiffs anyway, huh?"

"Funny guy, aren't you? Yes, it'll be a dead crowd." They both laughed. "Where's your aunt?"

"I think she went to bed. She was sure acting strange, asking me all sorts of crazy stuff. I think she's lost her marbles." Richard tapped the side of his head.

"What'd she say?" Uncle James frowned.

"Well, she was asking about work and the woman who was brought in today."

"What did you tell her?" Uncle James shifted his weight from one foot to the other.

"Nothing much. I tried to ignore her, but she kept asking."

"Don't worry about it. She's probably been sipping her sherry again. She's not much of a drinker—a little goes a long way with her."

"Right." Richard looked his uncle up and down again, wondering why he was acting strange, too.

A half-hour later, without a care regarding his aunt or uncle, Richard walked down the gravel road to meet Janie at their hideout, an old shack out in the woods. When he saw her flashlight up ahead, his adrenaline began to pump, making him feel jittery. "Janie?" he called out.

"Hi," she answered. Richard jogged over to meet her and, laughing together, they collapsed onto the blanket she'd brought. "Hey, look what I've got." She reached into a bag and pulled out a six-pack of beer.

"How'd you manage that?"

"Shoot, my dad's already passed out in his chair, and my mom's listening to the Rolling Stones, pretending she's some rock star."

"Sounds like your family's pretty messed up, too. My uncle is cool, but my aunt is a real drag."

"Hey, no one at school knows about my family. You know, me being a cheerleader and all. They think I have the perfect life, but I got them fooled, huh?"

"Yeah."

"That's why I like you. Everyone thinks you're so weird, and you are," she said, "but I feel like I can tell you anything."

Richard smiled. For once, being strange was good. "Are you close to your folks? I mean do you like them?"

"They're okay. Except when my dad gets mad, you know?" She opened a beer and handed it to Richard, and then took out one for herself. He'd never had any alcohol to drink before. The taste was bitter, but he swallowed it anyway, not wanting Janie to think less of him. His stomach warmed as the liquid fizzed on the way down. When it hit bottom, he belched loudly, and they both cracked up. She drank hers quickly, copying him.

Once they'd calmed down, Janie brought up his family. "What about your mom? I mean, were you close?"

Richard grabbed another beer from the bag. "Yeah, very. I loved my mother more than anything."

"Wow, so I guess you miss her?"

"Yep. I don't really want to talk about her, though." The pain of losing his mother still haunted him. The mention of her, especially by his aunt, pained him. His chest tightened, and he turned away from his friend.

"Hey, no problem. Do you still see your dad?"

"Never knew him."

"No way."

"Never."

"God, that's crummy. Do you know anything about him?"

Richard hesitated here. Anytime he'd told the story about his dad, people laughed. "So? Do you know who your dad is?"

"I never met him. He's dead too." Richard decided it was best not to reveal that his father was Mills Florence. He didn't want anything to threaten their friendship, and if Janie accused him of making up stories, he'd hate that.

"That's tough." Janie flipped back her fair hair. Her sweater slipped off her right shoulder; she wore a tube top underneath. Richard couldn't help noticing her small breasts.

"Well, did you bring the book?"

"You bet."

She clapped her hands. Richard opened Edgar Allan Poe's book of short stories. The book was old and the binding loose. Richard treated it with care, knowing how much it meant to his uncle. Tonight they planned on finishing "The Murders in the Rue Morgue." They'd been reading these stories together by flashlight for the past month. Richard was pleased that Janie liked them as much as he did.

The night creature noises halted and silence descended upon them, almost as if each living thing in the woods had waited for the storytelling to begin as well.

He read the gruesome sections in a scary voice, like Vincent Price. In the other sections, he imitated an Englishman, like his uncle did when he read. Janie listened, her eyes wide as she hugged her knees under her chin.

"'On a chair lay a razor, besmeared with blood. On the hearth were two or three long and thick tresses of grey human hair, also dabbled in blood, and seeming to have been pulled out at the roots.'"

"Ooh, yuck. God, Richard you're such a good reader."

Richard winked at her and continued. He loved her adoration, and went on, more enthusiastic than before. When he finished, Janie clapped.

"Wow, that's so spooky. Who would've ever thought an ape killed them?"

"An orangutan," Richard corrected her.

"Right. Kinda funny how all the characters thought the killer was either the French guy or the Italian. They had no clue."

"I know. That's how Poe hid who'd done it. My uncle says he was a master."

"His stories are pretty cool, even though they've got a lot of blood and yucky stuff. I'd hate to be killed like that."

Richard closed the book. "I like all the murder and gore."

"Yeah, I guess so. Just gross."

"I've seen grosser."

"Working with your uncle?"

"The other day a family was all bloody and broken up cause they'd been in a car wreck."

"Ooh, sick. I think I've had enough for the night. Doesn't it ever bother you?"

"Nope," he said, almost shocked that death would bother anyone.

"No wonder everyone thinks you're so freaky," she said.

He didn't like the remark, but since she'd brought up "everyone," he felt it was a good time to talk about school.

"Anyway, so...." He looked away from her. "I hope we get the same homeroom teacher this year."

Janie hesitated, then replied, "Yeah, I guess that'd be cool."

"Sure it would." Richard saw her down-turned lip in the dim light, and that she wasn't looking at him. "Don't you want to be in the same class?"

"Well, I said it'd be cool, didn't I? It's just . . ."

"What?" Richard gulped down the rest of his beer. "I thought we were best friends."

"Sure. Kinda."

"What's that mean?" Richard jumped to his feet.

Janie's eyes widened as she shrugged her shoulders. There was an obvious uneasiness about her that Richard had never seen before. "Oh, Richard, the thing is, well... I'm popular, and it's harder there at Roosevelt, with kids being bussed in from all over. You'll probably even meet people you like better than me there. For now, I'm kind of popular, you know. And, well everyone thinks you're…"

"A geek? So? We're friends! Doesn't that mean something? Popular? So what!" His head grew hot, as streaks of white anger blurred his vision.

"We'll still be friends, and we can meet like this on weekends— but not during school. It's hard for me at home, and the kids I hang out with make it easier for me to go home and deal with my parents. C'mon, you understand, right? You have to."

"I don't *have* to do anything. And I thought I made it easier for you to deal with your folks. I'm the one you talk to about them. You don't tell those boneheads you hang out with that your mom and dad are drunks. I thought you'd stick up for me, then everyone would be nicer to me. They wouldn't think I'm a geek if you told them that I wasn't. All you have to do is tell them that I'm really cool."

"It doesn't work that way. Not in this town anyway. And as far as my parents go, that's between us. Please. You of all people should understand that."

"I can't believe this." Richard, soaked in perspiration, paced around the shack. Janie was his best and only friend, and here she was dumping him so she could still be cool in school. "That's shit!" He stomped his foot and kicked the ground.

"Well, I better get going. You're mad now. Maybe tomorrow night you'll feel better and understand. We only have a week left before school starts. I am really sorry, Richard." She stuffed the beers inside the bag.

Richard picked up her flashlight and watched as Janie bent down, reaching for the book. No, tomorrow would not be any different. He would not feel any better about this. She'd said they were friends. He had treated her good, and this was what he got in return? His anger, far stronger than his conscience, was guiding him now. Richard would not allow Janie to do this to him. Friends? She was going to leave him, not talk to him, just because of what other kids said about him? Hardly!

He pulled his arm back, and whacked Janie hard on the back of her head with the flashlight, knocking her to the ground. Her shrill scream encouraged him further. Every part of him tingled. She turned, facing him. Seeing the fear in her eyes made his rage grow stronger, thinking how she planned to deliberately shun him. Richard swung with all his strength and hit her across the side of her head. Something warm and wet hit his hand. He heard the guttural sound she made as Janie Keaton, his *so-called* friend, collapsed. She made no more noise, no more movements. He swung the flashlight once more, giving her a final blow. The woods grew silent for the second time that evening.

Janie Keaton lay on the ground; blood smeared across her face and on her hands where she'd tried to protect herself. Edgar Allan Poe's book, opened to "The Murders in the Rue Morgue," lay next to her.

Richard dropped the flashlight, staring down at her. "Why did you have to do this, Janie? Friends! We were friends! Don't you know what that means? No, all you wanted was to be popular! I'm sorry, but not anymore. Now you'll always be my friend!"

He sat down next to her and cried almost as hard as the day he'd lost his mother. He didn't know what to do. Richard had only wanted her to still be his friend in school, that's all. Then none of this would've happened. If she'd only said, *Sure, we'll eat lunch together, and hang out after school*, she'd still be here.

But he'd killed her, and he had to do something—and quick. No one could know they'd been together. He thought fast as he wiped away his tears. He collected the book and flashlight, stuffing them down into the bag with the beer. It was almost midnight.

Richard hefted Janie up on to his shoulder, struggling under her weight for a moment. She was heavy, but he was strong. Uncle James had set up weights for him out in the garage, and he'd been working out with them all summer.

He made his way to the edge of the woods, and steadied himself. Richard knew exactly what to do. As quickly as his sadness had come upon him, it was gone, and now he thought with the mind of the orangutan in Poe's story—by instinct, and with fury.

Richard left her body buried under a group of bushes, wrapped inside the blanket they'd sat on earlier, then he walked to the back of the local market. The town was deserted, and he made certain to avoid any lights. He rummaged through a dumpster until he found a trash bag large enough to hold her. He went back and stuffed her body inside.

"I hate doing this to you," he said.

The mortuary was close by. No one was around, and he was sure he hadn't been seen. He made his way to the back of the funeral home. His stomach sank when he spotted his uncle's car. *Now what*? The bag was heavy, and he was afraid it might tear. He set it down between the building and some trashcans.

An hour later, his uncle exited the building humming "Blue Moon." Uncle James got into his car, and when he turned on the headlights, Richard's nerves jangled, his ears buzzing, afraid that his uncle would see him. Richard remained still until he could no longer see the car's lights. Though the air had grown colder, Richard's clothes were soaked with sweat.

He unlocked the mortuary and carried Janie through the back door. He took her immediately into the embalming station where he laid her down on the table. Although he kind of felt bad about what he'd done, he was excited about what he was going to do next. He knew he had to hurry, for fear his uncle would realize he wasn't in the house and begin looking for him.

After disinfecting Janie, Richard began the embalming process. Every fiber in his body pulsated. This was control.

"I'm sorry about your face Janie. I didn't mean to bruise you. But this isn't so bad. Is it? We'll be friends for eternity. Just you and me. And no one will think you're a geek. I can save you. Did you know that? I'll just put these fluids in your body, and I know you can't really talk to me, but I think I know you well enough to know what you'd say if you could."

Draining the blood and fluids from her, then filling her back up with chemicals was like being alive for the very first time. The power of it all! Power—that was exactly what he felt—Powerful! He moaned aloud as he continued with the process, the blood rushing to his penis. Maybe he should... No! He couldn't! She was his friend, but on the other hand she'd betrayed him—hurt him with her words. She had held all the power at that moment, and now, well, now he held the power. No one would know. He'd never kissed a girl, and he'd certainly never touched one in *that* way.

She was so beautiful, even with the marks on her face. He'd forgotten how upset he'd been only a couple of hours before. He stroked her face. His fingers traced the outline of her sweet lips. So doll-like. He had to feel them against his. He leaned over her, and brought his lips to hers, kissing her. Her lips were cold and rubbery, but to his body it felt like coming in from freezing weather to a warm home with a blazing fireplace.

Richard stood back from her. He had to do it. But how, how could he? It didn't matter; he had to have her. It was late, but so what, because Janie Keaton was about to become his very own. He pulled her tube top down around her waist. His body's physical reaction fueled him with desire for the dead girl. Her breasts were small nubs, but so very pretty. Richard had never seen anything so wonderful. He unzipped his pants. He was going to touch Janie. He was going to do *it* with her.

But then, something went horribly wrong. Janie's face—once pretty and fair—became hugely swollen and red emphasizing the bruises. He'd applied too much pressure, like his uncle had warned him not to. As this metamorphosis took hold and she rapidly changed into a hideous monster, Richard's instincts turned cold. His jubilant feelings and lustful thoughts were quickly replaced with anger and pain.

Richard knew that there was nothing he could do to correct the horrible mistake. He started to cry again. "Dammit!" he screamed. "Why couldn't you have just said that we could still be friends?" Richard knew he only had one option left.

Since Uncle James also provided cremation services, Richard went to the cylinder-type oven to light the fire. He waited until it was hot enough, and then placed Janie on the table and slid her inside.

He cried the whole time her body turned to ash. The room smelled of death. Richard sat next to the incinerator, balled up and shivering, even though the oven put off a great deal of heat. He lay down on the ground, once again feeling the loss of control.

Richard knew why he had done this terrible thing, and although it hurt, he felt he had been justified. Janie Keaton had chosen to get out, to leave. If she'd lived, she would have turned her back on him. And Richard couldn't go through that kind of pain. So, instead, he had had to kill Janie; it had put *him* in control of his destiny—not Janie.

When it was all over, he knew he needed to get home. He couldn't wait hours for the oven to cool. It would be morning before that happened. He'd have to tell his uncle that he had forgotten to clean out the oven the other day. He'd do that first thing in the morning.

Richard walked home, crying and stomping his feet, still not understanding why Janie couldn't have remained his friend.

CHAPTER TEN

HELENA SPED UP the Ventura Freeway to Santa Barbara in record time. Her knuckles were white as she clutched the steering wheel. She slowed down to pass a Highway Patrol car. The confrontation with Leeza had made her more anxious than she'd expected. Thoughts of a glass of wine crept to the forefront of her mind, but she shoved them away. Drinking would not cure a headache like Leeza, or anything else for that matter.

As she pulled into the expansive ranch, she sighed, relieved to be there for many reasons. She rolled down the window and breathed in the grassy pastures and nearby ocean. In the pasture to her right, a mare and her foal stood mowing down the grass. It was a beautiful sight and put an immediate smile on her face. She fidgeted with her hair, tucking loose strands back into her ponytail, wondering how Frankie would feel about her surprise visit.

Helena got out of the car and headed for the front door of the hacienda-style home—typical of the glamour and wealth of Santa Barbara. Frankie opened it, walking to meet her halfway. "Hi," she said.

"Hey, you," Helena replied, waving. "How are you doing?"

Frankie shrugged. "Okay." Even with her slight pout and taciturn attitude, Frankie was beautiful, and her mom knew that she was really soft hearted deep down.

"Good." Helena wanted to put her arms around her.

"Dad said you were coming up."

"I thought that after Leeza called you, maybe you could use a friend. I know how she can get to people. Is it okay that I'm here?"

With her trademark shrug, Frankie mumbled, "I guess so. Dad said to take you out for a ride. Pablo is down at the barn saddling up for us. I think Dad is down there, too."

A horse whinnied close by. "Great. I'm glad I wore my jeans. The only trouble is, I don't have any boots."

Frankie looked at Helena's white Keds. Finally she asked, "What size do you wear?"

"Eight and a half."

"Me too. You can borrow a pair of mine." Frankie went inside to get the boots.

Helena closed her eyes; heaviness weighed on her heart as she tried to envision Frankie as a little girl. She held back the tears, and her chest tightened, reminded of how much she'd missed, not to mention how lucky Patrick had been to see it all.

She headed down to the barn. She hadn't ridden in years. The last time was down in Mexico with Patrick; they were on location for a photo shoot. The weather had turned cloudy and muggy. The models complained that the humidity ruined their hair. So Patrick had given the girls the day off. He told Helena to prepare herself for an adventure.

"Where did you learn to ride?" she'd asked Patrick while she patted the sorrel mare he'd picked out for her that day.

"My father owned a cattle ranch."

"Really? How is it that you've gone from cows to models?"

"You could say that I have a little bit of my granddaddy in me. He was responsible for beginning the Kiley fortune. Being an Irishman, he liked whiskey, and knew how to still some good moonshine. He also liked pretty women. So he ran a club with dancers, featuring the best booze around. The cops eventually caught him, but he was smart and had hidden most of his earnings. My father inherited that money after my granddaddy mysteriously died. But Dad was honest. He moved us west, began ranching, and tripled the money he'd inherited."

Helena had been in awe of him and his family history. He was so charming and handsome. That was the day he'd told Helena how beautiful she was. He'd said it in a way that had made her truly feel it. He'd been her agent at that time and was very successful at it. Their affair ensued shortly after that trip. It was passionate but brief. When Helena became pregnant with Frankie, Leeza insisted Patrick sell the agency and focus on his other business ventures.

A more mature Patrick, with fine lines of crow's feet around his ice blue eyes, walked out of the barn as she approached it. The combined odors of manure and horse sweat made her wrinkle her nose. "Hey, you're early!" he called, coming over and greeting her with a hug.

"I still pretend I'm Mario Andretti." She pulled away from his embrace.

Patrick laughed, "Even in that big wheel you're tooling around these days?" His eye caught hers.

"Even faster." She ignored the butterflies dancing in her stomach, feeling like a schoolgirl at her first dance.

"So, have you seen Frankie yet?"

"She sent me down here. How's she doing, anyway?"

Patrick fiddled with the bridle he was adjusting. "She seems okay. She's got a strong spirit." He walked around to the crossties, where a stout gray Quarter horse stood. The mare lowered her head as Patrick unhooked one of the ties, slipping the bit inside her mouth and putting the headstall over her ears. "It's good that you came up—shows her that you care."

Helena crossed her arms in front of her, feeling her face grow hot. "Of course I care. I'm her mother."

"I know, I know. I didn't mean anything by it, only that it was a good move on your part, especially since you two are starting to bond."

"Did she tell you that?" Helena watched him gently place the saddle on the horse's back. He'd always been wonderful with animals.

Patrick tightened the cinch on the saddle, "Good girl." He patted the mare. "Duchess is a great old gal, she won't give you any trouble out there."

The knot in Helena's stomach tightened. "Did Frankie say she was feeling closer to me?" When Helena began stroking Duchess's face, she dropped her head so Helena could scratch between her ears.

"Something like that." Patrick paused and turned to face her. "She loves you, but she doesn't know how to show it. You have to lead the way. Look, she called you, didn't she? She didn't come to me first thing when Leeza called." He put a hand on Helena's shoulder. "All I'm saying is that, in your way, let her know that you're here for her."

Her way? What did he mean by that? But before she had a chance to ask, Frankie approached them with the cowboy boots in her hand. "I don't wear these anymore. I usually only ride English now." She set the boots down, then pulled her long hair back into a ponytail.

"Thanks." Helena struggled to get the boots on. They were tight, but she wasn't about to complain. Patrick winked at her, and she smiled back. Oh yeah, he still had that charm and, gray around the sides or not, Helena couldn't deny he was by far one of the most attractive men out there. However, good looks couldn't replace years of pain.

A few minutes later, they were ready to go. Patrick yelled after them, "Now don't be too long, say an hour. I've got some steaks to grill."

"What else is new?" Frankie mumbled.

Helena rode alongside her. She could tell her butt would be sore later on. Her horse wasn't named Duchess for her soft gaits. "Your dad still cooking only the basics?"

"Every night. He's a meat and potatoes kind of guy."

"There's another side to your dad, you know."

"Like what?" Frankie sounded indignant.

"He loves opera."

"Oh, I know. He plays that screechy stuff every night."

"He's also a big reader, especially the classics."

"I know that, too. He reads them all the time. Boring."

Helena wanted to turn this pissing contest around, make Frankie laugh some more. This wasn't supposed to be about one-upping each other. She wanted to build the trust between them. "Then let me ask you this: did you know that he loves escargot?"

"Snails?"

Helena nodded.

"Ooh, *sick*!"

They both burst out laughing. The tension dissipated as they rode along the green hills that looked as if they'd been painted from a scene out of *The Sound of Music*, set against the small beach community. A cool breeze blew up from the turquoise sea below them, while the late afternoon sun beat warmly on their faces, making them feel sleepy but good. Frankie talked about school and which teachers were weird and obnoxious and which ones were cool and how much she enjoyed her drama class. She told her mom about the friends she'd made, and how excited she was about the foals that were about to be born back at the ranch, and the one that already had arrived. They avoided topics that might cause friction, including Leeza.

Helena shared her plans regarding Shea House and what its purpose would be. "You see, the idea is to help these women get an education and get them out into the workplace so that they can begin to provide for themselves and their children. Like my friend Rachel. She's working on her G.E.D. right now, and once she's finished she'd like to go into some type of teaching. Shea House will help her to do that, while providing a home and childcare for her and her baby. Once she's on her feet in about a year, maybe a little longer, then we'll help her find housing and really help get her out into the real world."

"That's pretty cool. But can I ask you something?" Frankie said.

"Sure."

"Are you doing all of this because you feel guilty about me?"

Helena pulled up on Duchess's reins and stopped. Frankie

halted her mare, too. Helena looked out at the ocean as if searching for the right answer. Tears formed in her eyes. She brushed them away. "I guess in a way, you could say that I am. Shea House gives me a chance to be around babies and young children. I missed that with you. But it's deeper than that. These women need my help, and although I wasn't pregnant with you when I got so bad on the drugs and alcohol, I was grateful there were people willing to help me. If I can make some amends in this life by helping these girls and their children, that'll be great. But the goal is to try and provide those in need with a second chance. I got one, and I feel fortunate I did. Look at us. You've given me one." Duchess pawed at the ground. "I think she smells the hay back home."

"I'm glad I gave you one, too," Frankie replied.

By the time they got back to the ranch, Helena felt good about things. After putting their horses away, she walked up to Frankie and hugged her tight, as she'd wanted to when she'd arrived. Frankie didn't flinch. "I want you to know that I love you. Because of the past, I'm sure you wonder, but I really do. Always have. I'm going to do my best to make things right between us."

Frankie had tears in her eyes when she said, "I know, Mom."

"I'll be here for you from now on." Helena hugged Frankie again. They were so much alike, with strong exteriors masking their vulnerabilities.

As they walked to the house hand in hand, Helena vowed to protect this girl—her daughter—knowing she was lucky to get this second chance.

CHAPTER ELEVEN

WHEN THE GIRLS came into the kitchen, Patrick saw that Helena's arm was around Frankie. Obviously things were easier between them. Seeing them like that together took the cap off the pressure-cooker of guilt he'd been feeling for so long. It didn't alleviate all of it, but enough to make him feel pretty damn good.

"This place doesn't smell like any steakhouse I've ever been in," Helena said, wiping her hands on her dirt-stained jeans.

"Yeah, Dad, what gives? It smells like Pepe's down the street."

Patrick held his hands up. "You caught me. Welcome to Pat's Place, where we make the best pasta in town."

"Ooh!" Frankie said. "Dad only makes spaghetti on Christmas Eve or for really special people."

"You know, Helena, she gets that from you."

"What's that?"

"The smart-alek attitude."

Frankie smiled. Patrick couldn't recall seeing his daughter this happy in a very long time. Having Helena in the house somehow felt right. He watched her as she and Frankie set the table. She was more beautiful than ever. The hard years hadn't defeated her, but he'd always known she was strong-willed.

When they sat at the table, he stretched out his arms and took Helena's hands. Her eyes widened.

"Prayer," Frankie said.

Helena's hand gripped Patrick's hand back. He bowed his head as an electric sensation traveled throughout his body. He closed his eyes, wondering if she felt it. "Dear Lord, thank you for this lovely day, this food, and for Helena's visit. Please bless this dinner and help it to nourish our bodies. Amen." He lifted up his head. "You start, Lena." Patrick handed her the bowl of pasta. She didn't take it right away—she looked at him, her brow furrowed.

"Like *today*, Mom? We're all hungry."

Helena took the pasta bowl. "I'm sorry," she whispered.

Patrick watched her hands shake as she scooped out the spaghetti. "You okay?"

She nodded, but he could tell she was upset about something. What could it be? She didn't say much during the dinner, and Patrick racked his brain trying to figure out why she was being so quiet.

"Will you excuse me?" Helena asked. "I need to go to the restroom."

"Sure," Patrick said. Once she left, he looked over at Frankie working on a second serving. "Did something happen while you two were setting the table?"

"What? No. Why?" Frankie made a face, her mouth full of spaghetti.

"It looks like your mom's upset about something. She seemed fine when you came in, but now it's like, I don't know. Did I say something out of the ordinary?"

Frankie shrugged. "Really?" She set down her fork and leaned back in the chair. "I don't know. I'm starting to feel really good about things. She's hip. Her charity thing is way cool, and she's a killer lady. I never thought that before, but I'm changing my opinion, you know."

"Well then, I can't figure it out, everything was going so well."

"Oh, duh, I might know. It's a no brainer, Dad." Frankie smacked her forehead with her palm. "You two want to hook up again. You're totally into her, that's obvious, and she's not sure what to do. I mean, you called her Lena during dinner."

Frankie rolled her eyes, making him feel dumber than he already did, knowing she could be right. The problem probably had been his calling her Lena—his pet name for her when they'd been lovers. It had slipped out. With her here in his home, the comfort of it all made the name fall off his lips with ease. "You really think that was it?"

"God, Dad. I'm not Dr. Laura, you know, but you caused her to remember the past, and there's still feelings there. Remember when I found the letter that you wrote to her right after I was born? Asking her to forgive you?"

"Yeah, the one I never sent."

"In it, you called her Lena, and I asked you about it. Jeez Dad. Why don't you ask her out?"

"We're just friends. It wouldn't be right."

"Whatever." Frankie averted her eyes.

Helena walked back into the dining room and sat back down, smiling at them. "I'm sorry. I had something in my eye."

Frankie started to cough and laugh at the same time. Patrick glared at her.

"You okay?" Helena asked.

"Yep." Frankie stood. "I'm done. Besides, I think you two need some time alone. I'll do the dishes."

"No, that's okay. I'll help," Helena protested.

"But you hardly even touched your food," Frankie said.

"I don't know what it is, maybe the ride, but my stomach is kind of queasy." As Helena walked past Patrick with her plate in her hand, he grabbed her by the other wrist. "What are you doing?" she asked.

"I'm sorry about earlier," Patrick said.

"About what?"

She was still a bad liar. "About what I called you."

"Oh Gosh, didn't even faze me. No big deal."

"You sure?"

"Positive." She stared blankly at him.

"Maybe we do need to talk. There're some things I'd like to say." Her lack of emotion was disconcerting. Was she simply trying to hide from the feelings he was sure were still there? At least he felt them.

"Patrick, not tonight okay? I'm enjoying myself and don't want to wreck it by discussing the past."

His gut sank. "What about the future?"

"What are you talking about? All I know is that we have a daughter to raise. I'm grateful you've let me back into her life, I really am. But if you think that includes you back on a level other than friendship, you're wrong. I did that once, and look where it got us."

Her blank look turned to one of anger. He dropped her wrist. Now it was his turn to feel like crying. Patrick hadn't realized how strongly he still yearned for Helena until tonight.

He remembered the first time he'd called her Lena. They'd been in Italy that night. They'd heard *La Traviata* at La Scala. He'd held her hand loosely, as if they'd been a couple forever, completely meant for each other. It was easy being with her, unlike his high-strung wife.

Each time he looked at her, he'd tried to forget she was only seventeen. He'd never felt happier. Leeza was at home running the business and partying with the LA crowd. Patrick spent most of his time in Manhattan. Only their fourth year of marriage, but he couldn't make her happy. He'd wanted a baby, thinking that might bring them closer, but he was in love with Lena. If it hadn't been for her age...

Patrick took his plate into the kitchen, wondering if Frankie was right. Regardless of what Helena had told him, there did seem to be feelings there. He knew that he had them, and if calling her Lena had caused such a stir in her, perhaps it proved that she also had feelings for him. Could he be that lucky? Could they be a family together? He hoped secretly it was a possibility.

CHAPTER TWELVE

ON HER WAY back home, Helena dialed Tim's number on her cell-phone. She needed to talk to someone who would understand. The night had been successful in many ways. She was overjoyed that she and Frankie had made a real connection. But she'd been disturbed that Patrick still had romantic feelings for her. It was a problem she was not sure she was ready for or could handle.

Tim would hassle her. He'd told her that he thought they should get back together, loving the idea of romances rekindled and one big happy family. He picked up on the third ring. She checked her watch. It was already ten-thirty—an hour away from home yet.

"Hey, lovey," he yawned.

"Were you sleeping?"

"No, relaxing. A friend of mine just left. He had to go home to the other half, if you know what I mean."

"Uh-huh." Though Helena knew full well the pain that cheating caused, it was Tim's life, and he reveled in all its sensationalism.

"What's up, cutie pie? You sound disturbed. Did something happen at the ranch?"

"You could say that."

"Did you get into your ex's pants?"

"Nothing like that."

"Then why all the tension in your voice?"

Helena paused before replying. "He called me Lena tonight." Tim would know the significance of that. They'd had many talks about her nights with Patrick.

"No! He still loves you! What are you going to do about it?"

"I don't think that's it. A simple slip up, that's all. I mean, what am I supposed to do?"

"Tell me something, and you know I'll never reveal your secret."

"What?" She was afraid to hear the question.

"How do you feel about him? Really? What is your gut saying?"

"Tim, I have no idea. I've spent so many years trying not to feel anything about Patrick. I'm pretty mixed up."

"I can see we need another therapy session. Do you want me to meet you at your house tonight?"

"Not this late. Besides, I've still got to run the dog. I didn't have time earlier today."

"Are you sure? I don't mind. I'm worried about that nasty ex of his sending out another goon after you."

"And that's why I love you so much. You're a wonderful friend. But no, get some sleep."

"I don't suppose I need to bother harping on you about caution, because I know it won't do me any good to try and help."

"Nope. You can chat me up about it in the morning."

"I'll bring the lattes."

"You'd better."

Helena clicked off the phone with the question of the day banging in her head—how did she really feel about Patrick?

No sooner than she'd set down the phone did it ring again. Surely, it was Tim calling back to razz her some more. "I said we'd talk about it in the morning."

"Helena?" It was a woman's voice.

"Yes."

"Hi, it's me, Lindsay from The Sober Living House, and we've been trying to reach you for the last hour."

"I'm on the road. What's up? Is something wrong?"

Helena could hear it in Lindsay's voice. It crackled when she spoke next, "Yes, yes, something is. A little over an hour ago, I received a call from the UCLA burn center. Rachel was burned pretty badly in a fire this evening."

"What? Oh, my God. Where? The baby? What about the baby? Oh God. Is she okay?" Helena tried hard to stay on the road as her vision blurred, not believing what she'd heard.

"The baby was here. I was taking care of him. She told me she was going to walk over to the new place, you know your place, Shea House, and check it out. She was all excited about it."

"I know, I know. Tell me what happened?" Her heart was beating so fast it hurt.

"Apparently she got inside somehow and was looking around when the building . . . when the building . . ."

"When the building WHAT, Lindsay?!" Helena screamed into the phone, a panic rising in her like she'd never known before.

"The front part of the building, the part Rachel was in, blew. It blew up, Helena. They don't know if she'll make it." Helena could hear Lindsey crying. "They don't know if Rachel is going to live."

CHAPTER THIRTEEN

CLAIRE'S DINNER WITH Leeza was anything but dull. The broad had *flair*, you had to give her that. Claire sat across from her wondering how much hairspray it took to get that huge heap of bright red curls to stay put.

"You know, I'm not totally heartless. I don't want the kid to get hurt."

Claire held back her urge to laugh, nearly choking on her Caesar salad.

Leeza must have read her thoughts. She leaned her head to one side, doing that sultry but innocent thing she'd become famous for. "I know what you're thinking, Claire. In the past, I've been pretty vindictive."

"Nothing short of a barracuda," Claire snorted gleefully.

"It's not like they didn't deserve it, especially that bitch Helena. But no matter what, I didn't want to hurt Frances." Leeza slowly sipped her champagne, staining the rim of the glass with her shell-pink lipstick. Claire could feel heads turn in their direction. Did Leeza feel the men's lustful glances and the jealous looks from their companions? For what Leeza lacked in charm, she made up for in the full-bodied sexiness department.

It wasn't as if Claire was some slouch. She had looks too, but in a cute, petite way. The magnetic seductress across from her licked the rim of her flute. Claire shifted uncomfortably in her chair.

Leeza set the flute down and looked directly at Claire. As she leaned over the table, her cleavage left nothing to the imagination. Claire caught a whiff of expensive floral perfume Leeza must've bathed in. It nearly bowled her over, causing her to sneeze.

"Now you have no reason to believe anything I say about this, because last year, when I brought you the story, I didn't care who got hurt, not even the kid. But I've thought a lot about that little girl in the last couple of months. And I've got to tell you, I didn't come from the easiest upbringing myself. I think a little of my spunk wore off on her over the years."

Claire shook her head trying once again to stifle her laughter. Was this self-deluded woman for real? Maybe she was beginning to believe her own lies.

"Sounds crazy I know. But I've read some of the snotty cracks she's dished out to the reporters. That kid's no dummy."

"What are you saying, Leeza?"

"Can you write the story I told you without involving Frances?"

Claire finally laughed this time. "Leeza, how can I? It's all about her birth mother threatening you if you don't leave the girl alone."

"Can't you write something nasty about Helena then?"

"I probably could, but it's not worth my time. Either I print the whole sordid conversation, or I don't do it at all. Anyway, what's your deal? Patrick paid you up the yang, you've had your day in the sun, beat him, her, and the kid to a pulp mentally. Now it looks like Helena's trying to do some payback for her mistakes with this new center she's having built. Why don't you can it for a while? Enjoy life. Get over your spite. Take some of your cash and spend a week at one of those hedonist places down in the Bahamas, or some place like that. You'd love it. It's right up your alley."

"All right then." Leeza rolled her eyes.

"All right, what?"

"Don't do it. I'll drop it."

The bill came, Leeza's cue to go to the ladies room. Claire was baffled by this turn of events. She paid the bill and weighed running the story anyway.

Waiting for Leeza to return, Claire ordered a stiff drink so she could at least ask her about her *Playboy* spread, reminding herself that sex sells.

She sucked back the drink and made a final decision not to run the story about Helena. She knew that she might hate herself later for not going through with it.

"Oh God," she thought. "Am I getting a conscience? What in the hell are they putting in the water around here?" She held up the glass, studying the liquid inside, then quickly ordered another drink. God help her if she truly was gaining a sense of moral decency.

CHAPTER FOURTEEN

1974

Before . . .

RICHARD LEANED AGAINST the headboard of his bead and
reread *Ligeia*, the poem about Poe's true love. It reminded him
of Janie Keaton every time he read it. For the first year after her
death, he couldn't read "Murders on the Rue Morgue" or any
of Poe's poetry. But as the years passed, so did the feelings of
contempt for himself and for her. He'd learned not to care or feel
anything at all about it. He knew that she would still be alive if
she'd been nice to him.

What a relief it was that no one ever discovered what really
happened to Janie Keaton that late summer night four years
earlier. He'd been stupid and careless then. Now at seventeen,
he was much wiser and far more calculating. He played dumb,
but Richard knew he could pretty much play any role required
of him. Acting came easily for him. He'd been lucky that no one
ever suspected him. Of course, no one had any inkling that he
and Janie had been friends.

Richard set down the book of poetry on the nightstand beside
him and laughed aloud, thinking what people around town
believed happened to Janie. Her ignorant drunk of a father made
himself look pretty guilty when, only two months after Janie's

disappearance, neighbors found the Keatons dead. Janie's father had murdered his wife in a drunken rage, then turned the gun on himself and blew his own brains out. It was the talk of the town for quite some time.

Richard used to sit in the deli and listen to people speculate about the murder/suicide and Janie's disappearance.

"Her dad did it. Everyone knows it. Poor Janie's probably buried out in the woods somewhere. You know he was a drunk? She sure hid that one. Mrs. Stone says he was probably raping her and he was afraid she'd tell someone." The rumor grew grander with each conversation, and soon his guilt was pretty much the consensus around town. Richard got off totally free.

Richard headed out the back door to have a look at his collection. After the incident with Janie, he'd been determined to get a few things right.

As the door slammed, he heard Aunt Valerie yell after him, "Richard! Richard, where are you going? Thanksgiving's tomorrow, and I need you to get that turkey for me."

Richard didn't reply. She kept on yelling. He kept on walking. During the six years that he'd lived with his uncle and aunt, he'd learned to ignore her. Uncle James never said anything to him about it, probably because Uncle James knew how cruel she'd been to him. She took every opportunity to knock him or put his mother down. She was a real hypocrite, always touting her undying faith while heaping abuse on him and his uncle.

At first Richard couldn't understand her contempt for him, but over the years he'd begun to understand it. Aunt Valerie had such disgust for Uncle James and his fetishes that she despised anything associated with him. Richard also knew the old bitch would never leave because of her screwed-up religion. Richard, however, knew there was more to it than what her good book of faith taught her. He had a strong feeling that money was involved, and if his intuition was correct, it was quite a bit. He figured that was why Uncle James never left. Secrets, lies, and blackmail—ah, such a tangled web.

He walked deep into the woods where it looked eerily dark,

and the only sounds were the buzzing, howling, and hooting of the forest creatures. It was exactly how he liked it. He hugged his jacket tight around him. Reaching his makeshift shack, he went inside. It was a small fort built with wood and stones, but it served its purpose. He took the cold metal key from his pocket and opened the good-size locker he kept there—for his collection.

He swung open the door, and the formaldehyde passed through his nostrils heading straight to his brain. This place was good. The jars and canisters held the fruits of his labors.

On the first shelf there were mice, rats, rabbits, and all sorts of rodents. Richard had chosen them to learn on. After that, he'd advanced to killing and embalming cats and dogs. Now he'd moved up to larger game—deer and sheep. There were times when he would bring an animal here after trapping them and drain their fluids while still alive. The way the little beast struggled and bellowed was always interesting. Richard would sit and watch the life drain from them, only to fill them back up.

He'd created a smaller version of the mortuary's embalming station in his fort, with intravenous tubes and supplies that he'd stolen from his uncle. The small pump he used for the fluids wasn't as elaborate as the one at the funeral home, but it worked.

Today, he would not have time to hunt, except for the freaking turkey the bitch wanted him to get. But what fun would that be? He couldn't add it to his collection. It would be great, though, if he could. How nice to add Aunt Valerie's prize turkey, then tell her that it must've escaped.

He laughed looking at Whiskers—Aunt Valerie's cat—its eyes all bugged out, only the whites showing. Whiskers had been quite a treat. He'd screamed for mercy with his annoying howl, but hadn't gotten any. Maybe for Christmas he should tell her he'd found Whiskers and give her the gift of a lifetime. Wouldn't that be a riot! "Hey there, kitty kitty, how you doing? Love to stay and chat, but I've got a turkey to get. No more turkey for you, I guess. Huh, kitty kitty?"

He could smell the apple pie as he approached the house. At

least she could cook—Aunt Valerie's only redeeming quality.

The years had been hard on Uncle James. He'd had heart problems recently, which Richard attributed to the bitch in the kitchen. Today, she'd sent James to the market and Richard outside to catch the turkey so that she could come out and chop its ridiculous head off.

"Richard," she screamed. "Where have you been?" Richard didn't respond. "Richard! I've been waiting and waiting. I've asked you to do this for me all morning. But I should know better. You're as rotten as your uncle and that mother of yours."

Richard put his hands inside his jacket. His body shook. He was so damned tired of her beating him down. She only hated his mother because Elizabeth had been beautiful and sweet. He stared down at the ground, refusing to even acknowledge her.

"What in the world? My God, do I have to do everything?" She came storming out the front door, her fat ass trailing behind.

God, how did Uncle James stand it?

"You are so incompetent! That's what happens, I suppose, when your mother's a no-good whore and you're a bastard."

"I'm not a bastard," he said quietly, raising his eyes before lifting his head. He glared at her.

"Oh, yeah, I forgot. You're the son of the legendary Mills Florence. Richard, for God's sakes, your mother never knew Mills Florence, and she never went to Hollywood. But what can you expect from a whore? Good for spreading her legs and lying—even to her only child. You're no one's son, Richard. Nope. I'm sick of all this deceit. It's time to face reality, boy. You're nearly a man now. I'd say it's time you knew the truth, and you know what? Your daddy is the same man who's been raising you these last six years."

Richard felt as if he'd been slugged in the stomach as the meaning of what she'd said came slowly over him like a morning haze clearing off the mountains. He shook his head, trying hard to rid his brain of this thought, but once Aunt Valerie had said it, he knew that she was right. Uncle James was his father. Of course he was. It all made complete sense now.

"Thought that might get you. That's right, son, your precious mama was a whore for her own brother. No decency whatsoever, neither one of 'em. Lustful and disgusting, and you and that man you call "uncle" are lucky I obey the Word of God, for I do not forsake my husband even when sinned against. I have always been true. I will be welcome through those gates of Heaven, but you, boy, you've got dirty, sinful blood flowing through your veins. You can only go to hell. Now that you know the truth, quit standing there dumbfounded and get that turkey! We don't have all day. Your *father* will be back from the store soon."

Aunt Valerie turned to go back in the house, muttering how ungrateful Richard was. Richard's breathing became labored, his chest ached, and the burning behind his eyes was immense. His vision blurred as his heart raced. He needed to silence her.

He looked back over by the turkey's coop where the axe rested against the shed. He walked over and grabbed the handle firmly. He crept up behind her, raised the axe.

Aunt Valerie turned around, "Richard? What are you . . ."

He swung like a ball player up to bat, and connected. Aunt Valerie's head didn't come all the way off, but the blow severed the jugular vein and her head fell forward, half-on, half-off. Blood sprayed out of her neck. Richard jumped out of the way as she slumped against the doorjamb.

Richard leaned down to where it looked as if Aunt Valerie was simply taking a rest, and lifted the lolling head up, her dead eyes meeting his. "*That's* what I'm thankful for, y'old bitch," he said. "Don't have much to say now, do you?"

When Richard murdered Janie Keaton he'd felt bad, not so much because he'd killed her, but because he didn't have a friendship with her any longer. He'd had to kill her to control his destiny. No one was allowed to leave him, unless he said so.

Aunt Valerie was his second human victim, and this time he felt no remorse, none whatsoever. But he did not want to go to jail, so he'd have to act fast.

Richard went inside and pulled on some cleaning gloves, then dragged his aunt's body over to the wood-chopping stump.

He stood her up, then pushed her down hard across the stump, crushing her windpipe. The turkey made his insane gobbling noises inside his pen. If Richard were not in such a hurry, he'd go shut that fucking thing up, too. No time. Besides, the damn bird was part of the master plan, here.

Richard located a rock large enough to trip someone chasing a turkey around the yard. Richard let the turkey out of the coop. He wiped down the axe, then placed her hand on it so her fingerprints were the only ones on it. He put the axe down on the stump, as if she'd laid it there while trying to trap the turkey and then tripped, the blade sticking up and catching her just so across the throat.

He covered his tracks where he'd dragged his aunt's body across the ground, and then surveyed the scene. It looked good. It appeared as if the turkey had escaped and Aunt Valerie had set down the axe in haste, and while chasing the turkey she'd tripped on a rock next to the stump and fallen onto the axe, nearly decapitating herself.

Richard clapped, pleased with what he'd accomplished. "I'm brilliant. Whoopee, I am brilliant! I am fucking brilliant!"

He went back inside, picked up the apple pie, which was still warm, and sliced a piece. After eating the tasty treat, he turned on the television and propped his feet up on her sofa. He took a nap. Creature comforts, how liberating!

Uncle James's screaming shattered the silence. He ran inside looking like a crazed man as Richard rubbed his eyes, and stretched.

"What happened? What have you done?" James yelled.

"What are you talking about?" Richard yawned.

"Your aunt! What did you do to her?"

"I didn't do anything." Richard walked out the door pretending to know nothing. "Oh shit! What in the . . ."

"You didn't know?" Uncle James turned away from Aunt Valerie.

Richard could see his uncle's whole body shaking, as he leaned against the wall. He thought James would've been happy to be rid of her. "God no. Of course not!" Richard shook his head vehemently. "Aunt Valerie told me to go catch the turkey, but the darn thing kept getting away. So she got mad as usual, and said she'd do it herself. I came in and turned on the TV. I must've fallen asleep. I kinda had a headache."

"You didn't hear anything? Not the turkey, no screaming?" Uncle James pointed his finger toward the yard.

"No, sir. Nothing."

Uncle James—the man Richard now knew was his father—stared at him hard, as if studying him for the first time. Richard did not recognize this look, and his palms became clammy, as he cocked his head from side to side, popping his neck.

"Do you know what this looks like, Richard?" Tears welled in his father's eyes.

Richard was confused and started pacing the floor. "It looks like she tripped and fell on the axe. If that's what you're asking me."

James walked inside and collapsed on the sofa, his face in his hands. He shook his head and rubbed his temples for a few minutes as tears streamed down his face. When he looked up with reddened eyes, he said, "I can't believe you would do this. I know she was awful to you, but she took you in, and what you've done is damned horrible. I don't think I know you, son. You killed my wife!" he yelled.

"What the hell are you saying?" Richard continued to pace, throwing his arms up in the air, as his anger consumed him, making anything possible. Anger was power. And at this moment, the anger fueling him was coming from his very own flesh-and-blood father.

"Don't act stupid. I've loved you. I cared for you. I've done everything for you that I could, but I know there are things you hide—terrible things. I know about your animals, and God, I wanted to talk to you and ask you why, and try to help you. I hoped that you'd stop it all—but this! This is madness—you've killed your aunt!"

Richard knew that he couldn't continue to lie. His father had it figured out, and if he did, so would the police. So he formulated a plan. "For good reason," Richard said. "If I were you," he shook his finger at him, "I'd be thanking me."

"Oh, Richard, no!"

James sobbed and Richard watched him like a baffled child. He didn't like seeing his father crying with such agony, but at the same time he was angry and shocked, too. The room was still except for his father's sobs. The apple pie on the counter suddenly smelled sweetly putrid to Richard, turning his stomach sour.

James's next words chilled Richard. "I know you were the reason that little girl went missing a few years ago."

Richard glanced at him. His body went cold. He wanted to cry. The sourness in his stomach worsened and hurt so bad he thought he might puke.

"I also know what you did with her. I found ashes in the oven the night after she'd gone missing, and I knew we hadn't used the oven for some time—and I knew you'd cleaned it when we had. I watched you do it. Remember? You said that you hadn't, that you'd forgotten, but I knew that was a lie. I also found the bag of beer and her sweater in the dumpster out back. But I didn't tell. I figured you had a lot to work out about your own mother's murder. We all got secrets, Richard—and I kept yours, because I love you.

"Then with the animals, when I discovered what was going on with that, I let *it* go too. But this has gotten out of hand. You need help, son—you really do. This is much more than about your mother. You're sick. And I don't know what to do anymore." James took out a handkerchief from his jeans pocket and wiped his face.

Richard could not believe what he was hearing. This man whom he loved and trusted wasn't going to help him. "No. Please, you've got to cover for me, *please*. I can't go to jail. I didn't mean to do it. I'm sorry. I'm really sorry. It's just that I got so mad, and she was talking trash about my mother again. And you don't understand about what happened with Janie. She was my friend and she betrayed me. You wouldn't understand.

I won't hurt no one else, I promise." The desperation in his voice made him sick, but Richard was playing this one for the Academy Award. He refused to be locked away to rot in some prison cell. James owed him for his own lies and transgressions.

James sighed, then leaned back against the sofa and stared at the ceiling. "What can I do?"

"You promised to take care of me. Do it for my mother."

"You've got to leave, then. That's all I can say, and I don't want to know where you go. I never want to know! Do you hear me? Go away, far away. I can't be responsible for you anymore. I can't take it if you kill someone else. But I do love you, and couldn't bear to have you in jail, or worse yet, if the state killed you for these crimes. So go." The old man started to cry again.

His tears infuriated Richard even further—having to leave was ridiculous. "It's not like you loved the old bag. All she ever did was nag you. You know, for a while there I was too young to figure out *your* dirty little secret—the secret she had on you. But when I got a little older, it wasn't too difficult. I can't say that I blame you with some of the corpses that came in, *Dad*." The power was once again Richard's. That one little word infused him with more power than he'd ever known. He had his father right where he wanted him. He watched closely as James's entire body language changed.

James's head snapped back into place. "What are you talking about?" His red eyes turned into tiny slits.

"I now know why you kept her around. First, dear Uncle, is that you're my father. Secret is out. The bitch told me the whole sordid truth, before I . . ." Richard made a gesture with his finger sliding across his throat while making a gurgling sound. James tried to protest, but Richard wouldn't let him speak—not while he had the spotlight.

"Yes, Daddy, and old Aunt Valerie also knew that you were screwing the corpses. I can understand why you'd want to keep your fetish a secret. Hell, I can understand why you wanted to keep me a secret. You're a pretty sick old buzzard, aren't you? Like father, like son. Don't fall far from the tree and all that jazz, right? So maybe I should be telling you how it's going to go. If I wanted to stay, and you made a fuss, it could get kinda ugly. Know what I mean?"

"Richard, I . . ."

He could see his father sweating and raised his hand in protest. "No need to explain. Your necrophilia thing never stopped me from loving you. Actually, I understand. I really do. But I'm not too happy about this whole *daddy* thing. It's a pretty sickening thing you two were up to—I sure don't want to think you raped her. Since you are my daddy, though, I'll try to be real understanding. But the understanding has to go both ways. Of all people, I thought you would support me. I kill this woman who has been awful from the word go, and you want me to leave? You can't take the pressure? Man, who can? I'm shocked, to say the least."

Richard rubbed his forehead. He was sweating. But he was in control, and he knew it. He would feel his father's abandonment later, but now he needed to be cold. It was easy—like turning off a TV, he could turn off his feelings. He pushed down the hurt to the same place he'd put all the feelings about his mother so long ago. He ignored his nerves and the pounding in his chest. Why did everyone he ever loved wind up betraying him? What was real emotion anyway? Maybe his had died along with his mother.

"Be thankful," he told his father, "that I've loved you so much that I could never do what you're going to do to me—and don't worry, I could never kill you. But you will have to suffer for this."

James said nothing. Richard could see the fear on his face, could even smell it coming off him—quite a stench, nasty really. He sighed.

Richard paced the floorboards, which creaked beneath his feet. "I'll go. And since you won't have Miss Tightwad looking over your shoulder, you'll set up a bank account for me with unlimited funds. I know you have it, Dad."

His mind was buzzing. He couldn't see the room clearly; everything felt so out of place. He would never have imagined that he and this man would have ever come to this. They had always gotten along so well, agreed on nearly everything, loved each other.

James nodded slowly. "Whatever you want. Whatever you want." He held up his hands as if giving up. The look on his face was a mixture of confusion, contempt, sympathy, even love.

Richard knew that his father still loved him, maybe he felt ashamed that he did. In his father's eyes, he must be a mixed up monster that he felt sorry for. It was the other way around, as far as Richard was concerned.

"I hate doing this to you. I didn't figure it would happen like this. I never meant to upset you, but there was no other way. If you could only understand."

James nodded, bowing his head. He never looked back up at Richard.

"Well, since this is only business between us now, I need you to make me your sole heir when you die." James continued to nod. "Good. Better call the police—they've got a mess to clean up."

James did everything that Richard told him to do. It was in Richard's favor that James was highly regarded in their community, and the police believed his every word without much investigation. For once, Richard was glad this was a small town, with a small town police force, with an even smaller mentality— murder never crossed their minds.

Richard left on the bus that evening. James concocted a story that Richard was already up north visiting friends for the Thanksgiving holiday and had decided to get an apartment up there and wait tables until he started college the next fall. Richard wanted to get out quickly before the cops changed their minds; he knew his father wouldn't change his. As awful as he felt about what he'd done to his daddy, he'd had no choice. Life must go on. Hell, Richard had no doubt that life was just beginning.

CHAPTER FIFTEEN

TYLER LIT A fire in the fireplace and poured himself his third cup of coffee. He grabbed the large dossier of files he'd brought home, and then collapsed into his leather recliner. Stirring the sugar in his coffee, he stared at his pile of work.

Those files contained the proof that pure evil existed. Although he was agitated, he was compelled to read through them. Analyzing the criminal mind was his nature, his job, his life.

On the drive home he'd been jittery, thinking that maybe in tonight's chamber of horrors he might find something to help him make some sense of his Jane Doe case.

He leaned back in the recliner and flipped open the file: Elaine Myers. She'd also been a Jane Doe case for quite some time, and the killer had never been found. Also, this new Jane Doe had been found close to where Elaine Myers's body had been discovered. His intuition told him that Jane Doe was not his UNSUB'S, otherwise called the unknown subject's, only victim. There'd been others; maybe Elaine Myers was even one of them.

Tyler read the file on Elaine Myers, carefully studying the photos taken at the dumpsite. The deep feeling in his gut told him that the killer had not returned here to the original grave. Many serial killers would, as if to pay homage to their victims or relive the experience. Tyler didn't receive a vibe that his UNSUB necessarily wanted to relive the fantasy of the killing. There was something more to it than that for him. This guy had buried Elaine just like Jane Doe, which meant it was a personal thing with him. He didn't need to visit the grave or leave the body in the open to get himself off. If Tyler was right, then the perp probably kept a souvenir, maybe jewelry or a wallet, or maybe even panties.

He concentrated on the photographs of Elaine's skeletal remains, then the pictures the forensic art team developed as the woman's identity began to emerge through their skilled work. Once CSI had come up with a good impression, they searched the missing persons' banks where Elaine's identity was finally matched.

Elaine Myers was twenty when she was abducted in 1994 from a rural area outside of Los Angeles. She'd been pulling into her driveway when the perp made his move. When her boyfriend arrived later, he found the car in front of the mailbox with the door open, motor running. The police had targeted him at first, but not for long. He'd had a concrete alibi.

Tyler read and reread the report. *This guy sees these women and wants them, but why? What is their commonality? There has to be a particular characteristic that he targets.* "It's more than sexual, if that even equates into it at all," Tyler said aloud. No way of telling if Elaine had been sexually assaulted, as her remains were mere bones. The same was true with Jane Doe.

Tyler finished his coffee. He knew he should get up and make himself something to eat. He patted his stomach, feeling his ribs. Nothing tasted good anymore. Susan had been a wonderful cook. Now, he ate simply to survive. His mainstay was usually macaroni and cheese or a can of soup, if he didn't go out or order in.

Samuel Paul Nelson, Susan's killer, had ruined his life. This Jane Doe and the related cases were personal because of what they meant to him—reminders of Susan and her murder. Unlike Nelson, who left his victims in the open, this killer appeared to go to great lengths to find burial ground. This spoke volumes to Tyler. The killer was to some degree ashamed of what he was doing. That's why he hid their bodies. It also meant he could probably blend fairly well into society, because he did have some type of conscience, even if it was rather tiny. Elaine had been found wrapped up in a blanket and buried. This guy had a need to depersonalize the women. But Tyler believed that before he went through the ritual of depersonalization, he owned them in some way; he wasn't convinced that it was entirely sexual.

Tyler looked at his aquarium. He didn't have a television—too much noise. Instead, his large, fascinating fish bowl was his one source of solace. He watched the blowfish puff itself out and the pretty coral fish dance around each other.

He stood up, shaking his finger at the aquarium. "I don't think these girls were the beginning. I think there are more. And when we find out who Jane Doe is, I think it'll be like Elaine Myers. This girl has been missing for a long time. But he's doing something different. I know it. His fantasy game is escalating—has escalated. He's killed since he was a kid and will keep on killing until he's stopped. Mark my words." The blowfish deflated.

This wasn't voodoo, nor was it a psychic process, although Tyler knew that many would say that it was. They called him "Voodoo Man" under their breaths at the agency. He'd heard defense attorneys use that exact term when trying to get their sicko clients off. But when it came down to it, they all knew and respected Tyler for the profiling he did.

He stretched out his palms as if weighing something. Was this personal for the killer or not? *He's gone from one extreme to the other, developing a persona, building on his fantasy, his scheme. Personal or not? Tell you what, man, as far as I'm concerned, it's personal.*

He watched the fish for a while longer. He was missing something here. What was it? He sprinkled fish food into the tank, fascinated as they swam to the top, fighting over the food like gluttons.

Gluttony. A vision of a velvet sofa, candles lit around it, poetry from somewhere, read out loud to someone. The listener afraid— female. She is blonde, tears flow down her face, smearing makeup. Champagne glasses sparkle in firelight. A flash in front of Tyler's eyes and the vision—gone.

"He likes the finer things in life," Tyler said out loud. "Bastard thinks he's royalty, special somehow. Well, my friend, your term on the throne is about to end."

Tyler sat back down in his chair, finished his coffee, and started to re-read his files, determined to uncover the missing link.

CHAPTER SIXTEEN

HELENA DROVE STRAIGHT to the UCLA Medical Burn Center where Rachel had been taken by a life flight helicopter. Pressing buttons to take the elevator up, her mind and heart raced as the words Lindsay had spoken to her played over again in her mind, "Rachel burned. Shea House blown up." None of it made any sense. The palms of her hands were sweaty. She was nauseated almost to the point of vomiting, but knew she had to keep everything in check. Her needs were of the least importance right now.

The doors to the elevator opened. She stepped out. Blurred images in white flitted past her. Perspiration formed at the top of her forehead. She sneezed from the smells of rubbing alcohol and other sterilizing agents.

"Can I help you, Miss?" asked a male nurse. He was bald, in shape like a body builder, and his hazel eyes met her with scrutiny through wire-rimmed glasses.

"Yes, I hope so. I'm here to see Rachel Winters. I was told she was brought in here."

"Yes, she's here. However, only family is allowed to visit her." The nurse squinted through the glasses. "You aren't family, are you," he stated more than asked.

"Technically I'm not." She shifted her weight from one foot to the other. "I understand your policy, but you see, she doesn't have any family, not really anyway. She has a son, a baby boy.

But I am like family to her, as she is to me." Helena realized how
dumb she sounded. It was difficult to get any words out. Her
hands shook as she shoved them into her jeans pockets. "I'm
Helena Shea."

"Oh, ho, ho, excuse me," the nurse said. "Sure, sure. I
recognize you now. But celebrity status won't do much for you
here. Sorry."

"That is certainly not my intention. Rachel is my friend. I care
a lot about her and her child. We've spent a lot of time together.
Please, please let me see her."

Hearing the desperation or perhaps the sincerity in her voice,
the nurse relented and, changing his attitude somewhat, said,
"Hang on, and let me see what I can do."

He walked back down the corridor towards the nurses' station.
A few minutes later he came back nodding his head. "Okay, but
only for a few minutes. I'm afraid that you'll only be allowed
into an observation area. If she's awake at all, she'll be able to
hear you. We can't take a chance of any type of contamination.
Infection is what we're worried about now."

Helena choked back her tears. "Thank you. Can you tell me
how bad she is, please?"

He lowered his voice. "She's pretty lucky. When they brought
her in, she went into cardiac arrest, but the folks downstairs in
E.R. were able to resuscitate. Her burns cover the lower half of
her body. Right now, it's hard to say. Every second counts. Like
I said, the main thing is to keep her from getting any kind of
infection."

"I understand."

"Follow me."

The nurse led her behind two swinging double doors. He had
her scrub, put on a gown, gloves and mask. He then took her
through another door where she was able to stand behind a plate
of Plexiglas. Fluorescent lights beat down on her. She could see
Rachel through the glass. The young woman looked even tinier
than she normally did. Bandages covered her burns, her lower
half wrapped like a mummy. Intravenous lines were hooked into

several veins.

"Oh, sweet girl," Helena gasped. The tears she'd fought back now readily trickled down her face. She didn't bother to wipe them away.

Rachel turned her face towards the glass. A severe look of pain shone in her eyes as a tear fell from her face. She appeared much older than her eighteen years. Helena placed a hand on the glass. Rachel mouthed the word, "baby."

"He's okay. He's good. Lindsay has him. I'm going over after I leave here. He'll be fine, but you have to hurry up and get well." Rachel closed her eyes. "I'm so sorry. I am so sorry this happened to you. I wish there was something I could do to change it."

Rachel opened her eyes again, looked at Helena. They caught each other's gaze for a long time. It pained Helena to see her that way. She wanted to scream, cry out. There was no explanation for any of this.

"Lots of prayers okay, Angel?" Rachel said in a barely audible voice coming over the speaker piped into the room.

"You got it, my friend. All the prayers in the world. And don't forget, you're my angel and so is little Jeremy. You're gonna be fine, just fine."

The nurse tapped Helena on the shoulder. "It's time to go. She really needs to get some rest."

As they walked out Helena asked, "Can you tell me anything else about her condition?"

"Each twenty-four hour period she makes it through without contracting any type of infection will raise her odds significantly."

"Okay." Helena left the hospital and drove straight to The Sober Living House. Walking in, she quickly noticed the silence and the absence of the usual buzz of activity. The atmosphere was somber. No one was in the game or TV room. Helena went to Lindsay's office and tapped lightly on the door. A man with a slight paunch around the waist, wearing a tweed jacket, and smelling faintly of cheap men's cologne opened the door.

"Hello," Helena said.

"Helena Shea?"

"Yes," she replied cautiously, sensing something wrong, knowing it was odd for a strange man to be at The Sober Living House at a little past eleven at night.

"I'm Detective David Collier."

"He's here about Rachel," Lindsay said, her arms crossed in front of her long denim dress. Helena knew how much Lindsay disliked the police, a prejudice held over from her peace and love-in days during the 60s in Haight-Ashbury. She still wore the trademark braid; once strawberry blond, it now snaked down her back in a silver streak.

"I just came from seeing her, actually."

"How is she?" Lindsay asked.

"She's hanging on."

"Ladies, I'm sorry about your friend, but I'm here looking into why the fire happened." He pulled out a small notepad and pen.

"That's a good question. I'd like an answer myself," Helena said, having wary feelings about the cop. It was her motto not to judge too quickly, because she knew how it felt to be on the other side. However, Detective Collier was not what she would consider gracious or tactful.

"Yeah, uh, huh. Ms. Shea, were you aware of any gas leaks in the center?"

"Are you kidding? We haven't even opened. We've had workers in and out of there for months. We've passed several inspections. We were just getting ready for a final inspection."

"Do you have insurance on the center, yet?" The detective jotted something in his notebook.

"Of course I do. To obtain permits to even build a place like Shea House, I had to present proof of insurance up front."

"Do you know how much the policy is worth?"

"I have the paperwork at home. But I can tell you that there are quite a few different types of coverage I had to get." She really didn't like the way the detective was looking at her, like a hawk waiting to swoop down on its prey. "I was opening a center for women and babies, and for pregnant women. You can bet I've had to purchase a great deal of insurance. Not to mention, these women are recovering alcoholics and drug addicts."

"What about your personal finances, Ms. Shea? Have you put a lot of your own money into Shea House?"

The nauseating discomfort she'd felt earlier from her grief turned into a pit of anger as if she'd been socked in the gut.

"What's with this line of questioning?" Lindsay interrupted. During the eighties, Lindsay had decided to give up the Birkenstocks but keep the braid and get a BMW, a house in the burbs, and a law degree. But she'd lost it all after investing everything she had into one case defending an embezzler who she'd fallen in love with. She'd successfully gotten him acquitted, following which he repaid all of her hard work and affection by cheating her out of every penny she had. She turned to drinking to ease the hurt and anger, eventually made her way into recovery, and then began counseling other women who'd been down the same dark tunnel. Helena watched her turn from therapist into attorney mode, glad to have her on her side.

"There's reason to believe that the explosion tonight was caused by a pilot light hooked up to the stove. No one lit the stove, but the gas was on, and the arson team says they found a pack of matches lying only a few feet away. Looks like this fire was deliberate, ladies. Someone wanted to see Shea House come down in flames. We may even be looking at a homicide here, if your friend doesn't recover from the serious burns she's suffered."

Helena's dislike for this pompous ass deepened as his insinuations sunk in. But she was not afraid of him and replied looking him straight in the eye, "Yes, I have put quite a bit of my own funds into constructing Shea House."

"Like how much, say a hundred thousand or so?" he asked.

"You know you don't have to answer his questions," Lindsay said.

"I have nothing to hide. I can tell you right now I had nothing to do with blowing up my own recovery center, and I love Rachel Winters like my own daughter. To see her in so much pain and not knowing if she's going to make it just about killed me tonight. So, if you want to know how much I've put into my center, try close to a million dollars. Charitable funds have covered the rest."

The detective let out a low whistle. "Pretty penny, especially if your modeling agency isn't doing so well."

"My agency is doing just fine."

"That's good to hear. It's also good to hear how much you love Miss Winters. Like your daughter, you said?" The Detective arched his eyebrows, glaring at Helena.

"That's right."

"And, we all know how much that is." A sardonic smile spread across his face.

Helena's body shook, her balled up fists at her side.

Lindsay interrupted, "Detective Collier, I'm going to have to ask you to leave now."

"No problem. I'll be in touch." He closed the door behind him, leaving his Irish Spring scent wafting in the air behind him.

Helena slumped down in a chair across from Lindsay's desk. Lindsay placed her hands on her shoulders. "Oh, my God. I could never do what he's suggesting."

"I know. We all know that. He's a real ass, typical tough cop bullshit. Forget about him."

"I'll try." She shook her head. "Jeez, Lindsay, seeing Rachel like that was awful. She's in so much agony, and I can't help but feel it's my fault," Helena cried.

"It's not, hon. You have to know that it's not."

"What about the baby?"

"He's asleep. By law I've had to contact social services."

"Are they going to take him?" Helena closed her eyes, praying that wouldn't happen.

"I suggested that I take on temporary guardianship until we see what's going to happen. That way he'll be around people he knows and in a place he's already beginning to feel comfortable in. He's had so many changes in his short life. The last thing he needs is another disruption."

"What did they say?"

"They didn't give me a definite go, but let's face it, not a lot of foster parents out there want to take on crack babies, and an African-American baby at that. As ugly as that sounds, we still live in a fairly close-minded society, my friend. They're sending someone out tomorrow to interview and survey the premises. I doubt they'll take him. They know I run a good operation here."

Helena nodded, rubbed her eyes. "None of this makes any sense. Who would want to destroy my place? Why?"

"Who knows? Maybe the cop is wrong. It's possible one of the construction guys screwed up."

"What about the matches he said they'd found?"

"Lots of construction guys smoke. There's an explanation, Helena. There always is. You need to trust that."

"I can't believe it. It's gone."

"It can be rebuilt."

"I know, but I already had women waiting to get in. Where will they go? And what about Rachel? What if she doesn't survive?" Helena buried her face in her hands.

"She will. She's bullheaded. You know that. She'll make it through this."

A baby's crying from the other room brought a smile to Lindsay's face. "There's Jeremy. Time for a bottle. You want to say hi?"

Helena shook her head. "Not tonight. I don't think I can take much more. I feel horrible that his mother can't be here with him. It's probably better right now if I go home, see my dog, and get in bed."

"I understand."

She hugged Lindsay, then left. She was sure this night was the longest one in history. Who would've ever known at the beginning of the evening, being with Frankie with everything so wonderful between them, that it would end this way?

Helena walked to her car, got in and started to drive home, but first she headed towards Shea House. Passing it, she saw a couple of fire trucks still outside and an unmarked car. While she was stopped at the corner ready to turn into the parking lot, she saw Detective Collier. She stepped on the gas. Everything about his demeanor and ugly questioning made her want to stay far away from him. It was like he actually had it in for her. She started to dismiss this kind of thinking as pure paranoia, but when she remembered the way he'd spoken to her and glared at her, maybe she wasn't paranoid. She knew that Lindsay saw it too. In his mind, he'd already convicted her of torching her own place and trying to murder a friend. Helena had seen the certainty in his eyes.

She quickly drove past where Shea House once stood, its doors ready to be opened to receive those in need. What remained was nothing like the white clapboard building reminiscent of the Victorian era. A lovely swing had graced the front porch—now gone. Arched windows, their sills filled with planters of colorful flowers meant to enhance the place—now all gone. Some of the framework still stood, but everything else had been burned to the ground. Once again, the question *why?* rose in her mind. She had no answers.

CHAPTER SEVENTEEN

1995

Before . . .

RICHARD LIVED IN the Fairfax district so he could get as close to Beverly Hills as possible without going over his budget. The nineties, so far, had been decent to him. Dear old Daddy James had made good on his promise to supply him a meal ticket for several years. When the old fucker died of a heart attack while enjoying his favorite pastime, Richard became a very rich man. What a sight for the good ole officers back home: Their favorite mortician sticking it to the corpse and then croaking right on top of her. Beautiful. Might even make good porn. Maybe a bit too scandalous for the general public, though.

Scandal was not something Richard craved. He'd chosen not to return for the funeral. He'd hired an attorney to sell the farm and make sure he received all of his monies. To be on the safe side, he'd done all the legal transactions from an apartment he'd rented in Utah. Richard didn't want anyone to know his exact location, and he always used aliases. One had to be cautious in his line of work.

After murdering his aunt, it had taken him awhile to muster up his courage to do it again, but he had to, needed to. It was in him now, like a wolf that has had its first taste of blood. That taste—

so delectable—would never go away. He'd tried to rid himself of it, knowing that it wasn't in his best interest as far as society went to go around killing.

But it was his mother, really, who'd called to him from the grave to do these dark but necessary deeds. She wanted him to find a good girl, a beautiful, sweet, and kind young lady—one worthy of him. One like Herself, and he had tried. Oh, God, how he had tried. Yet each woman he met had been nothing but a bitter disappointment. None of them were even close to worthy. He'd meet them, court them, and then they'd turn on him, scorn him, ridicule him. Ugly whores, they'd all turned out to be, filled with hatred like that bitch aunt he'd done away with. So, he simply obeyed his mother's wishes and did what she'd demanded of him—killed them. However, parting with them was another matter entirely. He knew Mommy didn't like it, but there were some things he just wasn't willing to give up.

He'd attended cosmetology school to further learn the art of makeup application and was currently working in the entertainment industry. He loved women's lips, and Bridgett Core had beautiful ones, absolutely lovely. She was nineteen, and they'd met on a film set only a week before.

"My friend Patty says you do great makeup," said the platinum blonde, blue-eyed, perfectly proportioned girl. She definitely had that Pamela Anderson thing going on.

"Really?" Richard liked her looks and the compliment. Maybe Bridgett was the one. When he met the right girl, he knew his bad desires would die. Mommy told him so.

"Well, I'm kinda new, starting out in the biz, and I need a portfolio. Do you think I could convince you to do my makeup?" She tilted her head, hand on one hip, and with those pouty lips, it all got to him.

Richard glanced over at the three other young women seated at a table drinking cheap champagne and swallowing different colored pills—probably ecstasy. They were waiting to film "Lesbo Love," wearing nothing but their thong panties. Richard had gotten the gig doing makeup for porn stars from an ad on the bulletin board at the beauty school. It didn't pay well, but the money wasn't what he cared about.

Being with women sexually proved difficult for him, but watching sex acts in person enabled him to go home and satisfy himself with fantasies from the day's filming. If he could find someone like his mother, he was certain he could overcome his problems.

"Okay. When did you want to do this?" he asked, noticing the large areolae around her pointy nipples.

"I've got a photographer lined up for next Tuesday. He's supposed to be super good. Do you think you could do it? I couldn't pay much. I'll get a little money from this gig, but you know how money goes."

"That's okay." Richard felt perspiration trickling down the back of his neck. He hoped she wouldn't notice how nervous he was. Man, she was gorgeous. Maybe she was the one who could save him. Maybe Mommy would like her. In many ways they were exactly alike—Bridgett and Mom.

"Hey, I was thinking that we could do a practice run this weekend, you know, try different colors. See what we like?" She winked at him.

Was she coming on to him? "That would be good."

"Say Saturday night? Why don't you come to my place?"

"Sure. I think I can manage that." He couldn't believe it.

She jotted her number and address on a piece of paper and handed it to him. "I'm looking forward to it, Rich."

"Me too." With this crowd, he thought, "Rich" sounded cooler than Richard. He'd had a thing about names ever since Aunt Bitch had made a point of calling him Ricky like some goddamned TV sitcom Mexican dude. He certainly didn't love Lucy.

Saturday couldn't come soon enough. He'd been thoroughly aroused several times thinking of Bridgett. Maybe he'd be able to overcome this time. On Friday night, he couldn't wait, thinking maybe they could get together a day earlier. He was sure that Mommy would like this one, so he decided to drive by her place. If she was there, he'd say he was in the area and thought tonight might work out if she wasn't busy.

As he passed by her apartment building, he saw her walking to a nearby car with another man, a *Baywatch* looking kind of guy. He watched as the Hasselhoff character grabbed Bridgett by the crotch. She laughed. Something twisted inside Richard. He looked away. He was sure she'd been coming on to him the other day. *Is this how she is with all men?* He knew it should come as no surprise. She was, after all, a porn princess. But he'd fantasized all week that maybe she really did like him and that her nasty job wasn't what she was truly all about. Maybe it was all just a means to an end for her, being as young as she was. Richard had decided she probably didn't enjoy what she did at all. But now, watching her with this guy, he could see she *liked* being a whore.

Richard couldn't take it. He squeezed the steering wheel of his silver bullet Porsche, pressed hard on the gas, and sped away. Bridgett was another manipulative bitch, just like his aunt; but Bridgett was worse because she was beautiful, knew it, and used it. Tomorrow night he would set the score straight. Bridgett would get exactly what she deserved for her betrayal, for all the betrayals he'd ever suffered. He knew Mommy would approve of that.

****

He arrived at Bridgett's apartment Saturday night by seven as they'd agreed.

She opened the door. "Hey, hi! Come on in."

Richard looked her up and down. She wore leather hot pants and a white crop top, emphasizing her huge breast implants.

"Want something to drink?"

"Gin and tonic, please." He looked around her small place, plastered with posters of her favorite models, Van Halen, Led Zeppelin, and the two movies she'd "acted" in. He sat on what looked like a thrift store sofa.

"Here you go. It's not Bombay or anything. Like I said, I have a hard time making the cash thing work. Hope it tastes okay."

She sat next to him. On the coffee table were a few lines of cocaine she'd already prepared. She leaned over and snorted up. "Want some?" She wiped her nose with the back of her hand.

"No thanks." Richard said, repulsed. He'd seen plenty of drugs smoked, swallowed, and even injected in his day, but refused to take part in any of it. He liked his drink. A few gin and tonics a night and he felt perfect. He also liked an occasional glass of champagne on special nights. On this particular night, he'd bought a bottle of Dom Perignon.

"I know it's kind of shitty to do. But I'm always so tired, and a little pick-me-up never hurt."

"Right." Richard was careful to remember everything he touched, so he could wipe off his fingerprints.

"Wow, hey I just noticed." She perked up. "I'm like such a dope. It looks so good—your hair, I mean. Like totally good. You look like that Brandon guy on *90210*, you know. What's his name? Not Luke Perry, but the other dude." Richard shrugged. "Anyway, I never pictured you with dark hair. Cool."

"Thanks. I kind of did it on a whim, I guess." It had been part of his plan. If anyone saw them together, they would remember him with dark hair rather than his normal dirty blonde, which he would return to by the next morning. He'd even driven the van tonight. He only brought it out for these occasions; otherwise, it stayed inside his cabin's garage.

"Like I said, it's totally cool. That's great that you're so free like that. So many guys would think that dyeing your hair was like gay or something."

"I'm not gay," Richard said. His head pounded from her incessant chatter. Blah, blah, blah. Now that he'd witnessed her tramping around, she was no longer his vision of beauty. Her lips were still nice. He stared at them.

"No, I never thought you were. But some of the others, you know, at work. 'Cause like you're in your thirties and not married and stuff." She paused, taking a sip from the Chablis she'd poured for herself. "They're just stupid."

Richard nodded. "Did you tell anyone that I was coming by tonight?"

Bridgett sheepishly shook her head, "No, I'm sorry. I know that probably would've stopped any rumors about you—I mean you with me for a night—but, Rich, I hate to say it but some of them think you're kinda . . ."

"Strange?"

She looked away. "Not me. I kinda like it that you're different. I think you're totally cool, like I said. And your makeup jobs are so awesome. You do such a kick ass job on some of those chicks. I know how skanky some of 'em look, but when you're done with them, wow! But I didn't tell anyone my plans tonight. Too strange, I guess—me and the makeup guy they all think is a fag," she laughed. "Oops, sorry, didn't mean it. That's some strong stuff," she said, pointing to the line of powder left on the table. "Sure you don't want some?"

"Totally," he mocked. He was pleased at how much easier it would all be since she hadn't told anyone. He was also thinking of all his tubes of lipstick that he'd collected over the years for evenings like this. He would choose the perfect color for the perfect moment. A pearly gloss came to mind, painted on a woman who should've portrayed an innocent, not a tart.

"I didn't mean to offend you. I apologize if I did."

"No, you didn't." He downed the gin, burning the back of his throat as it sailed to the pit of his stomach. He had to get her out of the apartment. He couldn't accomplish what he needed to here. It was time for him to turn on the charm. "You didn't offend me at all. You sure look beautiful tonight. Did I tell you that?"

"No." She blushed. "You're sweet."

"Listen, I was thinking about the makeup, and you know, before we do that, why don't I take you out? Some place nice?"

"Really?"

Unlike the other day when his nerves were a mess, he had transitioned into a secure zone where nothing could touch him and certainly never conquer him. It was Richard's world, a good place to be.

"Get your coat."

"Should I change?"

"You look great. In fact, you look perfect."

As they got into the van, Richard said. "Oh, damn. I left my jacket up there."

"No problem. I'll get it."

"That wouldn't be very gentlemanly of me. You stay right here. Give me the key, and I'll be right back. Why don't you look through the cassettes in the case there, see if there's something you like. I'll only be a sec."

"Sure, okay." She nodded and handed him her key.

Richard ran back up to the apartment, took out a cloth from his coat, and wiped anything and everything he'd touched. Once done, he locked the place back up and wiped the handle of the front door clean. He ran back down.

"Sorry it took me so long. I called the restaurant to make sure we could get in."

"No problem. I put in your Pearl Jam tape. They're pretty cool. So where are we going?"

"Oh, a little place I know up the coast."

"Super."

They drove up the Pacific Coast Highway. Richard's head pounded as he tried to ignore Bridgett's singing along with Eddie Vedder. He had to think, needed some peace. He felt the hypodermic inside his pocket. He would wait until the next light and do it quickly. They came around the bend passing Pepperdine University. The light turned yellow. Richard slowed down. His heart raced, sweat formed on his brow. He squeezed the needle, and carefully removed the cap. Bridgett was looking up at the college.

"It's sure pretty. I wish I could've gone to school." She continued to stare out the window. The light turned red.

He stuck the needle in her arm and squeezed the tranquilizer into her.

She squealed. "What the . . ."

Richard floored the accelerator, timing the light, knowing that she might try to escape when she realized what he'd done. The drug would take a few minutes to work.

"What was that, Rich? What are you doing? Why are you driving so fast? That hurt. Why did you hurt me? I don't like needles. I'm not into that junk." She slurred her words. "You're supposed to ask, and besides it's not like you got me in the vein. Man, I don't like this. I would've tried other shit if you wanted to, but man you're supposed to ask. I don't like this . . ." Her words were getting harder to understand. "I want to go ho . . ." She slumped over.

"Yes, sweetie, I know you want to go, and go you will, for a very nice ride." He reached across her seat and leaned it all the way back. Even though it was dark, he didn't want anyone seeing her. He placed his jacket across her and continued up the coast to his palace—the castle of his dreams and horrors, where only he was king. His collection was now beginning, and what a fine a collection it would be.

As he pulled onto the long dirt road that led to the thick woods where the cabin stood, Richard's nerves came alive, knowing how clever he was, feeling how superior he was. There was no other like him—nor would there ever be.

He stepped out of the car, breathing in the fresh, crisp air. Oh, happy, happy day. Mommy would be pleased tonight. He looked over at Bridgett, still out of it, and grabbed his jacket. Before escorting her inside, Richard walked around the cabin making certain that nothing had been disturbed since his last visit. Then, like a child on Christmas morning, he unlocked the door and entered.

Ahh. He could breathe again. The outside world was so stifling, but here he could live and breathe and be himself.

He flipped on the light and rubbed his hand across the back of the scarlet antique sofa—so very Goth—exactly how he loved it. Everything in the cabin was classy—rich brocade fabrics and damask silks. Mommy would've approved. Too bad she couldn't see all this, but Richard knew there would be another like her. Soon he would find that perfect girl, and she would live here with him.

The lemon oil he'd used to rub down all the wooden pieces

reminded him of home. Cleanliness was next to Godliness, and Richard was very tidy. His guests would feel more comfortable in a clean home.

He went into his bedroom where an elegant four-poster bed stood encased in gold velvet drapes. He moved an Oriental rug in the center of the floor and unlocked a door beneath the rug. He danced down the stairs whistling show tunes as he entered the embalming station. But his prize waited for him back in the van. How foolish he was being. He ran back up the stairs and out the front where, thankfully, Bridgett lay still passed out. He picked her up and carried Bridgett into his domain, where she would be eternalized.

He laid her down on the sofa, fanning her long hair out across a silk pillow. He placed a strip of duct tape across her mouth, in case she woke up before he was ready. He flipped on the stereo, and *The Moonlight Sonata* flowed out into the room. He took out the chilled Dom Perignon, uncorked it, and poured the expensive potion into two fine crystal flutes.

Richard then picked up Edgar Allan Poe's book of short stories. Tonight he would read to the lovely Bridgett, helping her to expand that ignorant mind of hers. After all, she'd said that she'd wished she'd gone to school. This was her chance to gain a little culture.

Richard lit dozens of candles in the cabin's main room and put a log on the fireplace. His victim slept soundly as he made everything perfect. Now the evening could begin!

He walked back into his room and turned down the crushed velvet duvet and the silk sheets. The dark walnut vanity held all his tools, including his favorite shade of red lipstick—like his mother's. He'd changed his mind about the lipstick he'd use on Bridgett, deciding that the innocent gloss wouldn't work on such an elegant evening. In the bathroom, he put paraffin wax in a crock-pot. It would melt slowly and be the perfect temperature when he was ready.

With the champagne poured, the sonata playing, the candles lit, tools ready, and the wax melting, everything came together.

Last but not least, he went to the medicine cabinet and took out a syringe and medication. Ready at last! So excited, Richard could barely contain himself staring at the blonde beauty lying across his sofa, her features lit up by the fire. The scene was really very romantic.

He opened the book. Walking around to his companion's side, he inserted the IV. He placed the bag on a metal push stand and watched its contents slowly drip into her system. Round one. The first drug, Narcan, roused her and eased any effects of the sedative he'd injected as well as with the drugs she'd used earlier at her home.

"Hello, sleepyhead," Richard said softly. He removed the duct tape from across her mouth.

Bridgett looked around, eyes blinking. Then she saw the needle in her arm. "What the hell?" She began to struggle immediately. "Look, I'm not into weird games. I just like to party a little, you know," she said, her voice quivering.

"Shh, shh, hush." He held a finger up to his lips. "This isn't a game. I don't like games. I like real fun. You'll see, and enjoy. I've been watching you. I've come to realize what a true whore you are. I can't believe I foolishly thought that maybe you liked me. But you like to fuck and get fucked. And I don't really approve of that. My mother, although a little indecent herself, wouldn't approve of that either. Not for me, anyway. But since you like to fuck so much, later, after the real festivities are over, I'll fuck you myself."

Tears of fear welled in her eyes. "Oh, God," she sobbed. "Who are you?"

Richard had no sympathy for her. He laughed, taking one more step into his fantasy. "Me? Hmmm. Why don't you call me Poe? Yes. That's good." The name suited him. He relished becoming the fine author of gothic horror.

He sat in a chair across from her and crossed his feet on the ottoman. He opened his favorite book and announced the title: "The Murders in the Rue Morgue."

Bridgett screamed. Richard dropped the book, and brought his hands to his ears, covering them. "No, no, no! That's no way to act in my home. You are a chosen one. You should feel privileged that I've allowed you here. And you are the *first*. That's right. You are the first one who has come here to be eternalized. There have been others, but they weren't as lucky." He clucked his tongue thinking about the others he'd tortured and killed, but he couldn't remember them all. What a shame. He wouldn't forget again.

Richard studied her as she sobbed harder, her entire body shaking, and her eyes wide. She continued to struggle, but to no avail.

Shaking his head he gently told her, "Please don't. You'll only tire quickly, and we have an enjoyable time ahead. No one can hear you, so don't bother screaming or struggling. It will only make it worse. Okay?" She nodded. "Good. Now, ask me to read to you."

She looked up at him. "What?"

"You heard me."

"I don't under . . ." she shook her head.

"Ask me!"

"Will you read to me?" she muttered.

"No! Once again, you do not realize the gift you've been given. Okay, let's try it again. Say: Mr. Poe, will you please read to me?"

She bowed her head and trembled. His rush had begun and he tingled all over. "Mr. Poe, will you please read to me?"

It was such a delight to hear those words. "Yes, of course." He opened the book to his favorite story, the one he'd read to Janie Keaton so long ago. Tonight, however, he could finally achieve what he'd botched so badly with Janie.

Upon finishing the story an hour later, he looked back at Bridgett. Her eyes were closed, but he knew she wasn't asleep. Tears continued down her face. Tears! He walked over to her and lifted her chin. She opened her eyes.

"Please, please don't hurt me. I'm begging you. I'll do anything you want. Let me go, please. I don't know where we are. I won't tell anyone. Please."

"Bridgett, I can't do that. I wish you could understand." He picked up the champagne flutes and held them up. "In your honor. To the first of the collection, the first to be eternalized, and remain with me. My lovely girl, you shall never feel pain again." He clinked the flutes together. "Ah, isn't that a pretty sound? Crisp. I love good crystal. Now take a sip." He held it up to her lips.

Bridgett spit the champagne back at him. "You're fucking crazy! Why are you doing this? What the fuck did I ever do to you?"

Richard wiped the alcohol from his face. "You didn't have to do that. Now I'm perturbed." Richard caressed her face. It was soft and wet. She struggled to pull away from him. Standing behind her, he reached his hands down across her breasts. They were large and hard—plastic. But touching them caused him to harden.

"I'm sorry. I didn't mean it," she cried. "Do you want to do it? We can, you know. I will. I'll suck you off if you want. Anything."

Richard sighed, bored with her pleading. He also knew that he could not finish what he started with her while she was alive. He'd discovered this before, and the women he'd tried to make it happen with had endured great torture from the anger he felt about it. No, there was only one way Richard could get himself off.

He knelt in front of her. "Do you want out?"

She nodded, her eyes begging him. "Yes, please."

"And we can make love?"

"Yes. I'll do anything."

"I know you will." He stood and walked behind her.

"Thank you."

She obviously thought he was going to free her. In a sense he was. He took out a plastic bag from his coat pocket and placed it over her head. Bridgett struggled and writhed, muffled screams coming from her for about a minute. Richard was strong. He held tightly, but carefully, so as not to bruise her. Blood rushed to his extremities as the adrenaline charged his body. Richard focused on the music to calm himself. He didn't want to climax, yet. If he did, the fantasy would be destroyed.

Bridgett fell silent, no more attempts to be free. In Richard's mind she was free now—free to be his. Her body slumped over. Richard didn't take the bag off right away or let go of the grip. He had to be sure she was gone.

When he removed the bag, there were no signs of life. First he untied her and laid her out on the couch. Mixing the wax from the crock-pot, he carefully spread it across her face with a paintbrush. He let it cool, then peeled back the wax, which was now a mask. He set it on the dining room table where he could finish it later with plaster of Paris. But first he needed to have her.

Richard carried Bridgett into his bedroom where he stripped her clothes off, further arousing him. He climbed on top of her, and as his evening's fantasy was finally completely fulfilled he climaxed inside the corpse. Yes, he knew his mother would approve as he called out for her, "Mommy!"

CHAPTER EIGHTEEN

ALTHOUGH RACHEL HAD made it to the weekend, it was still touch and go. Helena visited as much as possible and checked in on the baby with Lindsay. Thankfully, Social Services had allowed the baby to remain in the center.

Even with the trauma, Frankie had come down for her weekend visit. Helena wanted to spend all the time she could with her daughter, but this next AA meeting was too important for her to miss. She was to receive her yearly coin, a symbol of uninterrupted sobriety despite the maelstrom of gossip about her past, and Tim insisted that she go. She'd asked Frankie to attend, but Frankie said that she was tired and didn't want to.

Tim met Helena at the meeting and seemed to know at once how worried and distracted she was. "Okay, lovey, what are you thinking? I can see that tick-tocking in your brain and know something's up," Tim said.

"There's a lot going on in my head. First and foremost is seeing poor Rachel in so much pain, and the fire, not to mention that detective who seems to have it in for me. And then there's Frankie. I wish she'd have come tonight. I thought she might understand how much it meant with the horrendous week I had. I thought she'd be more supportive." Helena shrugged, letting out small sigh.

"Goodness, Helena, she's fifteen. Supportive is not an operative word in her vocabulary at this stage. You were once fifteen; narcissism flows through their veins. I seriously doubt that many teenagers attend AA meetings with their folks, even on an anniversary. Think about it. I'm sure it would make her uncomfortable. The poor kid has been through the media war zone. She doesn't need any other pressures, especially from you."

Helena dropped Tim's hand. She was almost offended, but then, Tim's style was pretty straightforward. "Maybe you're right."

"You know I am. And, as far as Rachel goes, the docs are doing their damnedest to help her, and you've told me how tough she is. She's made it through nearly three days. Tonight is supposed to be a positive moment for you, girl. Look how far you've come. Try and turn it around and think of your own progress tonight. Live in the moment, okay? Now, let's lighten the conversation and let me hear some dish about old Paddy Poo?"

"Patrick? That's lightening the subject?"

"No, the Pope—yes Patrick, and yes, love always lightens things up."

"It isn't love. Not at all. When he brought Frankie down yesterday, we talked basically about nothing over a cup of coffee, then he left. So, I don't know where he is, and why would I care?"

"Oh, boy, you do have it bad. Isn't love, my ass."

"What?"

"Helena Shea, after all these years you still hold a torch for Patrick Kiley."

"Please."

"Please is right, girl. It's so obvious. You can't tell me that having Frankie in your life hasn't stirred up those old feelings."

"That's the past. I was naïve and vulnerable."

"Sure. You've never been naïve, love. And as far as vulnerable goes, your shell's as hard as a damned tortoise. Give it up, friend. He's still got you hooked good, and now that you've got the kid back in your life, I have no idea what you two are waiting for. Why don't you hurry up and screw and get it over with?

Come on, let's get back together already and have one big happy family."

"We're not exactly June and Ward Cleaver. Will you let it go, at least for tonight? Right now I have to focus on my sobriety, Frankie, and Rachel. Then I have to figure out how to get Shea House back on track. Since the explosion and fire have been classified as arson, I'm not sure how private backers are going to feel about throwing more money into it. And I'm running pretty low on cash. I've spent a good amount of my own money already."

"Okay, I can tell you want to change the subject, talk about more depressing things, but I won't stop until I wear you down. I want you to be happy, and I think *he* makes you happy. You're in love, sister, 'cause you never stopped loving him. I'll back off for a nano-second, though. I know this is an important eve, darling."

"Gee, thanks."

"Hmmm. So that creepy detective is still telling you it was arson over at Shea House?"

"That's what he said the other night. He hasn't called since, and I'm not too eager to be in touch. I've been talking to the arson team and the fire marshal, and they all agree that someone started the fire. The marshal told me that it's possible it could be gang related. You've been down there. The area isn't exactly prime real estate. Gang bangers don't necessarily like the idea of someone coming in and helping the community get sober. It's bad for business."

"Have you thought about moving the location?"

"I have. But where it is, is where it's needed. The women I'm trying to help have nothing, and no one's helping them get an education, stay straight, and learn how to parent. I meet with the insurance people next week. I'm going to have to do some fast-talking. At this point we're at least another year out from starting a new center. It's possible I'll have to re-apply for permits, and who knows if I'll even get insurance. Everything is iffy right now." Helena hung her head.

"Hey, hey, it'll all work out. You'll see. Relax, okay? Now let's find somewhere to sit."

People milled around the center, chatting with each other and vying for the best seats. She and Tim found two good ones up near the front. Helena's nerves trembled, not only from their conversation, but because the difficult portion of the evening had arrived. She'd have to speak tonight. She was glad Tim was there to hold her hand.

Even when she used to strut down the catwalk during her modeling days, she wouldn't get this nervous. Her face flushed, and she broke out in a cold sweat.

After the third speaker, she'd gathered enough courage to stand and tell her story. Helena shifted her weight from one foot to the other. She owed this program so much, but standing alone before the group never seemed to get any easier. Even though she knew many of these folks and a lot of them were Shea House supporters, all she could envision were strange faces in front of her—judging her.

For her, retelling her story was like waves hitting the shoreline at full speed—not the normal rolling motion a calm sea makes, but a wild, stormy one, always crashing against sharp and painful rocks. There was no easy way out of these icy waters, so she simply took the plunge and began.

"My name is Helena Shea, and I am an alcoholic. I started drinking heavily right before my dad died. But when alcohol wasn't enough to ease the pain, I added Valium. Once Dad died, I really got out of hand. I was just so lost and lonely, and partying took my cares away, for a little while at least. Luckily for me, or so I thought at the time, the fashion world fit my lifestyle, making it easy to score whatever I needed: pick-me-up, bring-me-down, anything. So . . ." She took a deep breath and exhaled before beginning again. "Before I knew it, I was doing drugs and drinking more with each passing day. I'd wake up with a Screwdriver or Bloody Mary, and a line of coke. It escalated from there." She vaguely remembered those mornings when she prayed that her choice of venom would ease some of the pain of losing her father. She'd adored him. He had loved her through so much, especially through the difficult decision to give up Frankie.

Helena fidgeted with her tennis bracelet, twisting the diamonds around her wrist. "Regrets and past mistakes were catching up with me, and I started to experience growing consequences of my alcohol and drug use. I started my own agency, but because of my addictions, it wasn't doing very well. You may have heard or read about it in the media. Take my word for it, *The Scene* and *Entertainment Tonight* don't know nearly as much as they think they do about my life."

Low, sympathetic laughter erupted from the crowd packed inside the auditorium. They all knew that her life had been dissected and travestied as the paparazzi invaded any privacy she and her family had tried to maintain.

"Then," she laughed, "I got offered a major motion picture which was to star a big-time screen actor, who shall remain nameless. I thought my life would change! I'd no longer be considered a dumb model, but a high maintenance actress instead." Laughter once again lightened the mood of the room. "Not to be, I'm afraid. We started shooting, but I kept messing up my lines. So, on a break, I figured I'd do a couple of lines to speed things up." She rolled her eyes. Talking about it made it seem so distant, as if it had happened to a good friend, not to her. She couldn't believe she'd done those things. Her life was so very different now.

"Well, the director kept making not so subtle remarks about my aging body. You could say he pissed me off when he suggested a body double for the nude scene. So I cracked him in the nose. Before long, the police showed up and escorted me off the set. *Permanently.*

"So of course, I did what every good alcoholic does in a crisis: I bought some more coke and other 'necessities' to party it up at home alone.

"I bottomed out. Partying alone just doesn't have the same appeal as hanging with a friend, or *ten*. But I had reached the point where nobody wanted to be around me." Tears welled as she remembered that feeling of isolation and utter despair; imprisoned by booze, powders, and small, round pills. "My friend and assistant at the time, Brianne, found me rolled into the fetal position, pretty much out of my mind the next day. I'm surprised I wasn't dead. I should have been. I was pretty delirious though. I don't even remember her putting me in the car and driving me to Palm Springs. I lost a big chunk of time there somewhere. I just blacked out."

Heads in the crowd bobbed, understanding that loss of time and memory, like being in the Twilight Zone. The room was silent, except for the occasional sniffle from someone connecting with her story—and people *were* connecting with her story.

"But I do remember arriving at Betty Ford and trying to convince everyone there that I was totally fine. Of course, that wasn't the case. They got me sober and introduced me to the twelve steps of Alcoholics Anonymous. I thank God today for the program and those folks out in Palm Springs who didn't give up on me when I'd given up on myself. Because of them, loving friends, and this fellowship, I'm pleased to announce that today is my one year anniversary of uninterrupted sobriety." She wiped her eyes with the back of her hand. "My life, though still pretty hectic and by no means perfect, is a hundred times better— no, more like a thousand times better. I've gotten to know my daughter, begun putting my agency back on track, and am learning to deal with the media—all without drugs or alcohol. It's good to be sober, taking life one day at a time." The crowd applauded as a long sigh escaped her lips.

Sitting down, looking at all the people in the auditorium— from men in business suits, to kids far from twenty-one, to the homeless—she realized that alcohol and drug dependency happened in all walks of life, all ages. No one was immune. As a drunk, she wasn't any more special than the next person. She was simply Helena Shea, alcoholic and drug addict. Somehow, that was a comforting feeling to have.

She leaned into Tim, who smelled like his signature clove

cigarettes. "Well, how'd I do?"

"Wonderful, wonderful! Very courageous." He made a fist for emphasis. She laughed. The release of tension felt like a gift.

Helena smiled at Tim. He'd helped her through so many rough times over the last year. He truly was a loving friend.

Turning her attention to the next speaker, she heard him say, "Take it one step at a time." The words affected her now more than ever as she thought about Rachel, Shea House, Frankie, and even Patrick.

Helena returned home later than expected, hoping Frankie wouldn't be upset. The meeting had gone on for quite awhile. As she walked through the door, Ella whined, alerting her that she needed to go out. Helena could hear the television on in the other room and figured Frankie fell asleep watching it.

She peeked into the family room and saw Frankie curled up with a blanket and pillow on the sofa. She knelt by the sofa to study the innocent face, wishing she'd seen her like this as a young child.

Frankie stirred, as Helena kissed her cheek and stroked her hair. "I love you, sweet girl. So much." The puppy nudged her elbow. "Okay," she whispered.

Helena took Ella for a quick run. It was nearly eleven-thirty. There was something in the air that bothered her. The ocean was writhing as if awaiting a storm, and there was something dead close by. The stench nearly made her gag, and she tried to hurry Ella.

Her cell phone rang from inside her sweater pocket and startled her. Frankie must've awakened and was now looking for her. "Hi, baby," she said as she flipped open the phone.

"A bit too assuming, aren't you?" That voice again, from the other night.

"Look, jerk-off, I know Leeza Kiley put you up to this. I sure in hell hope she's paying you well, 'cause frankly, when I find out who you are, you'll need the money for a good attorney."

"You through ranting, bitch?"

Helena was about to hang up, when he said, "Your daughter is so beautiful when she sleeps and quite tasty, I'm certain. I love that she's wearing nothing but a white T-shirt and panties."

Helena dropped the phone and Ella's leash. She ran as fast as she could, fighting the sand that bogged her down. Ella barked loudly, following behind. Helena stumbled. She stood up, her ankle burned; she continued to run. She was screaming Frankie's name before she reached the house. Terror tore through her body as she hunted for the key in her pocket. It was gone. She'd lost it in the sand. She pounded on the patio doors. No one came. She screamed Frankie's name again. She frantically searched for a rock large enough to break the window. Finding one, she threw it against the sliding glass door. It cracked all the way down, but didn't break. She picked the rock up again and threw it harder. This time the window came crashing down as shards of glass cut Helena's arms. She climbed through the gaping hole. "Frankie! Frankie!"

She wasn't on the sofa. Helena scanned the room still illuminated by the television set. She felt sick.

"Mom? What the heck? Why did you do that?" said Frankie, pointing to the door. She stood in the hall doorway rubbing her eyes.

Helena rushed over and threw her arms around her, sobbing. "Oh, God. I thought, I thought…"

"Thought what?" Frankie looked at her as if she were mad. "Oh man, you haven't been drinking?"

"God, no!" Helena tightened her grip.

"What's wrong?"

"Where were you just now? Didn't you hear me banging and yelling?"

"I was trying to pee, Mom. You were making so much racket you couldn't hear me yelling back at you from the bathroom, and then you broke the door. What were you doing?"

Ella ran up and whined outside the broken glass. Frankie wiggled out of Helena's arms to help her through.

"No, don't!"

"Mom, she wants in. She's afraid of the glass. She'll cut

herself."

Helena tried to regain her composure. She wiped the sand off her clothes and face. "I'll do it. I don't want you to get cut either." Helena gently picked up Ella, her ankle killing her, and brought her over the glass and into the house.

"What is wrong with you? And you're limping? What happened?"

"Here, help me move this." Helena went over to an armoire she used as a bookcase, hastily removing the books while Frankie watched, horrified.

"Mom?"

"Hold on a minute, just help me please, and then I'll explain." It took the two of them a few minutes and quite a bit of effort to move the piece of furniture to cover the gaping hole where the patio doors once stood. When they finished, Helena got a sheet and pinned it up against the window. She then took an ice pack from the freezer and sank onto the sofa to ice her ankle. Frankie stared at her. She patted the seat next to her, inviting Frankie to sit. She didn't want to alarm her daughter, but she also knew that Frankie was old enough to be made aware and cautious. She told her everything, beginning with the incident with the van and her thought that Leeza was behind it.

Frankie brought her knees up, wrapping her arms around them. "So, someone was watching, seeing what I was wearing tonight. Like, you think from outside the window?"

Helena nodded. "I think so." She grabbed a blanket draped over the sofa and covered Frankie's bare legs.

"Sick. It could still be her. Leeza, I mean. She might have some creepazoid keeping tabs on us. She's psycho, Mom. It sounds exactly like something she would do."

"I know, honey. But do you think she'd go that far? That's pretty damn brazen. It's even crossed my mind that she's the one behind the fire at Shea House. I don't know anyone who hates me that much, unless its gangsters like the fire marshal has suggested. If not, then it could be Leeza."

"I think she'd do about anything to get even with you. You

blew up her world when you and Dad made the decision to tell me the truth. The only pleasure she got out of it was that she beat you to it by telling the tabloids and divorcing my dad. She loved that."

"This might even be too low for Leeza. I'd like to call your dad. I'm a little scared. It might be best for us to head back up to Santa Barbara in the morning. You'd be safer there, I think, at least until we get this figured out, find out who's behind this."

"Mom, you promised we'd go shopping for my birthday."

"I know, and we can. I'll take you in Santa Barbara."

"But Rodeo Drive is so cool. Please."

"Frankie, someone was watching our house tonight. He might still be. We have Ella to warn us through tonight, and I'll call my security service to have them keep an eye on the place. If I call the police, we'll wind up on the front page of *The Scene*, and that's the last thing we want, especially following the fire. Word is that Claire Travers is already snooping around, seeing what dirt she can dish."

"Mom, I'm sorry all this is happening."

"Me too, baby. We've got to keep our chin up though," Helena said trying to sound reassuring. "And, whether or not Leeza is behind this stunt, at least up at your dad's she can't have her creep watching you."

"What about you?"

"I'm a big girl. I'll be okay. Maybe I'll have Tim come and stay for a while. I'm needed here with Rachel and Shea House."

"But you're the one that nearly got killed by the crazy in the van the other night. Even if it is only Leeza acting like her usual witch self. I do think she's psycho enough to hurt you."

Helena brushed tears from Frankie's face. "No one's going to hurt me."

"We just found each other, and I'm finally beginning to feel like I really do have a mother who's there for me. I've never had that. Daddy was always great, but it's not like having a mom. And Leeza was a real bitch, certainly not very motherly." Frankie frowned.

Helena pulled her close. "It's okay." She held her, rocking her like she would a baby, tightening the blanket around her. The only difference was, this baby had grown into a young woman filled with pain—a pain that Helena blamed herself for causing. "It'll be all right," she whispered. "I promise." Helena sang softly to her child as Frankie drifted off to sleep.

The thought of eyes still watching them never left Helena's mind as she let Frankie's head rest in her lap. Helena would stand vigil all night, refusing to allow Leeza's hired hand—or anyone else, for that matter—get to her child.

CHAPTER NINETEEN

LEEZA NEVER STAYED the entire night at a man's place. It didn't matter if she dated him for a while or not. It was one of her rules. She needed her beauty sleep. Something she couldn't get with a man snoring next to her. Besides, they often kept her awake. They liked her too damn much.

So, she left the Brad Pitt look-alike she'd hooked up with at the restaurant where she and Claire had eaten the other night. He'd turned out to be somewhat goofy. A couple of hours with the future Ms. March was all he wound up getting. Ms. March! She relished the sound of that and hoped it would grind into Patrick's nerves and burn like acid.

Thank God she'd divorced him. *To hell with him!* He couldn't appreciate a real woman, anyway. He liked little girls, like his precious Helena and the kid. Now everyone in America would soon see that *she* was beautiful, too. That scandal brought misery to all those who'd deserved it, but it brought her nothing but joy. Still, she couldn't help but feel for the kid. She had to admit that she did love her, in her own way.

Leeza's day had played out fantastically, taking all those photos for the March issue of *Playboy*. The scandal and being famous, or infamous, depending on how one looked at it, had also helped to land her the spread instead of some younger "twenty something" model. And the money was yummy icing on the cake. She laughed out loud, loving the idea of bringing more grief to Patrick and that bitch.

She headed up the Santa Monica Freeway in her Burgundy Jaguar, a perk from the divorce settlement. Her hands gripped the smooth steering wheel; it still smelled of new leather.

She was slightly buzzed from the champagne she had drunk only hours before. Too bad she had another photo shoot the next day, or she could've played a lot longer with that guy, goofy or not.

Helena may have been a super-model in her youth, but Leeza knew that the perfect age for a sexually uninhibited woman was thirty-eight. The proof of that was evident on any given night with men lusting after her gorgeous body.

Winding around the bend before her house, a few miles up from Helena's shack, she snorted and tossed her flaming red tresses behind her shoulders. Minutes later, she pulled into her garage.

Once inside the house, she rushed to turn off the alarm only to notice it wasn't on in the first place. *Damn that maid! She's been told a million times to set that thing when she leaves.* Leeza did it herself and headed for the bar to pour a nightcap before going upstairs, kicking off her heels as she walked.

She mixed herself a dirty martini, squeezing the olive juice into it. She flipped on some Luther Van Dross, which she adored. So sexy. She and Patrick had loved listening to him when they were together. At times, she missed Patrick, loved him and hated him at the same time. This was one of those times, when an empty, cold house reminded her that she was alone. Her shrink told her she was obsessed with him. *Que sera, sera.* She opened her French doors and stepped out onto the balcony, toasting the wind and sea.

She shut her eyes and sang along with Luther.

She thought about Patrick. Maybe if she'd tried harder to love the kid, this would have never happened. Could they have been a family? Well, neither regret nor tears could change things now.

Her eyes shot open as a strong arm wrapped around her, pinning her arms to her sides. Another hand covered her mouth, silencing her scream. "Shh, shh," a man's voice whispered in her ear. He finished singing the Van Dross song. He knew all the words. She began to relax, thinking he must be an old lover. The song ended. She couldn't help but be turned on. This had to be one of her lovers. If only she could figure out which one.

"It's so sad, but this has to be done. You are so beautiful. Poe would've loved you. In fact, Poe does love you. I am Poe. I would love to read to you, but tonight there is no time. I have so much work to do."

The words didn't coincide with the idea of his being a lover. And as he squeezed her harder, Leeza realized this brute was here for more than a romp in the sack. She struggled, but was no match for him. He was strong, very strong.

"No, no. Don't do that. If you would cooperate, it could be so much more pleasant."

She tried hard to kick him in the shin. She wished she hadn't taken off her stilettos. She continued to struggle, refusing to give up. Hell, she was Leeza Kiley. Born to fight, all the way from the trashy trailer park she'd dragged herself out of to her recent ugly divorce.

But as he whispered in her ear again, her blood froze from his icy words. Fear overtook her. She tried to bite his hand, but couldn't. Leeza realized that she was in mortal danger.

"You *are* feisty. I like that, but you're beginning to bore me. I was hoping we could have a little chat about Helena. I hate her as much, if not more than you do. I could destroy her like I have so many. But I've conjured up a much better idea. Once I killed for fear of abandonment—such power in that realization. Abandonment is very scary. But in Helena's case it's all about revenge. You know about revenge, don't you?" He kissed her on the cheek. "Well, beautiful, I could enjoy playing games with you, but you're not the one I want. Don't you fret, sweet thing, because I'll take care of that bitch once and for all, for all the pain she's caused so many of us. Good night, beauty."

Leeza felt a rope tighten around her neck, and she struggled as he squeezed the life from her. She gasped for air as the pain grew intense, and she started to lose consciousness.

Ironically, Leeza's last thoughts were of Helena. For the first time in her life, she felt sorry for her. She knew from the hatred in this man's voice that what this psycho had in mind for Helena would be far worse than the way he'd chosen to kill her. Leeza felt the ground beneath her slip away, and within seconds all was gone.

CHAPTER TWENTY

WHAT A SPLENDID night. Although it had deviated from Richard's usual ritual, it was almost better—beginning with the scare he'd put into Helena.

He did, however, wish that he could've preserved Leeza. The last one was getting a bit ripe. It was time to bury her. The embalming process was not indefinite. But there were other reasons why Leeza couldn't join the collection. It would've ruined the plan. Yet, he had taken the time to make a wax mask of her face. Upon returning to the cabin, he would go to work on it, to recreate the face of the woman. Then it would forever be available to help him remember her, as he did each of his beauties, even after he disposed of them.

He hoped he hadn't been too hasty or careless in removing the paraffin from Leeza's face lest he leave any traces of the wax behind. But he figured she probably had facials all the time, maybe even gave them to herself as a part of her own facial routine, so he needn't worry. Besides, Richard was certain that he'd removed all traces of the mask.

Everything was about ready to go. It was all beginning for Helena. Richard loved it. He would enjoy her demise almost as much as if she were seated in front of him, begging him to read to her.

There had only been one who'd entered his life who loved to be read to, who had stuck by him. Richard knew as soon as they met that she would've never abandoned him. She was the reason he hadn't killed for so long. She had filled that void left by his mother. Mommy had approved of her. She had carved a light in his soul where there had been none. When he'd found her, he knew his aching need to conquer and collect had been satiated, that she alone could take pain away. Because she was faithful. And she had.

However, Helena Shea single-handedly destroyed that for him. She was responsible for turning him back into his old haunted self. She *took* Brianne from him, *forced* his love to abandon him. And now, just as he had paid, Helena Shea would pay dearly. But she wouldn't pay with her life, oh no, not that, not yet. She would begin by losing the people and things that meant the most to her. It was a damn shame that crack addict Rachel hadn't keeled over yet. It would be a perfect start to things if she'd do that. The beauty of her involvement was that Richard hadn't known she was in the center when he'd watched it blow. His mother must have planned that for him. She would have had the insight to do such a thing. Mommy hated Helena as much as he did.

By tomorrow morning, Helena would be paying with her freedom. And from there, it would only get worse.

CHAPTER TWENTY-ONE

HELENA FINALLY DRIFTED off to sleep on the sofa. Visions of Leeza entered her dreams again, swinging a pendulum directly in front of her, laughing and mocking her, telling her what a horrible mother she was. In her dream, Leeza set Shea House on fire, and oh, my God! Frankie was inside. Just as her dream state began to allow the velvety darkness of real sleep to take over, the ringing of her doorbell—followed by a loud knocking—awakened her. Ella went berserk, barking her head off.

Frankie stirred. "Mom?"

"It's nothing, baby. Go back to sleep."

Helena checked the clocks in the kitchen. It was almost seven in the morning, later than she thought. A dull light came through the pinned up sheet. The front room was goose-bump cold without any glass to block it. Who could be at her door at this hour?

The doorbell rang again. Ella continued her earsplitting barking. "Okay, okay," Helena muttered. She reached the door, her hands shaking from being abruptly awakened.

"Police, Ms. Shea. We need to speak to you."

"Police?" she whispered, "What the . . . !" Maybe it had something to do with the incident last night. But how could they have known? Or possibly it was about the fire? She peered through the peephole and saw a uniformed officer standing next to Detective Collier, wearing that tweed jacket and bad Elvis hairdo. "Yes?"

"It's me, Ms. Shea, Detective Collier with the LAPD. We spoke at The Sober Living House the other night. I'm here with Officer Keen. I need to ask you a few questions."

Helena opened the door. "If this is about the fire couldn't we make an appointment to speak at a more appropriate time? It's only seven on a Saturday morning."

"I'm aware of the time. But this can't wait. It has nothing to do with the fire at your center, Ms. Shea. There's been a murder. We're hoping you might be able to help us out."

"Murder? Who?" Helena watched the detective shift his weight from one foot to the other.

"Leeza Kiley," the detective said. "Can we come in now?"

Helena gasped. She could barely speak. She eyed the cops suspiciously. "You're really twisted, Detective Collier. I told you that I didn't start the fire at Shea House. What kind of game are you playing with me?"

"I can assure you that I am not toying around." The detective and officer walked into Helena's home. Addressing the uniform behind him, he ordered, "Secure the place. It'll be a zoo around here before long."

"My daughter is still asleep. Let's go in here." She led the officer into the living room, while Ella stood in the hall, growling at the detective. Helena had to lock the dog in her room.

"Mom? What's going on?" Frankie appeared in the hall, too.

"It's nothing. Go lie back down in your room."

"But Mom, what's wrong?"

"I'm not sure yet. There's a policeman here who needs to speak with me. I'll let you know after he leaves."

"Is this about last night?"

"I don't know. Now go back to bed. You can watch TV in my room if you like."

Frankie reluctantly did as she was told. Helena went back into the living room.

The detective was on her sofa, pad and pencil in hand. "What happened to your door, there?" he asked.

"You wouldn't believe me if I told you." Helena weighed the possibilities of telling him the truth. The possible negative consequences of doing just that made her lie.

"Try me."

"I lost my keys last night while taking my dog for a walk."

"So you broke the window? Little rash, isn't it? What about your daughter?"

"She was sleeping, and you know teenagers, they can sleep through anything. I tried to break in and when I couldn't, I got pretty flustered and angry, so I busted the window."

"Boy, you certainly have a temper, don't you Ms. Shea? That's interesting. You wouldn't mind if I corroborated your story with your daughter, do you?"

"No, not at all." Her stomach tightened. "So now, what's this about Leeza? I simply can't believe what you're telling me," Helena stammered.

"Believe it. The maid found her dead around an hour ago," he replied. "I understand that you knew Mrs. Kiley quite well."

Helena didn't know how to respond. Feeling weak in the knees, she slowly sank into an oversized chair opposite him. "Yes, I suppose you could say that."

"And you weren't exactly the best of friends?"

"You could say that, too."

"Ms. Shea, where were you last evening between ten and twelve?"

"I was at a meeting with a friend. I got here around 11:30 and then took my dog for a walk on the beach, like I said. I came back home, and after my fit with the door, I fixed it the best I could and stayed up for a bit with my daughter." Helena felt as if she were in a fog, bogging her down. She couldn't fathom that Leeza was dead.

"And your friend and daughter can verify your time table?"

"Of course."

"What about when you went for a walk? Were you alone?"

"Just me and my dog. Why do you ask?"

"How long was the walk?"

"I don't know, ten, maybe fifteen minutes." Helena thought briefly about the phone call, but her gut told her to remain silent, even though she knew he wasn't buying her story about the glass door. "You could ask Ella, my dog." She smiled hoping to get a laugh out of the detective. He couldn't seriously be thinking that she was involved. But he remained sullen.

"Ms. Shea, did you kill Leeza Kiley?"

"What?" she asked, horrified. "Of course not! I can't believe this!"

"Just doing my job. I read the papers."

"You made that clear the other night. But I wouldn't consider an *Enquirer* or *The Scene* reliable sources of news. There was no love lost between us, but I certainly did *not* murder her. I'm actually starting to feel harassed by you."

Collier nodded his head. "Do you mind if I have a look around?"

"For what?"

"As I said, I'm doing my job."

"Am I a suspect in your investigation, Detective?" she asked, her voice turning hostile. Her face burned as anger churned in her stomach.

Detective Collier did not answer her question. He stood and glanced around. He stared at her living room drapes for quite some time. What was he thinking? He walked over to the edge of the window and looked down at the floor. Helena couldn't see what he was looking at, but he pulled a plastic baggie out of his coat pocket and bent down to pick up something. Turning around to face her, he held out the knotted rope that held the drapes back. She'd forgotten to get a replacement tie back when she'd noticed it missing the other night.

"Problem with your drapes?"

The question caught her off guard. Why would he be concerned with her drapes? She answered him anyway, not wanting to make the situation any worse, especially with Frankie only a few feet away. "Yeah, I guess you could call it that. I noticed it a few days ago. My dog probably knocked that down. I think she must've chewed off the rope and hid it someplace. She's a puppy. They do stuff like that."

"Did you know that Mrs. Kiley was strangled? Your drapery rope looks like the one she was strangled with. Ms. Shea, you'd better get yourself a good attorney."

"You're kidding, right?"

"If I were you, I'd do it pronto because within minutes I'll have a search warrant. It looks as though you might be taking a ride with me today. Oh, and by the way, I'd come up with a better story for your lawyer about the broken door and the drapery cord. 'Cause I ain't buying it."

CHAPTER TWENTY-TWO

WITHIN AN HOUR, a swarm of reporters stood outside Helena's home. On the basis of the missing drapery cord, Detective Collier had called in for a search warrant, and now her home crawled with police. She heard a helicopter hovering overhead and wondered which news crew was filming her roof, expecting something exciting to happen. She hated those bastards.

Helena figured that Patrick had heard by now and was probably worried sick. But the phone lines were tied up with reporters trying to get their scoop, and her cell phone, even if she could use it, was somewhere in the sand where she'd dropped it last night.

She was certain their images were fixed on television sets all over the city at this very moment—busy reporters concocting their cockamamie stories. Maybe the police were putting Patrick through the same paces. If there was a hawk like Detective Collier at his place, there was no telling when she and Patrick might be able to communicate. If the press was outside her home, they had likely surrounded Patrick's ranch as well. Helena hated the thought of that. She wished Frankie were with her father instead of having to see this. From the scare Collier had given her, Helena wasn't sure how this morning would end.

She crept into Frankie's bedroom where a youthful looking police officer rummaged through Frankie's underwear drawer.

"I hope you're getting off on that," Frankie said.

Helena heard the vehemence in her daughter's voice. "Frankie," she warned.

"But, Mom, he's touching my panties. What are they looking for anyway? This is lame."

"Yes, it is. But I don't think we have a choice." Helena tapped the officer on the shoulder. He smiled sheepishly. "Can I have a word alone with my daughter?"

"I don't know if that's okay, ma'am."

"It's fine. I asked Detective Collier."

"You sure about that?"

"Positive. Why don't you go and ask him yourself."

"I suppose it'll be okay for a few minutes."

Helena shut Frankie's door behind the rookie. In a hushed tone she spoke quickly. "Has Detective Collier talked to you yet?"

"No."

"He will, and I lied about how the glass door got broken." Helena told Frankie everything she'd told Collier. "So if he asks you about it, I need you to agree with my story until I can speak with an attorney."

"Why, Mom?"

"I don't have time to answer that now, please just do it. The other thing is that I need to reach your dad, but our phone is tied up and I lost my cell last night. Did you bring yours?"

Frankie nodded. She opened the closet and got out her gym bag, rummaged through it, and pulled out the cell phone Helena had bought her so they could always keep in touch. "Wouldn't leave home without it."

"That's my girl."

Frankie handed the phone to her. Patrick's number was busy. She then dialed his cell phone, to no avail. Helena sighed.

"Page him, leave my number, and type in 911," Frankie suggested.

"It's true what they say, I guess, about teenagers being smarter than their parents."

Helena paged Patrick. She and Frankie both crossed their fingers hoping he would call back. They got their wish momentarily.

"Jesus, Helena, what's going on down there? I've been trying to get through to you. I've even tried this number, but Frankie's had her phone off. I got a call from the LAPD saying that Leeza was murdered and that they'd sent some men to your house. What is happening?"

"I don't know, Patrick. They think, they think…." She refused to choke up. She had done nothing wrong, and she wouldn't let the police and reporters get the best of her. "They're considering me a suspect in Leeza's murder."

"What? That's crazy. My God, Helena, on what basis?"

"I don't have time to go into it right now. I've only got a minute. We've got to get Frankie out of here. There's a detective with a huge chip on his shoulder, and he's talking about taking me to the station."

"Don't worry. I'll call and have the jet fueled. Let me throw a few things together, and I'll be down there within two hours."

"I may not have that long."

"Hang in there. If they take you anywhere, have Frankie stay in the house. We'll get all this straightened out."

"Okay," she said, trying to sound reassured. The detective banged at the door. Helena whispered, "Gotta go." She tossed the phone to Frankie, who stashed it back in the closet.

"Ms. Shea!"

"Coming, Detective." She opened the door wide. He glared at her suspiciously. They both stared at each other for a few seconds, then looked over at Frankie who was wiping her eyes pretending, or maybe not, Helena wasn't sure, to be wiping away tears. "I was trying to calm my daughter down. She's a little shaken. I'm sure you can understand."

"Your attorney is here," he grumbled.

Helena followed the detective out. She smiled back at Frankie, then said, "If I have to go with them, you stay here, okay? That's what we need you to do. Your dad will come for you. I don't want to leave you here alone like this, but that detective might not give me a choice."

Frankie nodded and Helena could see then that the tears hadn't been phony. "It's okay, Mom. I'm almost sixteen remember? I can take it."

"I know you can." Helena followed the detective out of Frankie's room, preparing for whatever was about to happen next. She saw her attorney standing in the living room, looking fully aggrieved.

James Wingate, over six feet tall, unmistakably Irish with his pale complexion contrasting the vibrant golden red hair framing his face, was yelling at anyone who'd listen. Then he saw the man in charge, Collier himself. His thin mustache, trimmed to resemble a bar brawling cowboy from the mid-nineteenth century, curled up at each end. His pale blue eyes matched the color of the ice that settled on the shores of his ancestors' country during a deep freeze. However, rather than speaking in an Irish brogue, he had a southern accent that revealed his childhood had been spent in the heart of Texas.

"Don't say a word, Helena. Let me handle this jerk, okay? This search-warrant rigmarole is a crock. He used what he could to get inside your home." He pointed at Collier. "I've already talked to some pals on the force. There's no way you could've strangled that woman—you don't have the strength. They're blowing smoke. They need a scapegoat. They don't want the Malibu community up in arms about a murderer on the loose, and you look like a good way out. Don't worry; I'll get you out of this."

Helena nodded, her hands shaking. His fast-talking and confidence reassured her. James was savvy, as well as being a friend from AA. She trusted him. She knew him to be a man of his word.

"All right, Detective, pack it up," James interrupted the search party. "You've got nothing here. You're harassing my client and building a good case against yourself and your department."

Collier turned on his heels, his eyes red, and hands on his hips. In a booming voice, he said, "Your client had motive and time to commit this crime. And when I get my lab results back, I guarantee that the rope around Mrs. Kiley's neck will match your client's drapes!"

"Ms. Shea did not do this. You know it, and so do I. You're barking up the wrong tree. The DA will laugh you all the way back to a desk job. If you know what's smart, Collier, you'll take your posse and head on out."

Collier and James had a stand off of cowboy-days proportion. A minute into it, Collier, the first to blink, looked around and nodded to his troop. "This isn't over, counselor. Not by a long shot," he said, shaking a finger at them.

"You're right about that, Detective. You're right about that. Before the end of the week, you and your department will be begging my client to drop her lawsuit."

James escorted the police to the door. When he opened it, hordes of reporters and cameramen standing at the edge of the Pacific Coast Highway shouted questions. "Did she do it?" "Did Helena Shea kill Leeza Kiley?" "How did she do it?" "Are she and Patrick Kiley lovers again?" "Is the kid there?" James slammed the door after the last policeman left.

"You need to make a statement to get them off your back for awhile," he said, speaking of the reporters. He walked around the house, closing shutters and drapes, turning her light-filled home into a dismal tomb. She felt trapped, as if she couldn't breathe. He looked questioningly at the broken door. "That might need some explaining."

"I can."

"Good." James looked at Helena and asked, "I'm right when I tell these folks that you're innocent? You had nothing to do with any of this, did you?"

"Of course not!"

"I'm sorry, Helena, I have to ask. I know that you couldn't have done this yourself, but there'll be accusations about hired killers and so on. You and Patrick both have the financial means to hire someone. And we all know things weren't exactly kosher between you and Leeza."

Helena poured herself a cup of coffee and found her cigarettes. Lighting one, she took a long drag, savoring the nicotine's soothing effect. She wouldn't be giving up her bad habit today. "Let me ask you something, James."

"Shoot."

"If the police find that cord from my drapes does match, what does that mean?"

"They'll have probable cause." He shifted his weight from one foot to the other, never taking his eyes off her. "It won't be good, I can tell you that much."

Helena stared at him through angry eyes. "I'll tell you what it *really* means. It means that whoever murdered Leeza has been in *my* house and is trying to frame me for murder."

CHAPTER TWENTY-THREE

DETECTIVE COLLIER WAS back within an hour, and this time he wasn't leaving until Helena came with him. "I have a warrant for your arrest," he snarled, just before cuffing her.

"What?" James yelped in amazement. "This is preposterous! Is it necessary to cuff my client, Detective?"

"Yes, Mr. Wingate, this is necessary. We have reason to believe that your client was involved in the murder of Leeza Kiley."

"Helena, don't worry about this. I'll take care of it," James said.

James had been reassuring her of that since Collier and his crew had left. But none of his phone calls worked, at least not yet. She refused to let any of these creeps see her break down. She'd lived through too much shit for that. As the detective read Helena her rights, she felt like she'd been jabbed in the stomach.

"Mom!" Frankie cried. "What are they doing?"

"It's okay. Stay here. Dad will be by soon. I promise, sweetheart, it'll be fine." She tried to sound calm for Frankie's benefit.

"Mom? Can I go with you? Please?"

"You're better off here. Stay in the house, Frankie, and don't talk to anyone!"

Helena couldn't look at Frankie anymore. She knew her daughter was crying, and there was nothing she could do to stop it. She hoped Patrick would arrive soon, as he'd promised.

With James leading the entourage, the front door was flung open. Immediately, flashbulbs popped in her face, as a tidal wave of accusations slammed into her. The reporters pressed against her like a swarm of jellyfish, their tentacles out and ready. Under siege, she bowed her head and let James speak for her. Drenched with sweat, she struggled to swallow the bile pushing up from her stomach.

"Helena, did you kill Leeza Kiley?"

Helena recognized Claire Travers's voice amongst the voices of reporters shouting questions at her.

"How did you do it, Helena?"

"Are you and Patrick Kiley lovers again?"

"What about the cord they found her strangled with? Is it true it matches the drapery cord in your home?"

Helena couldn't believe they already had that information. They were all ravenous vultures, jostling each other for the tiniest piece of her flesh.

She heard James say, "Ms. Shea did not murder Leeza Kiley or hire anyone else to do so. We will prove that she had nothing to do with this crime, and that the LAPD is in violation of Ms. Shea's civil rights. Please, that is all I have to say. You're trespassing on private property, and we ask you to cease and desist, or every one of you—and believe me, I'll find out who you are—will have lawsuits filed against you for trespassing."

One of the cops shouted, "Okay, people, show's over, back off. Get off this property."

James opened the cruiser's back door and told her that he'd be following in his car. "I'll get this handled in no time."

She watched him flip on his cell phone again, already working on getting her out of this horrible mess.

The ride to the station was silent except for the jargon coming over the police radio and the drone of the chopper flying above them. Helena hoped that Frankie was all right and that the vultures had left her alone. Thank God the child had such moxie and common sense. There was no way she'd talk to any of them. She knew that Frankie would wait for her father to get there. As she left, she saw that several policemen remained, continuing to search her home.

Helena also knew that the media would be waiting on the front steps of the police station. James met her there and continued to defend her as she was guided through the crowd and escorted inside. There, at least, she found some respite from the shrieking reporters.

James held up his hand. "Not a word, hear me, nothing. They're going to take you down to booking. By the time you get back, I'll see what I can do. Okay? Trust me."

"Booking? They're actually booking me for this? For murder? Aren't they taking this a bit far, James?"

"I agree. That Collier's a real ass. By the time I'm through with him and this department, they'll wish they'd never bothered you. They're concocting some kind of conspiracy theory that's a load of crap, and they probably think you'll crack and expose the actual murderer."

She nodded. She wanted to check with Patrick, make certain he'd gotten to Frankie, but for the moment, she was being brutally shuffled through the system as if she'd actually committed this hideous crime.

Anxious and with a pounding headache, she nearly fell down when a large female officer pushed her through a door. "What, are you drunk, too?" said the burly woman. "You are known for that, aren't you?"

Startled by the officer's callousness, Helena grew weary. The pounding in her head turned to a numbing, dull ache. The events of the morning were catching up with her. Tired—very, very tired, was what she wanted to answer, but she reminded herself not to say a word. These people were her enemies. Keeping mum may have made her look guilty, but she followed her attorney's orders, not wanting to jeopardize herself any further.

After showering her down and thoroughly frisking her, even probing the most private areas of her body, the woman gave her prison grubs to put on. Then she was taken to the booking area where she was sure the mug shot they took would be shown on that evening's newscasts.

More humiliated than she'd ever been before, even on her worst bender, she still refused to cry. After the "photo session," the officer escorted her into a closed-off room, where James sat waiting for her.

Seated across from her, he looked grave. "Listen, I've pulled some strings. I can get an arraignment on the docket for tomorrow morning."

Helena's jaw dropped. "Are you saying I have to spend the night here?" His silence answered her question. "My God, I can't believe this is happening."

"Tomorrow morning, you'll be out of here. I refuse to allow you to spend more than one night in this place. I tried everything, I really did. But because they're charging you with Murder One, we're talking huge dollars for your bail—and one helluva scandal. That shithead detective is still trying to somehow tie you into the fire over at your center. He's got nothing, though. They can't detain you after tomorrow. I've looked into this. Leeza Kiley was two inches taller and twenty pounds heavier than you, confirming my initial suspicion that this is a witch-hunt. Anyone in his right mind will know that you couldn't have committed this murder. Collier is bloodthirsty. The cops are looking for a patsy—and I'm sorry, kid, but you're it," he said in his southern drawl.

"So what happens now?" She bowed her head.

"I'm going before the judge in twenty minutes." He looked at his watch. "Can we count on Patrick to put up the cash to get you out of here?"

"I think so. That'll sure get people talking, his bailing me out."

"People are talking anyway. You'll have gone national by the time *Entertainment Tonight* and *Access Hollywood* is over this evening."

"Terrific. I'm a real Robert Downey Jr." Helena looked down at the cuffs rubbing her wrists raw. "I need some protection, James. I'll need to get out of the media's scrutiny. We've got to get my daughter away from this, too. Maybe I could go to the ranch with Frankie if Patrick wouldn't mind. What do you think? Will they let me out of the county? No one can get onto the ranch, and I'll at least have some privacy."

"I'll see what I can work out with the DA."

"I need to call Frankie and see if she's all right. Can I do that? Also, would you call over to The Sober Living House and ask for Lindsay? Tell her who you are and find out how Rachel is doing and the baby. Please?" She cracked a weak smile.

"You get one phone call, so call your kid. And yes, I'll speak with your friend and find out about Rachel." He leaned across the table and kissed her on the cheek. "You'll be out of here in the morning. I promise. I've got to go talk to the DA and the judge." He winked at her and told the officer to allow her to place her call.

Frankie answered her cell phone. "Mom?!"

"It's me, honey."

"Are you really in jail? I didn't believe it when they took you away. I thought they'd just ask you some more questions. But a reporter said they'd booked you for murdering Leeza. Is she really dead, Mom?"

"Yes, Frankie, and I'm sorry. I know she wasn't the kindest to you, but I'm sure, knowing you, that you must've loved her in some way." Frankie didn't answer. "They did book me, but it's all a mistake. I'll be out soon. I need to talk with your dad. Has he gotten there yet?"

"Yeah, he took Ella out to go to the bathroom while I finish getting my things together. He told me that he heard you'll be there overnight."

Helena sighed. "Yes it looks that way. Where are the two of you staying tonight?"

"With some friends of dad's. They said that Ella could come along, too."

"Oh good, thank him for me." Helena was relieved to know that Patrick had a handle on everything and that her puppy would also be in good hands.

"I'm scared for you."

"Don't be, honey. I'll be fine. I have to hang up now, Frankie, but we'll get through this somehow. I promise you, we're going to be ok."

"Mom?"

"Yes?"

"I love you."

"Me, too," Helena whispered back.

The female officer took her to the row of cells. Other women prisoners hurled out crude, rude remarks at her as she followed down the passageway. "Ooh, look at the glamour girl! Kiss, kiss, kiss for me, pretty baby."

"Hey beauty queen, got a place nice and warm for you to taste." Laughter resounded down the long corridor of cells.

"Ooh yeah, we've got all sorts of treats for a pretty thing like you. Bet you smell like a rose."

She shuddered at the comments, thinking that she'd hit rock bottom once before, but as the cell door slammed shut echoing down the corridor of the prison, this felt far worse.

The catcalls continued. Helena closed her eyes and leaned against the cell's stonewall. A sudden thought crossed her mind, and her eyes opened wide. With all the hoopla, she hadn't remembered last night's phone call from the man she'd thought had been hired by Leeza to frighten her and make her life miserable. Now she had doubts whether Leeza had been involved with the events that had occurred over the last week—serious doubts.

Was she being set up by someone else? She didn't think there was anyone out there who could possibly have hated her as much as Leeza. If she had an enemy she was unaware of, could this same person be behind all the frightening developments of the last week, including the fire and Leeza's murder for which she was being framed? If so, then it was more than likely someone Helena knew, someone who had access to her home. The thought sent an icy chill down her spine as she racked her brain wondering who could *possibly* want to destroy her like this. The only person she could think of was already dead, and Helena was charged with her murder.

CHAPTER TWENTY-FOUR

THE SMELLS OF stale body odor, urine, and vomit had obliterated Helena's appetite by the time dinner arrived: mashed potatoes, with a piece of dehydrated meat, and a few thin green strings that must have been green beans. Even though she hadn't eaten all day, she decided to pass.

"Hey, bitch, ain't you eating your grub? 'Cause I will."

The woman in the cell next to hers must've seen Helena set her plate aside. Helena slid the plate through the front of the cell over to the other woman.

"I like a willing servant," the woman laughed. "I wonder what else you'd like to do for me—fine little piece like you." She said it loud enough for the rest to hear. Whether the woman meant it or not, Helena knew the women reveled in her discomfort.

She sighed and curled up on the small metal cot, the mattress no thicker than cardboard, and the blanket like a layer of tissue paper. She was cold, hungry and humiliated. If ever she could've used a drink, it was now. No, that wasn't true. Helena reminded herself that drinking would just make things worse, never better. Her *worst* day sober—and this might just be it—was better than her *best* day in the hell of active addiction.

She ran over again in her mind how she had wound up here. The police had to realize that their evidence was flimsy at best. But what if they did convict her? What if a jury somehow believed that she was guilty? What if Collier found some way to tie Helena into the fire, and what if Rachel didn't live? Oh, God, if Rachel didn't live . . . It was too difficult to think about. All she wanted to do was be there for both Frankie and Rachel. Instead, she was here in this miserable cell, while some psycho got off on threatening her and now possibly setting her up. If he was a murderer, what did he have in store for her next? Maybe he'd already planted more evidence to further implicate Helena in Leeza's murder or the fire. She wished she hadn't gone storming over to Leeza's house the other day. Claire Travers was probably pounding out more vicious lies that could figure into a trial, if it came down to that. Who knew what Leeza had told the gossip columnist.

Shivering from the cold and fearing she might never get out of this place, sleep finally overtook her exhausted mind and body.

"Shea! Shea! Get your ass up!" A voice shouted into her ear, abruptly waking her. "Your bail has been posted." Someone shook her. She rolled over and saw the guard standing there, hands on her hips. "You gonna get up, or what?"

She stood and followed the guard out. Once she signed her release papers, her clothes and personal belongings were handed back to her. She quickly changed, hoping that her own clothes would erase some of the stink of jail.

When the steel doors swung open, there stood her lawyer and Patrick, who looked as worn out as she felt. She walked straight into his arms. He held her tight as she wept.

James laid a hand on her shoulder. "The masses await. Are you ready for this?"

Helena nodded. "Just get me out of here."

As the three walked through the front doors of the jailhouse, Helena was not as prepared as she thought. Dozens of reporters and camera crews surrounded the place, once again pushing cameras and microphones right in her face. The story must have hit big last night. This morning she was bombarded with the same slanderous questions, but keeping her head down, she did what she could to ignore them.

"Ms. Shea, did you hire someone to do it?"

"What about the rope?"

"Did the two of you conceive this plan together?"

The insults stopped when James held up his hands, as if he were a preacher in church. "There is no story here, folks. Ms. Shea had nothing to do with Ms. Kiley's death. We will prove this. The LAPD has made an enormous mistake by detaining my client. If anyone should be on trial, it is the LAPD for their clear harassment of an innocent citizen."

"What about Mr. Kiley? Did he post bail?"

"How is he involved?"

"No further comments at this time."

Patrick held onto Helena as he and James ushered her to the waiting car. She looked out as the driver shut the door, observing the chaotic scene around her, catching a glimpse of Claire Travers. Their eyes locked for a split second before Claire lifted her camera and took a shot. Helena closed her eyes, attempting to dissolve those images. This horror was not going to end any time soon.

CHAPTER TWENTY-FIVE

CLAIRE BREEZED INTO the criminal investigation department of the police station and headed for Collier's desk. Reporters were, as a rule, considered a nuisance by cops, but that never deterred Claire. She was sure that Collier would be happy to see her.

The room stank like coffee, and old cigarette residue stained the walls, which obviously hadn't been painted since the days when smoking was tolerated in the office. Papers were strewn everywhere across desks stained by coffee spills, stacking up as crime strained the department's resources.

She saw Detective David Collier talking with some of the other detectives outside the evidence and records office. He looked up at her and shook his head, knowing that trouble stood before him—but he had to admit that it was good looking trouble: a great ass, bright green eyes, blonde hair, and a feisty spirit. Claire knew that her ass had expanded an inch or two after she'd hit thirty a few years ago, but several butt tightening exercises a day seemed to keep the men looking, including David Collier. Claire watched David excuse himself and walk over to her. She'd known David for almost five years on a business basis, but he was always trying to make it something more.

"What are you doing here?" he asked, his eyes squinting into a suspicious glare.

"As if you didn't know. I'm getting dibs on the hot story of the day."

"Ah, well of course you are, Claire." She didn't like his smile.

Claire could smell his breath. He liked onions on everything but ice cream and cake. "So, what do you know? Is Helena Shea guilty? Did she do it? Did Kiley? Got any more word on that fire? What about the girl in the hospital? Is she gonna make it, or is Helena going up for more than one murder?"

"Whoa, slow down Miss LA Times. Dinner tonight at seven? We can talk then," he replied coolly as he escorted her into a private interview area, shutting the door behind them.

"What do you have besides the drapery rope, David? I hear the DA's office is saying they don't have enough of a case to continue. Some say you're barking up the wrong tree. Some are even saying Helena Shea was framed."

"Dinner first?" he insisted.

"David," she sighed in exasperation.

"You're not the only reporter looking for a story here, Claire. I'll be on my best behavior," he said with a wink.

"You're married," she reminded him. How did he consistently seem to forget this obvious detail?

"What's the harm in a dinner between friends?"

"David, come on, help me out. Give me this story, please. Are there any other suspects?"

"No one is above suspicion." He arched his eyebrows flirtatiously. "In fact, we know that you met with Leeza Kiley the other night. So I do need to ask you a few questions. We can either do it here at the station, or later over dinner. As you can see, I'm pretty busy right now."

Claire knew he had her trapped. "Come on now," she begged. "How could Helena Shea have strangled Leeza?"

There was a tap on the door. Collier hollered, "Yeah?"

Another detective cracked the door and said, "We need you."

Collier told Claire he'd call her later. Thank God for caller ID and answering machines. She didn't need any trouble with married men.

She left the station, remembering her last dinner with Leeza.

She had thought Leeza might have had a shred of humanity somewhere in her. But Leeza's past cruel actions made Claire wonder how many more had a score to settle with the vivacious redhead. Surely Helena Shea couldn't be the only one.

What about Patrick Kiley? He'd paid Leeza large sums of money just to be free of her. Then he'd faced the scandal, along with the rest of his family. It must've been awful, knowing what pain he'd brought to the women in his life. According to the record, though, he had an alibi: dining out with business associates until very late. So if he was involved, he hadn't been the actual perp.

Claire had a hard time believing that Patrick Kiley would be stupid enough to risk his life and security to have his ex-wife killed. Then there was this arson business with Shea House. Something wasn't clicking. The puzzle was not fitting together as neatly as what the police were obviously hoping for. But her story was hot again, and Claire was determined to squeeze it for every cent it was worth.

CHAPTER TWENTY-SIX

TYLER LEFT THE office early and headed to the bar down the street from his house, a little hole-in-the-wall with dim lighting and tattered vinyl seats. He needed a drink tonight, and he liked this quiet little place. The bartender knew how to make a stiff one. He also remembered his patrons' names, a practice that Tyler appreciated.

He couldn't get Jane Doe out of his thoughts; he even dreamed about her. He could see her dark eyes pleading to the madman who had unleashed his evil upon her. Tyler thought he could smell her when he slept—like lilies. The asshole who killed her enjoyed her scent too, reveling in her sweet freshness. She had been a girl bordering on womanhood—at least that's what her actions and emotions in his dreams suggested.

Forensic investigation had put her age at around twenty, give or take a couple years. He hated the man who'd savagely murdered her, robbing her of a long life filled with love and family, as his Susan had been deprived. Tyler still sensed that like Nelson, his wife's killer, this guy considered his kills as prizes. If only Tyler could connect another victim to this UNSUB, he could gather enough information to put together a real profile. Tyler knew this guy who'd killed Jane Doe had killed others as well, so maybe it was about a collection. But why did he need to collect, and where did he keep them?

When the toxicology report had come back on Jane Doe,

traces of formaldehyde had been detected in the bone, just as with Elaine Myers. "He's preserving them," Tyler said aloud. The bartender glanced down at him. "Another Stoli tonic," Tyler ordered and then went back to his thoughts. "And once the chemicals wear off, he dumps them."

Tyler picked up his cell phone and called his boss, Loretta Frey. She wasn't available, so he left a message. "Listen, we need to get on the national database and search out victims with exposure to formaldehyde and other chemicals used to preserve bodies. I'd also like to get a list of mortuaries located in the areas where Jane Doe and Elaine Myers bodies were found. I think I've figured out a link. I'm pretty sure he likes to hang on to them for awhile, and he's got a helluva fascination with death." He hung up, shot back the Stoli and ordered another one, wanting to get drunk and forget all this shit for once. But he couldn't stop thinking about his collection theory now that this idea of preservation was beginning to clarify things.

Tyler knew that hunting this madman would be taxing—they all were. But the echo of his wife's murder was so strong that his will to hunt him had grown as well. Tyler sucked back another drink, slammed the glass down on the bar, and pronounced, "The hunter has now become the hunted."

CHAPTER TWENTY-SEVEN

THE GULFSTREAM TOOK off from Burbank heading for Santa Barbara. James was able to convince the judge to allow Helena to leave LA County. After all, she had nowhere to run, since her famous face was known throughout the western world. Patrick had decided to take her to his ranch, knowing that the media would spin it but not caring. She was relieved, wanting only to escape their oppressive intrusion into her life for as long as possible.

Frankie remained quiet and withdrawn during the flight. Ella hid under Helena's seat. She'd insisted that the dog come onboard with her rather than ride in cargo, and neither Patrick nor the captain had raised objections.

Helena was grateful that Frankie was all right. She still hadn't had the opportunity to tell Patrick about the phone caller and how he might be tied into this. She didn't want to tell James until she conferred with Patrick. She knew how the revelation of a possible third party's involvement might sound to her attorney and all who were watching through critical eyes, especially after withholding this information for so long.

James made up for everyone else's silence by talking incessantly about matters Helena wanted just for a moment to forget. "This rap won't stick, Helena. There is no way the DA will take this case without anything more conclusive to go on." He tapped his foot against the floorboard. "But listen to me, they may try to work the conspiracy angle. Patrick has a strong reputation in the business community and a solid alibi on the night in question, thank God." Then in a hushed tone he added, "The police haven't questioned Frankie thoroughly yet. Plan for that."

"They won't put her on the stand, will they, James?" Helena said.

"We're a long way from that," Patrick cut in. "As far as I'm concerned, they won't put any of us on the stand."

"Mark Rogers—the DA—is a jerk, I won't deny that," James said. "If he sees an angle, he'll try to work it. He's full of political ambitions. This case is exactly what he needs to get his face out there."

Patrick squeezed her hand. Normally, she would've pulled it from his grasp, but right now she found it comforting. She smiled gratefully at him. "Do you really think they'll try to concoct some conspiracy theory?" he asked James.

"It's the stuff that makes great movies, and face it, gang, your story plays out like one," James said. "But I can't really say at this point."

"In the meantime, the cops are investigating everything about us, while the real killer walks free." Helena shook her head, a bitter taste rising in her throat. She was tempted to reveal her theory, but with Frankie so close, she thought it best to wait.

"Afraid so," James sighed. "The good news about your friend is that she's doing better. She's still in critical condition, but from what I understand, they believe that she'll pull through."

Helena closed her eyes, thankful to hear of Rachel's condition but also feeling horrible knowing that her friend would be scarred for life.

The plane landed twenty minutes later. A car waited for them on the tarmac. They were taken out to the ranch, where, sure enough, more camera crews and lookie-loos were camped by the main gate. But there wasn't much to report other than that a limousine had pulled into Patrick Kiley's ranch, presumably with Helena and their daughter inside.

As they settled in, Frankie came to the guestroom where Helena unpacked. She sat down on the end of the bed looking more like a frightened little girl than a budding young woman. "Mom?"

"Yes?"

"Are you okay? I was pretty scared for you. I thought that I was never going to see you . . ."

Helena stroked Frankie's long dark hair. "Nothing's ever going to keep us apart again." She pulled Frankie away and looked into her claret eyes. "I promise." Frankie nodded and hugged her once more.

Helena hoped that was the case, but her gut shouted that the evil which had seemingly crept into their lives was like a poisonous snake waiting to strike again—slow, low, quiet, and filled with venom.

CHAPTER TWENTY-EIGHT

"ALL RIGHT, COLLIER, where do things stand on the Kiley case?" Claire sat across from the detective at Hooley's Irish Pub, a favorite watering hole. It attracted a regular police crowd. She'd had to succumb to his pleas of meeting him for dinner if she expected any answers from him. He'd left her two telephone messages that afternoon, and she'd finally agreed. They downed their first pitcher of ale while waiting for their fish and chips.

"Claire, this is official police business. I can't discuss this case with you." His eyes gleamed, full of mischief.

"Look, I came to dinner, didn't I?"

"I didn't know it would be so horrible for you," Collier said, smirking.

"Sorry, I didn't mean to offend you."

He waved her off with his hand. "Nothing like shutting a man down to turn him on. But anything I tell you puts my career in jeopardy. I could lose my job."

"Never. You'd only be an unnamed source. Don't you think I subscribe to the journalistic code of ethics?"

"Good one, Travers. A tabloid reporter with ethics? Ha!" He burst out laughing.

"Yeah, well at least I'm always obviously good for a chuckle. Ready for some more brewski?"

"Hey, are you trying to loosen my lips?"

"Whatever it takes." Claire smiled, knowing she'd get her

information before the night was over. Their platters of fish and chips were set down in front of them while they ordered another pitcher. Nothing like fried fish and French fries to make a girl's stomach happy. Claire poured malt vinegar over her fries and dug in, while Collier continued his flirtatious banter over the upbeat Irish melodies playing on the jukebox.

"I'll tell you what it'll take."

"Are you sexually harassing me, Detective?"

"I wouldn't call it that." He filled their mugs.

"Because if you are, you could be getting into some really hot water."

"Threat? Or would that be like bath water?" He held up the mug, ready to toast the meal.

"Call it whatever you like."

"All right, since you wanna play hardball, sleep with me." He set the mug back down.

She knew that, although he was joking with her, he was also serious. "Overt sexual harassment."

"I'm honest."

"I like you, Collier, I really do. You're cute, funny, and, oh yeah, what is the word I'm looking for? You know, the one that's synonymous with commitment? Married, that's it."

"Claire, I'm separated."

She didn't know what to say, so she cracked a joke. "Better yet. I'm the rebound girl until you and wifey figure things out and hook back up. Sorry, not interested. The gal in the middle never has much fun."

"It wouldn't be like that. You've caught my eye for some time now, and you know I've never crossed the line. Oh sure, I flirt, but who wouldn't? You're a beautiful lady. But I've always been faithful to my wife. She left seven months ago for a stay-at-home type. We've had some problems over the last few years. I don't really want to get into it. I suppose I haven't had the balls to admit I've been traded in for the new, improved model. I'm only now beginning to tell people."

Claire studied his face. She heard him try to swallow back

his shame. The strength it took for him to confront this demon made her fidget. Claire had heard from a couple of other cops that Collier and his wife had lost a teenage daughter a few years back. She'd never asked how the girl died, but was sure her death also had something to with their break up. It was difficult for couples to recover from that type of loss and see eye to eye again. She wasn't good at intimate conversations, so she didn't bring it up. Vulnerability was something she found unattractive and weak, but on Collier it wore well, and stirred her. "I'm sorry, I had no idea."

"So, spend the night?"

Claire slugged him softly on the shoulder. They laughed and finished their second pitcher before she mentioned the Kiley murder. "Do you think Helena did it? Or did she hire somebody?"

"Not gonna let up, are you?"

"What did you expect?"

When Collier slurred his words, Claire figured she had him right where she wanted him. "Want my opinion?"

"You know I do."

"I think that Helena Shea is probably guilty in some capacity. She had plenty of motive to kill Leeza Kiley, and she had the means to make it happen. Do I actually think that she did it herself? Hardly. A man had to have done it for her. A lot of brute force was involved in that strangling. The bruising was severe. If Ms. Shea had done it herself, she probably would've gotten shot. I also think she hired someone to torch that rehab place she was building. Ms. Shea's bank accounts aren't as filled up as they used to be thanks to all the cash she's been putting into that place. There's a huge policy on it. Maybe she decided to back out, get her cash back, and let the government take care of the druggies. Maybe her do-gooder thing was simply an act. Now, I don't think she knew that girl was gonna be in the place when it went to embers, but if I can hang her on that one too, I will."

"Why do you hate her so much?"

"Why do you?"

"I don't."

"You could have fooled me with your sleazy stories."

"My stories aren't sleazy, and I'm only doing my job."

"Me, too."

"I think there's more to it."

"Nope. It's a job, like yours is a job."

"Whatever. Let me ask you, if she couldn't have strangled Leeza herself, why'd you haul her in?"

"The DA and I are pals. I explained to Rogers that Ms. Shea had to be in on it in some way. We figured that by giving her a taste of prison grub versus that gourmet stuff she's used to, letting her try an orange jumpsuit on for size and showing her what it's like being intimidated by some hard cons hungry for a pretty piece of ass—we might just get her lips flapping. But she's tough, and she's gotten lawyered up with a high priced attorney. She's not talking one bit." He motioned for the waitress, pointing to the empty pitcher. "I'm thinking they definitely hired a pro. They've both got enough money to do something like that. But I knew going for Kiley wasn't the answer. She could break under pressure. He wouldn't, and then he might just hang the whole department out to dry. I don't think Kiley had anything to do with the fire either—only her. Another thing that ties her in is that drapery chord—very stupid on her part."

"But couldn't that all be a setup? I overheard some guys talking about a frame-up job. Helena Shea must've made a few enemies in her time. Not to mention that if she's behind the arson at her place, why now? She sets a fire and then murders her archenemy? I know the model stereotype says they're not exactly geniuses, but how stupid could she be?"

"I've seen dumber. Anything's possible, but I gotta go with what's in here." Collier pointed to his gut. "And I know that no one could've hated Leeza Kiley more than Helena Shea. After all the grief that siren caused her last year? I never thought we'd hear the end of that story."

"Apparently we haven't."

"Hell, no. It's hot again, and that's why you need me—to give you the insides. I know that Leeza's murder wasn't a random attack. Now all I have to do is dot my i's and cross my t's, and you watch, it'll all come together."

"It's that easy, is it?"

"Sure is," Collier replied, his smugness growing with every gulp of brew.

"Wish I had your confidence," Claire said. Although Claire had never been a Helena Shea fan, she hadn't been her enemy either. She'd been the lucky messenger who caught a great story that had incidentally earned her some decent cash and given her some notoriety in the tabloid pages. It had even prompted some interest from a big media gun into Claire doing her own thirty-minute magazine show weeknights on one of the networks. She was still negotiating that. If anything, she had to be grateful to Helena. Without her juicy life to exploit, Claire wouldn't have climbed the career ladder as quickly as she had.

"So tell me, what did Leeza want with you? What was your dinner date all about the other night?" Collier asked, leaning in closer to her.

Claire paused for a moment, deciding how to handle this. She knew that she couldn't keep information from the police. But this was more personal, wasn't it? Fancying herself as an amateur sleuth, she didn't want to reveal everything to Collier just yet. She wasn't convinced of Helena Shea's guilt. By telling him about the confrontation Helena had with Leeza a few days before Leeza was murdered, she would definitely be dumping fuel on his investigative fire.

"I'm sure it's not news to you that Leeza was nothing less than a drama queen. She wanted to talk about her upcoming spread in *Playboy*. She was quite proud that at thirty-eight she'd gotten the centerfold. The scandal was partially responsible for her getting that spread. Leeza always knew how to work the angles."

"Scandal or not, she *was* pretty damn hot. I'm nearing fifty, and she was one of the best-looking women I'd ever seen. Reminded me of Melanie Griffith. It was a bitch seeing her dead like that. So, nothing else you need to tell me about the dinner?" His eyebrows rose skeptically.

"That was it. I left her at the restaurant to flirt with all the men wanting to get into her pants. The next thing I hear, she's dead." Claire could feel the alcohol going to her head, but poured another for each of them anyway.

"All right, Nancy Drew, I'll give you the benefit of the doubt for now. But you'd better expect me to have a few more questions if I find out you're keeping anything from me."

"I've got nothing to hide, Hardy Boy. What do you say we down another, and you tell me your woes?" Claire knew she might regret the evening, but with her beer goggles on, Collier was beginning to look a little like Elvis, for whom she had a certain fondness. Besides, he was sweet, lonely, and she was sure he held the key to unlocking this story. What could be the harm in having one more, anyway?

****

The harm turned out to be that a half-dozen beers and one persuasive detective found Claire's leg draped over Collier's—at five in the morning. With breath that would embarrass a dragon, Claire pulled the sheet around her as she got up quietly and made her way to the bathroom in hopes of finding an extra toothbrush. The sight of the one-bedroom bachelor pad—not to mention the stench coming from something rotting in the kitchen— confirmed to her that Collier and his wife had indeed split. No extra toothbrush meant that Collier hadn't entertained any other overnight guests recently. Feeling ashamed by the evening's events, she dressed quickly and quietly snuck out of Collier's bachelor pad before he could lift his head.

An hour later, after stopping by her home for a shower and her usual two-cup-caffeine-jumpstart, she headed to her office at *The Scene*. She rolled her car window down, letting her wet hair dry in the morning air. It was also an attempt to shake the pounding headache that reminded her of her poor judgment in last night's escapade. How could she have let it happen? *Oh, but Collier was really, really cute—well, last night he was, anyway. Ugh, cute schmute, you schmuck! You crossed* way *over the line between professionalism and sheer stupidity!*

All day at work she tried hard to shake off the memories of the night before. She left early—a rarity for her, especially at the beginning of a big story—taking the work home with her. One of her hobbies was developing her own photographs, and she'd told the tech that she'd do these herself, hoping she'd gotten that shot of Helena looking directly at her. That shot, she was certain, would make its way onto the front pages of millions of newspapers.

Her answering machine blinked obnoxiously as she walked in, signaling what Claire figured was inevitable: another call from Collier. He'd left messages that ranged from courteous and professional to nasty and obscene. On the last two, he'd sounded quite perturbed.

As she started to play back the messages, the phone rang again. She decided it wouldn't do her any good to avoid Collier; in all likelihood it would make things more difficult. "Hello?"

"Busy day?"

Claire heard disrespect tinged with anger in his voice. "Actually it was. I'm sorry I couldn't get back to you. It's just I've . . ."

"No worries, Claire. I thought that maybe you really liked me. Maybe, hell, who knows? But I see that pumping information is your deal. And I mean that literally. You truly are the all-American-career girl."

"No, Collier, that's not what it was about, I swear."

"You broads are all the same. Don't bother."

Claire could tell that he'd had a few. She also realized that she'd better handle this situation with care. Otherwise, last night's poor decision could have severe consequences. She did need Collier for the information he could give. He'd given her the inside scoop on several stories in the past concerning the jet set and their criminal side.

"Come on, David. I did enjoy being with you. And I like you. It was just kind of weird. We've been friends for so long. And I was busy today. I'm sorry I left so early this morning. I guess I didn't know how to face you."

A long pause on the other end; Claire could hear voices and

laughter in the background. "All right, so maybe it was a bit weird. But nice weird, huh?"

"Definitely."

"Well, do you think maybe you could meet me tonight?"

"I'd like to, but I've got to finish my article." He didn't reply. "What about tomorrow for lunch?" That was safe.

"Yeah, okay. I'll call you in the morning."

"Great." Claire mustered all the enthusiasm she could, then hung up with a sigh. She went into her hall bathroom, which she'd turned into a darkroom. Visitors rarely stopped by, so she could keep it set up. Like a frustrated child, she purposely banged her head several times against the wall, repeating, "Stupid, stupid, stupid. Forget about it for now, and handle it tomorrow. Forget it," she said staring at the painting on the wall facing her—a Picasso replica.

Claire's home projected her enjoyment of life's simple things. It was a small end-unit condo, all in white, offset by her bright and colorfully eccentric art. Art was her one extravagance, besides the plants which occupied any vacant spot in every room. She liked contemporary.

Coming from the CD player in the other room, Billie Holiday sang the blues as Claire developed her photos. The red light shone on the tray solution. There it was. Helena Shea, looking out the door of the limo just before it closed and right into the lens of her camera. Her eyes appeared sad, frightened and tired. Guilt swept through Claire as she strung the photos up to dry and stared at the picture of the beautiful woman who was obviously so worn and confused. This photo wasn't just worth a million words; it was also worth a lot of money.

It was a living and it paid the bills. Her readers could come to their own conclusions. *I only write the stories*, she argued with her demons, as she looked at a broken-down Helena Shea. She'd seen the woman come through scandal after scandal: the loss of her dad, a life shattering bout with alcoholism and drug addiction, a very well publicized trip through rehab, and to top it all off, the public revelation about her daughter's birth followed by a tabloid war with Leeza Kiley. Now, she'd lost her rehab center and was facing a possible conviction for murder and arson. Claire's contribution to exploiting this woman's life made her feel pretty damn miserable. How much more could Helena take? Claire was not accustomed to thinking of the people she wrote about like this; she hated the feeling.

She walked out of her darkroom, needing some air. She left the photos behind, wishing she'd become a doctor or something that benefited mankind. For the first time in her career, she struggled with her responsibilities as a journalist. Was she doing the ethical thing? She couldn't help but wonder if, as her work hurt others, it could also be doing damage to her?

CHAPTER TWENTY-NINE

TYLER LISTENED WITH interest to the update on the Leeza Kiley murder on his car radio. Something about the woman's murder nagged at him. He felt sorry for Helena Shea and angry with Detective Collier, with whom he'd had the distinct pleasure of having a few run-ins with in the past. Collier seemed hell-bent on proving her guilty. But Tyler had far more important things to take care of. There was a dragon to slay. He was sure that Ms. Shea had a good lawyer who could get her off if she was innocent of the crimes she was charged with.

He made a right turn into suburbia and headed straight for his boss's home. Loretta had called earlier to say she'd gathered some interesting information for him, and that he could stop by her place to pick it up.

As he pulled into Loretta's circular driveway with his window cracked, he heard her Rottweiler barking in the backyard announcing his arrival. Her teenage son came out, a skateboard under his arm. He nodded to Tyler as he put the board down and skated away.

Tyler tapped lightly on the door, then let himself in. The house smelled of mothballs and fried chicken. Loretta was from the south, and though she was first and foremost a cop, she hadn't forgotten her southern hospitality.

Loretta Frey was fiftyish, with a few grays peeking through her otherwise dark hair, which was cut in a severe bob. She was taller than he was, making her at least six-feet, with clear blue eyes framed by finely etched lines.

"Hi, Tyler. I thought I heard you pull in," she sang out, peering around the entry from her kitchen. Her home felt like a Hansel-and-Gretel-cottage, with archways leading into various rooms. At a glance, one would never guess that Loretta Frey ran the Child Abduction, Serial Killer Unit, Los Angeles Division. Her charm as a hostess coupled with her perfectly kept home were deceiving, but after working several cases with her, Tyler knew that she, too, could be a hard-nosed agent who lived to put away the bad guys and did it very well. Though there were many in this male dominated profession who wished they could deny this fact, they simply couldn't argue with a career filled with successful arrests, convictions, and closed cases. Loretta had earned her job running his division.

"How's it going, Ms. Loretta? Something smells wonderful in here." He rubbed his stomach.

"Good, good. I fried us up some of my mama's famous chicken for lunch. She always made a fine fried chicken. I thought you might be hungry."

"Starving. I've learned to bring an empty stomach when coming here."

"You've learned well, then." Loretta winked at him and put together a heaping plate of the chicken, mashed potatoes and gravy, coleslaw, and biscuits. Tyler wouldn't leave hungry. That was for sure.

She made herself a plate of food as Tyler started in on the feast. "I checked out your hunch," she said, "and I came up with this." She set down her plate and handed him two files: *Bridgett Simons a.k.a. Bridgett Core*, and *Trudy Giles*.

"What's this?" He flipped one open.

"Vics showing trace elements of formaldehyde. The bodies were found partially decayed a couple hundred miles between one another. Bridgett, a former porn star, was found out in the Mojave just like your Jane Doe. Trudy Giles was found in a rural area outside of San Diego. UNSUB still out there on both cases, as far as we know."

"I knew it! We've got a serial killer here."

"Looks like a strong possibility."

"What's the time span? Why didn't the computer catch this?"

"Good question. Trudy Giles was found in the late 80s. San Diego PD thought it was an isolated case and the national mainframe, as you know, wasn't operating at that time. Bridgett was found in '95. Her porn star status led police to believe she'd pissed the wrong guy off. No one gave any thought to a possible serial killer."

"Any others across the board?"

"Well, haven't found anything yet, but if our man is a serial killer, he's been at this for at least fifteen years, maybe longer."

"What about funeral homes? Mortuaries? Medical schools?"

"I'm on that, too. We're looking for priors in that line of work and at the med schools. This could be some janitor who knew where the stuff was stored."

"I don't think he's blue collar."

"You have a profile going?" she asked.

"Working on it. I know this much: he's organized, practiced, maybe a professional. He's been at it for a while which means he can blend into society. If he's been at it for that many years, he's not in his twenties or even early thirties. He's probably at least forty. If he's preserving these women, then he's got some twisted fantasy going on that's most likely escalating."

"What are you thinking?"

"My guess is they're used as some sort of emotional or romantic partner, perhaps representing or tied to someone he's lost. Someone close to him."

"Maybe like a mother figure?" Loretta asked dipping her biscuit into the gravy.

"Could be. If he's saving the bodies for a period of time, he needs physical companionship, but fears intimacy. He needs to be in control. I think he adapts very well to different locales, maybe takes on a variety of personalities. Is there anything in the computers about rape?"

"By the time they found the Giles girl it was too late to tell. Minimal remains. We had to go off dental. But there did appear to be signs of post-coital on the Simons girl. Too many years to get a semen sample. They tried to get the DNA, but couldn't."

"That's what I'm saying! This guy's good, knows exactly how to do it—a true psychopath. The problem with these bodies being so dated is figuring out if he's still prowling, or maybe in jail for other crimes, or has changed his MO, or maybe he's dead."

"Like finding a needle in a haystack." Loretta put down her fork.

"But something tells me he's still at it. This needle's gonna pierce again, and I've gotta blunt him before it happens. I don't think he's dead or moved on down the road. Okay by you if I talk to the detectives on these cases?"

"Sure. You might have a hard time tying down the guy on that Bridgett Simons case. It's David Collier with LAPD."

"No kidding? The one and only? What's the deal with that jerk anyway—his career in so much trouble he's got to go around charging innocents? You've heard he's working that Leeza Kiley murder, haven't you?"

"Be careful what you say, Ty. We're not working his case. Messing with the local cops' jurisdiction will get us both in hot water. It just isn't considered politically correct. Don't question him about the Shea case. Off the record, I agree. She probably didn't do anything. Bad timing and the wrong enemy to have, maybe, but murder, I doubt it. But that's his mess, not yours. When you reach him, stick with the topic at hand."

"No problem. I can be politically correct, I suppose. It just doesn't sit well with me when a cop does the bullshit things that Collier does to get a conviction."

"It's not our case. *Please* try not to cause me any grief on this one? The chief of police can be a real ass to deal with. They don't like us treading. Oh, you might also want to talk to Claire Travers. She's a tabloid journalist."

"What would I need her for?"

Loretta took a drink, then wiped her mouth daintily with the napkin. "She writes a lot of that gossipy crap about the rich and famous. Apparently when this girl Bridgett went missing, Claire wrote an article about how the girl had been a small town girl with hopes and dreams, blah, blah, blah." She waved her hand back and forth. "She even took a trip to Idaho to talk with her mother. The cops chalked it up to the porn industry lifestyle, like I said. Shit like this happens all the time in that line of work. Girl doesn't show up for work one day and no one thinks too much about it. But apparently this girl had a spark, and after a few days, people noticed that she'd disappeared. No leads, nothing. But who knows, maybe this gossip columnist picked up something or will remember something that Collier won't."

"I'll see what I can do."

"I think you're on the right track, Ty. Stay with it."

The two agents finished their lunch before Loretta got on the phone to track down David Collier. Three hours after Tyler arrived in Pasadena, he had a tentative meeting set up with Claire Travers.

Tyler knew he was getting closer to this freak, beginning to figure him out. He also knew that the boys who played in this bad guy's league were very slick and dedicated killers. The only way he'd ever stop was when he wound up dead or behind bars. Either way, it had to be soon, before another girl became his trophy.

CHAPTER THIRTY

AS NIGHTTIME ROLLED around, Frankie switched on the television, then quickly turned it off when she saw her parents and herself on the screen. She couldn't go to school for a while or hang out with her friends. Her mother's lawyer said that even having friends over could be a detriment, since visitors might be subpoenaed to testify against her mother. Outsiders were no longer welcome. The family had to band together. Oh, to be a normal teenager with a normal family. Was it too much to ask?

Frankie sat on her bed, trying to get into the latest Stephen King novel. There was a knock on her door, and Helena came in without waiting for Frankie's permission. Frankie pulled her knees up to her face. Helena sat down beside her, not saying anything for a moment. Finally, Frankie said, "The reporters think you or Dad could've killed her, don't they?"

"That's one theory, but it's not true." Helena touched Frankie's dark hair.

"I know it isn't true, but they'll talk like it is. It's like before, but worse. I can't even see my friends. The reporters and your lawyer are ruining my life."

"We'll just have to get used to it, ignore them, and put up with these inconveniences, but it'll only be for a little while. Then they'll go find some other tragedy to exploit."

"Ignore them? Inconveniences? Are you kidding? There's like a gazillion reporters out there, and we're supposed to ignore them? I can't go to school. I can't even ride my horse, because the paparazzi might get a picture of me." Hot tears burned her eyes. She quickly wiped them away. "God, Mom! I mean, I'm happy that you're not in jail and I know you didn't do it, but when do I get my life back? This is what I get for having a famous model for my real mom?" Frankie watched Helena flinch, wishing she could take back her harsh words. She hated hurting people, and things had been going so well between them.

"You have no idea how sorry I am for all of this. I wish there was something I could do to make it better."

"Well, obviously you can't."

"Don't talk to your mother that way, young lady." Frankie saw her father standing in the doorway. "This is difficult for all of us. We love you, honey, and we're all going to get past this." He walked over and handed a mug to Helena. "Here you go. Thought you might like some tea."

"Thanks."

"What about you, Frankie? Want me to make you a cup?"

"No thanks. I want to be left alone. Just when you think it's all gonna be okay, boom!" She smacked her hands together. "It's not. Those people out there don't care what they say or do to us. They want to ruin you, Dad, me, everything. Exactly like before. It'll never end, I just know it."

"Listen sweetie, you've got a right to be angry, you really do. And we will get our lives back soon. Then we can go forward. But please know how much we both love you." Helena and her dad left her room

Whatever. If we ever get our lives back, Mom, it'll be like starting all over again. Gee, that sounds grand. More shrinks, more trying to prove to ourselves that we're as regular as the next family. Sure.

As soon as her parents were gone, Frankie reached for her phone. She needed to get the hell out of here. She'd sneak past all the jerks outside and at least see a few friends. It was Saturday night. After everything she'd been put through, she deserved a good time. And she was going to have it.

CHAPTER THIRTY-ONE

TYLER FIGURED ON his little *soirée* being fascinating. He wasn't disappointed. The meeting he'd arranged with Ms. Travers also worked perfectly into Collier's schedule—interesting, that anything would work in Collier's schedule. Such a busy guy. Ha! Tyler had worked briefly with Collier before, and no love was lost between them. Collier didn't have a clue about the intricacies of psychological profiling; he'd called it witchcraft, and had said some ugly things about Tyler Savoy. But Tyler wouldn't let an almost washed-out detective bully him.

He had no idea what to expect from Claire Travers. After leaving Loretta's house, he went straight to the library to read her articles on Bridgett Core. He found it interesting that her latest articles included several pieces on the Shea/Kiley scandal and a recent by-line on a news piece about the Kiley murder. Although tabloids weren't Tyler's thing, he'd discovered that Claire Travers was a good writer. Tyler remembered that Susie had enjoyed reading the gossip rags for fun, occasionally filling him in on the lurid lives of the rich and famous.

As was his custom, Tyler was early for their meeting, so he reread Ms. Travers' articles. He became so engrossed in the stories about Leeza that he didn't notice when the gossip columnist and the detective walked in. Ms. Travers certainly pricked his bubble of concentration.

"Another fan, I see."

Claire Travers was nothing like he'd imagined. She was quite pretty with green eyes and blonde hair, cut into a short pixie style; her black skirt showed off shapely tanned legs.

For a moment, he was speechless, until Collier growled, "So what's all this about, Savoy?"

Tyler looked square into Collier's eyes. "Nice to see you too, Dave. It's been awhile." Tyler stretched out his hand to Ms. Travers. "Hi, I'm Tyler Savoy. I'm with the CASKU division of the FBI."

"Very nice to meet you, Mr. Savoy."

"Call me Tyler, please."

Collier rolled his eyes.

"Call me Claire, Tyler."

"Nice to meet you, Claire."

"Okay, formalities over," Collier said. "Let's get this over with, 'cause I've got things to do."

"Right. You wouldn't want to miss a repeat of *Miami Vice*," Tyler said, and with a laugh motioned for the waitress, ordering three beers on tap. Before Collier could respond, Tyler spoke up again. "I understand you both did some investigating on a missing persons case back in '95? A young woman by the name of Bridgett Simons?" He pointed to a photograph from Loretta's file.

"You mean Bridgett Core?" Claire cut in.

"One and the same."

Collier shifted in his chair. "I worked that case, yeah. No real leads. You know, one of those things. Girl was in a nasty business, sometimes there are nasty consequences."

"Actually, that's not completely true," Claire said. "I found out that girl was fairly decent. She had a rotten upbringing and was only trying to make life work for her."

"Come on, Claire. I've seen this plenty of times. These broads don't wanna better themselves. It's all about the money."

"I didn't know you were such a chauvinist ass."

"Okay, I didn't call you here to discuss Miss Core's morals. I've found a connection with her murder and two others," Tyler interrupted.

Collier's face turned ashen. Wiping his mouth with the back of his hand, he said, "What? Are you talking about a serial case? Come on, man, don't pull that hoodoo voodoo crap you profilers do. The girl ran with a bad crowd, pissed someone off, and *that* was that. Curtains." Collier drew his finger across his neck.

"Were you aware of the formaldehyde found in Bridgett Core's remains?" Tyler asked.

"Could've easily been a mistake by the lab. Those techs use that stuff all the time. They're not infallible. Maybe it was on their hands when they did the autopsy. Hell, I don't know. They also found drugs. Who knows, maybe she was into some weird smack. You wouldn't believe what I've seen people take."

"That girl wasn't into weird smack," Claire said.

"She was a junkie, Claire."

"She was misguided. It was that simple. Yes she probably used a bit, but she wasn't a junkie. She wasn't a bad kid. Tyler might be onto something."

Tyler turned to face Claire. "Look, I'm working on a Jane Doe case. I think the two are connected, plus at least two more."

Claire leaned in. "What makes you think that?"

"We've found traces of formaldehyde in all the vics, and I have a hunch."

"Hunch?" Collier interrupted. "Aw, c'mon, Claire, Savoy here thinks he's the Miss Cleo of the FBI's Psychic Friends Network. He solves cases through his so-called feelings or visions or whatever the hell he calls them. It's bullshit, if you ask me."

"I don't think its bullshit. And I didn't ask you. It's been proven that profiling works. We aren't living in the dark ages anymore, Dave," Claire replied. "Besides, I did some research of my own today. I found out that Tyler has solved quite a few serial murders. He's truly a known asset to the FBI. Not only is he considered an excellent agent, he's renowned for his work in profiling."

"You gotta be fuckin' kidding me."

Tyler smiled. He liked Claire Travers, and he enjoyed how she handled Collier. However, he did get the feeling that there was some type of intimate connection between the two of them. He crossed his arms and leaned back in his chair. "Thank you very much, dear lady."

"Oh cut the chivalrous crap and tell us what you want." Collier asked checking his watch.

Tyler ignored the remark, remembering Loretta's pleas. "Information. Any information you two can remember. I need anything that might help me to connect these cases together."

"Savoy, I don't know if you read the papers, but I'm kinda busy these days. I'm the lead detective on the Leeza Kiley murder. I'm sure you've heard of it?"

"Oh yes, sir, and guess what? I got a hunch you're taking the wrong lady to the gallows, buddy." So much for being politically correct.

"Don't tell me you got a *vibe* about that murder, too, Savoy? I hate to tell you, but we've got it all figured out. It's only a matter of getting solid evidence."

"I thought you might say that. You're looking to shake down Helena Shea, or the Kiley woman's ex."

"I think that's obvious." Collier took a gulp from his beer.

"You're wrong."

"Oh shit, Savoy, what the hell did you drag us out here for? I don't need a lesson in how to do my job—past, present, or future, thank you. My record speaks for itself. Now as far as the Bridgett Core thing, I'll have one of my guys get back to you with the info. Like I said, I've got other fish to fry."

"Best be careful who you're putting in the pan there, Collier. You might wind up wishing you'd done a little better investigating before this Kiley/Shea thing is over."

"You know what, dickhead, that's my case! You can take your hocus-pocus bullshit elsewhere. Let a real cop do his work. Come on, Claire, we're out of here."

"Actually," she replied as she looked up at Collier, who was now standing. "I'd like to listen to what this man has to say."

"Fine. Then Prince Charming can take you home." Collier

turned on his heels and marched out the door.

They watched him storm out of the restaurant. "Something tells me he's not going to be much help with my case," Tyler remarked.

Claire shrugged and replied, "Doesn't look like it. I'll do what I can, though I'm not sure what that might be. I talked to Bridgett's mother and a few people she'd worked with. I'll have to check out my files and see what I can come up with. It'll take a few days, though. Anything written two years ago or more I've boxed up and put out in my garage. Can you wait?"

"I guess I'll have to."

"I don't think I can tell you much more than what you've already read in my articles."

"Try me. There's a real sense of urgency here."

"Why?"

Tyler didn't want to scare her, so he sugarcoated his answer with, "Because I like to solve cases at record speed."

"Yeah, whatever. Tell me the real reason."

"You're good." He weighed his answer and decided to drop the bomb. "By the way, this is all off the record."

Claire nodded. "On my honor."

"I need to solve this case because this guy does what he does well, and I'm pretty sure he does it a lot. And if I'm not mistaken, he's gonna do it again soon if we don't put a noose around his neck first."

CHAPTER THIRTY-TWO

FRANKIE'S FRIENDS WAITED for her at the cove at Summerland beach, anxious to hear her version of what was going on. Getting the real story made it worth their while to sneak out of their homes after the dinner hour.

For her escape, Frankie wore a black turtleneck, jeans, and her dad's Raider's cap. There were several security cops around the ranch, but one savvy teenager who'd combed every inch of the place, using a little ingenuity, could get out. The few media stragglers left outside were the least of her worries. Her father's ranch was huge, and if she played it right, she knew how to get down to the beach.

Next to her room was a guestroom with French doors opening to a patio. Her mom was staying there. Luckily her parents were still out in the family room talking with the attorney. Ella was lying on the bed. She lifted her head as Frankie entered, whining and wagging her tail. "Shh, girl, hush." Ella laid her head back down, continuing to eye her.

Frankie knew that motion detectors were set up all around the backyard. Just another challenge—not like she hadn't done it before. She made a game out of it, pretending she was some sort of spy-007, girl-power style.

She unlocked the doors and slipped out, staying close to the wall. She ducked low and crawled around the edge of the backyard. There were steps leading down to the pool, but she worked her way through the landscape. Once she'd slid down on her belly to the bottom of a small knoll next to the pool, she stood and wiped herself off. She hadn't triggered the motion detectors.

But as she stood up, a large Doberman came bounding along, his pal close behind. Damn! "Merlyn, Morgan, go back!" she whispered loudly. The dogs had triggered the automatic lights as Frankie sprinted for a large palm tree to hide behind. She heard her dad open one of the doors.

"Merlyn, Morgan, come here! No, no it's nothing, only the dogs playing, don't worry about it." Frankie heard her dad say.

Frankie breathed a sigh of relief and waited until the lights turned off. Next to the palms was the wrought-iron fence. This was where things could get dicey. Her next step was to scale the fence, by no means an easy task. She fell back once and nearly split her jeans, but with a little effort, she was off the property, having been noticed only by the dogs.

She made her way to the back road leading to the cliffs. Thankfully the reporters hadn't discovered it, as it was really only known to a handful of surfers. She knew her parents would kill her if they found out, but she had to get away from the house for a little while and hang out with her friends—people who didn't judge her or her parents by the news reports.

Once she'd reached the cliffs, she scrunched down to begin the steep descent. Part way down, she stood back up, brushing herself off. She took off her backpack for a minute to rest. She looked at her watch. Her friends expected her in twenty minutes. Sneaking out was fun. Getting away with it was even better. When she was much younger, her dad had called her his little Indiana Jones. Frankie had always enjoyed adventure.

She closed her eyes, breathing in the salty air, listening to the sound of waves crashing against the rocks below. She loved it out here. Her friends would hang out, talk, and some would drink beer, if any had filched some from their parents' fridge. Frankie wasn't into the drinking scene after knowing what her mom had gone through, but she certainly wasn't one to judge friends who didn't judge her.

Chris Highland was supposed to be there, too. He was cute and funny, and he played on the baseball team. Frankie thought that maybe he liked her as much as she liked him. Still fairly innocent, Frankie had only been kissed twice. And with trepidation and desire, she had to admit that she wanted Chris to kiss her.

She reached down to throw her backpack over her shoulder. As she did, someone stretched his arm around her neck and pulled tight, dragging her back. She choked. Her arms failed, trying to dig her nails into his arm. His strength was far superior to hers. She slipped on the loose dirt and rocks, but he held steady.

A cloth was placed over her face as he whispered, "Quiet, my sweet. It will all be fine. I knew if I came here and waited patiently that I'd probably get my chance to meet Helena's little angel. I'm pleased it happened so soon. You are a restless girl, I know. And because of that, I knew you'd eventually attempt to get out of that prison, and here you are."

Frankie tried to hold her breath, but his strength and persistence won out. She felt herself drifting off—the fumes of whatever covered her face nauseated her, stinging her nose and eyes. The world below blurred and then disappeared into a void. Seconds later she could no longer hear the crashing waves.

CHAPTER THIRTY-THREE

THE GRANDFATHER CLOCK in Patrick's living room chimed eleven o'clock, startling Helena. The effects of the past twenty-four hours had done a good job of shattering her nerves.

They'd talked with her attorney all evening after she'd phoned Lindsay and received an update on Rachel and the baby. The baby was doing fine, and Rachel was better but still in a great deal of suffering. Helena wished she could go to her. No chance of that. She had to get her information through Lindsay. The hospital refused to give it to her. Apparently there were people who believed she was guilty for both Leeza's murder and torching the center. She knew there was even speculation that she'd tried to kill Rachel. The whole thing was ludicrous, and Helena had never felt more depressed in her entire life, other than when her dad died. At least she'd seen that coming. This situation was more like a bad train wreck. She'd had no idea it would hit.

James, her attorney, finally left for his hotel, even though Patrick insisted he stay with them. He'd phoned once to let them know that most of the media had left the front gate, but the guards were still standing watch. Some comfort.

Morgan, one of the big black dogs, climbed onto the sofa with Helena, warming herself by the fire Patrick had lit. She looked over at him stoking the fire. The other dog, Merlyn, was lying at her feet. The smoky smell of burning wood made Helena think

of happier times, when a roaring fire would have brought Patrick
and her together, cuddled in each others' arms.

She scratched Morgan's head. "What did you do, chase my
poor puppy into my room? You ornery vixen." The large animal
wagged her stump of a tail. Although the fire blazed, nothing
seemed to warm Helena. Frankie's cold words had left a dull
ache in her heart. Patrick gave her a woolen blanket, which she
wrapped around herself.

"There we go. That should last a little while longer, at least."
He placed the poker back in its holder. Then he came over to her,
hesitating before sitting beside her on the sofa. She looked down
at her hands, fidgeting with the ends of the blanket as she tried
to hold back her tears. Patrick wiped them away. "It's all going
to work out."

She squeezed his hand. "I want to believe that, but I'm having
a hard time. It's not like we haven't dealt with all this before. I
guess I can go through a trial if I have to, because I'm innocent.
But this whole thing is so unfair to Frankie. She's just a kid.
To have to drag her through this media onslaught again makes
me sick. Then there's poor Rachel and little Jeremy. I feel so
helpless."

"Me too. But we had no way of knowing this would happen."

"I love Frankie. I can't lose her again."

"You won't. She's more resilient than you give her credit for."

He hugged Helena tightly, enough to make her feel slightly
uncomfortable in his arms. She pulled away, fearful that their
embrace might lead to more than a shoulder to cry on.

"Listen, there's something I have to tell you. It's something
I've even been keeping from James until I had a chance to discuss
it with you." Helena watched her grave words tug at his features.

"What are you talking about?"

"There've been some weird things going on lately, and well,
I didn't want to alarm anyone. I thought it was Leeza up to, you
know . . ."

"Helena, you're not making any sense. What're you getting
at? What weird things?"

Helena took in a deep breath and let it out slowly. Then she told Patrick all about the near hit and run with the van, the phone calls and her suspicions about the fire.

"And you didn't tell anyone?" Disbelief was written all over his face. "This is serious. What were you thinking?"

Helena choked out, "Well, I thought, as I said, that Leeza was behind it. And if she did hire someone to destroy me or Shea House, that could only implicate me further in her murder."

"Possibly, but you're innocent, and that would come out. I can't understand why you've kept this a secret."

"You can't? Why don't you try to go out in public right now, Patrick. You don't think people won't berate you, question you, doubt you? They've been doing that to me ever since Leeza started the ball rolling by telling Frankie the truth via the tabloids, before we had a chance to. Come on, you don't think that if I went to the police with this that there wouldn't be doubts, questions? If I had told them this, it might look even worse for me now, like I'd concocted this whole outrageous story of a stalker so that I wouldn't be a suspect." Her hands trembled as she wiped her nose. "Innocent yes, but believable? Come on, the tabloids in the past made me sound like a manipulative bitch who spent all her money on partying and didn't give a rat's ass about her child. Not to mention that I'm a husband stealer. I was just rebuilding a decent image, one in which people would see me for who I really am, not some self destructive, ego driven maniac. Now, what do you think people are going to believe? And that detective who's out for my blood, do you think he's going to believe me? No. People like to believe the worst, and I felt by hiding this I was at least protecting you and Frankie."

Patrick leaned back rubbing his eyes. "You're right. I'm sorry."

"Well, what should we do?"

"I think we have to go with it and hope for the best. We'll tell James tomorrow. He's good at what he does. He'll try hard to keep it under wraps. He's your attorney. There is something that goes along with passing the bar called confidentiality. Trust him."

"Okay. But I'm still not sure if it's the right thing to do. Right now, I'm too tired to worry about it anymore. I think I'll try to get some sleep. I'll check on Frankie one last time before going to bed." Anger churned deep in her stomach as she recognized skepticism in Patrick's voice, but she was far too exhausted to deal with it.

"Helena, the one thing I don't get is why you didn't call me when this psycho included our daughter in this game, when he said he'd been watching her?"

She closed her eyes, feeling as if she were already on trial. She shot back at him, "It happened so fast, I really don't know. Maybe I thought that for once I could protect her. You've been doing it all her life. And for once, just once, maybe her mother should do that too. I know it sounds stupid and selfish, and I'm sorry now, but it's how I felt." She excused herself and headed for Frankie's room. Her muscles ached as the hollow pit in her stomach swelled. Anger was not something she managed well. It had been something she'd always kept bottled inside. An unhealthy trait, one that allowed her addictions to control her life, but she could never go back there again, no matter how loudly the chemicals that dulled her pain called her by name. So for now, the ache raged on.

Frankie's light was still on, and Helena could hear the radio playing Jack Johnson. Good, she's still up. Maybe she'll want to talk. She knocked on her door. No response. She decided to go in and turn off her radio and light. When she entered her room, she saw that Frankie wasn't there. Helena checked the bathroom, then went down the hall to the kitchen, thinking that perhaps Frankie had gone there for a midnight snack. No luck. Where could she be? She double-checked throughout the house. The realization set in that Frankie was not anywhere inside the house. Panic rose like spewing lava from a volcano.

Patrick was locking the back door as she came into the kitchen. The look on her face must've told him something was very wrong. "What is it?"

"Frankie's gone!"

CHAPTER THIRTY-FOUR

PATRICK INSISTED THEY not call the police for the moment. "Listen, she's a savvy kid. She knows exactly how to sneak off this property, and I know no one got onto this place. It would've been impossible."

"If she was able to get out, someone could've gotten in," Helena replied.

"Like I said, she knows the ins and outs like nobody else would."

"So she's done this before?"

"Of course. She's a teenager. She probably snuck off to hang out with her friends. Think about it. Here we've told her that basically she's grounded, through no fault of her own. She took off to let off some steam."

"I still think we should call the police." When Helena reached for her pack of cigarettes, Patrick grabbed them out of her hand. She said nothing.

"Didn't you just say that by including the police in every aspect of our lives we were only inviting trouble?"

"That's unfair, Patrick."

"I really believe we have nothing to worry about. She's a

pretty pissed off fifteen-year-old right now. If we call the cops, our problems will escalate. Let's try to think logically. Here." He opened a drawer and handed her a leather notebook.

"What's this?"

"Frankie's personal phone book. After the last time she pulled a stunt like this, I insisted she keep it in the kitchen, just in case. Start calling. I'll go search the grounds. She may be out at the barn or at the cliffs, listening to the ocean. Don't jump to conclusions. It really could be that simple."

"But it's so late."

"She's looking for a little freedom, and I don't think it matters to her what time it is." Patrick knew it was late, and although his words sounded calming even to himself, he couldn't help but feel worried. Frankie knew the penalty for sneaking out: no driver's license until she turned eighteen. He'd felt that would be a sufficient deterrent.

He grabbed Merlyn's leash, the keener of the two canines, and headed out with him. Helena dialed the first number.

Patrick walked the length of the ranch. He peered into the stalls and the tack room, where Frankie liked to clean her saddle, absorbing the smells of the leather and saddle soap. Frankie loved that smell. Patrick had hoped he'd find her here taking comfort from her favorite horse. But, no.

Thank God the reporters were gone. They'd be back here bright and early, hoping to see something worth photographing or reporting. The silence made him feel uneasy, as he left through the back gate and headed for the cliffs leading down to the beach. It was very dark. *Should've brought the damn flashlight.*

As he began the descent down the trail, he stopped short when his shoe kicked something. Merlyn whined. Patrick bent to pick it up—Frankie's backpack. The hair on the back of his neck stood on end. Goose-bumps bubbled on his arms. He opened the backpack, finding one of Frankie's sweaters and her cell phone.

"Oh, God! She wouldn't have left this stuff behind. What if she's fallen? He screamed, "Frankie, Frankie, it's Dad!" No reply. He needed light to see. He stumbled back up the cliff with the dog following. On solid ground, he sprinted toward home. He pushed open the kitchen door.

Helena, her face etched with anxiety, looked up from the phone book as she was setting the phone back down. "What is it? Did you find her?"

Patrick shook his head. He was out of breath. "No—you?"

"Nothing. One of her friends confessed they had plans to meet at the beach, but she never showed."

"Call the police," he ordered, in between gasps for air. Logical thinking had fallen away. He now knew something horrible had happened to his child.

CHAPTER THIRTY-FIVE

FRANKIE TRIED TO shift her weight to one side, but couldn't. *Can't move my hands and legs*. She realized they were in restraints.

Tears choked the back of her throat, which was excruciatingly dry, when she discovered she was wearing different clothes. This psycho had put her in a white cotton nightgown, trimmed in an eyelet pattern. She wasn't wearing any panties. She cringed. What had he done to her? She didn't think he had raped her, because she didn't hurt between her legs. Her friends who weren't virgins had said that it hurt like hell for a while right after their first time. She also didn't notice any blood, but the thought of him touching her and seeing her naked made her want to vomit. She tasted bile rising in the back of her throat.

She shook her head, trying hard to regain her composure, to make some sense of what had happened. As her eyes adjusted to her surroundings, the room reminded her of her dad's ski cabin in Tahoe but much smaller, and, oddly, black foam rubber covered the walls. The musty smell of rotten wood and mothballs further nauseated her.

All around the room were pictures of a girl who looked a little bit older than Frankie. There were also magazine and tabloid clippings from the past couple of years about her family. Why had this man erected a bizarre shrine to their scandal? What had he done to that other girl? What did he intend to do to her? It struck Frankie as even odder that adorning the top of the walls, almost like a border, were facemasks. All women. They looked frighteningly real, even the hair. Frankie felt a shiver slide down her spine. One looked exactly like Leeza. She knew then what he'd done and what he planned to do to her. Her heart raced as blood flowed rapidly through her. Every nerve ending screamed with fear.

She closed her eyes when the door opened. He walked over to her. She heard him set something down on the nightstand. *The Gypsy Kings* bellowed Spanish melodies from a stereo in the other room. He gently wiped her tears away with a handkerchief. She flinched, a scream aching to escape, but she was too petrified to make a sound.

When he spoke, his voice sounded strange, as if he were speaking through a device that changed it, made it deeper. "Open your eyes, Princess Ligeia. I'm not that bad."

Frankie shut them even tighter, more terrified than ever to face the demon.

He raised his voice an octave, and it sounded like he spoke through clenched teeth. "I said, *open your eyes!* I don't like to be mean, but if I have to, I will."

Frankie did as she was told. The creep didn't look like a kidnapper or a killer. He was tall, at least six feet. He had brown eyes and a crooked nose, possibly broken in a fight. His gelled back hair was dirty blonde. He wore jeans and a white polo T-shirt. As twisted as the thought was, the man was good looking by most women's standards.

"Why are you doing this?" Frankie sobbed. "If it's money, my parents will pay it. Please let me go home. They'll give you whatever you want." When he ran his fingers through her hair, she wanted to kick him and smash his face in.

"You're so very pretty. You know that?" Frankie didn't answer. "I bet you do." He scratched the crook of his nose. "No, pretty girl, it's not their money I want. What I want is worth much more to me."

He looked over at the pictures of the model. "I've been lonely for so long now. It'll be really nice to have someone to come home to. Do you like movies? I got us all kinds. I got all *her* favorites. She's very pleased that you're here." He pointed to one of the pictures on the wall. "And so is Mother. I also bought some clothes you can model for me, and lots of CDs—all your favorites. I want you to feel welcome here." He stroked her face.

How did he know what she liked? Frankie had to go to the bathroom badly, but didn't want to move, fearful of where he might touch her next.

"Don't be frightened. We're going to have a good time."

"I like movies," Frankie whispered.

"Good girl. Then I'll let you pick the first one."

She hesitated before speaking again. "Can I go to the bathroom first?"

He studied her for some time. She knew he was wondering if she'd try to escape. "Will you be a good girl?"

"Yes." She tried to keep her voice from shaking. She realized that a man like this would enjoy her fear. He reached into his pocket and took out a ring of keys. He found the one he was looking for and unlocked her handcuffs, then her shackles.

They had to go into another room which didn't have the black foam encasing it. It was decorated to the hilt, kind of what a haunted house might look like from an era long past. Two windows looked onto a remote wooden area. There was a fire in the fireplace, and an antique red velvet sofa in the center of the room. A small dining room stood to the right of the front door, with an intricately carved table, along with two Gothic chairs with tall backs, like something from an old Hollywood horror flick.

The bathroom was at the other end of the house, next to his bedroom. Frankie quickly peered inside. There was a large four-poster bed with gold-colored curtains, more blown-up photographs of that girl. And more masks.

"I'll be right outside this door," he said.

It took her a minute before she could actually relax enough to pee. As tears clouded her vision, she wished she would wake up and find this to be just a horrible nightmare. She tried to balance her emotions, knowing that he would take further advantage of her if he sensed how frightened she was. At this very moment, Frankie was grateful Leeza had raised her. For if it hadn't been for Leeza's cruelty, Frankie wouldn't be as strong mentally or as manipulative as she was. Trust would be the key. The answer was to get him to trust her. The longer he did so, the longer she would stay alive. And if she stayed alive, she might be able to escape.

Frankie mustered all her courage before flushing the toilet, taking a deep breath, and leaving the bathroom. It was time to become friends with this psycho. It might be her only chance for survival.

CHAPTER THIRTY-SIX

THE RINGING PHONE jolted Tyler awake. His vivid dream about Jane Doe vaporized into the night air, as his eyes opened. The clock on the nightstand read three A.M. At this hour, any call had to be something bad. He picked it up. "Yeah?"

"Sorry to wake you." It was Loretta. "We've got a situation. Patrick Kiley's fifteen-year-old daughter Frances Kiley has been reported missing. Doesn't look good. Santa Barbara doesn't have their own profiler, so they called me for one. I've pulled some recent reports, and a couple of girls have gone missing in the same area in the last two years. This thing is going to be huge by morning. There's already a team of Santa Barbara agents on this, and if you want to take any of your own CASKU team on up, I'll give the go-ahead."

"Shit," he muttered. "Kiley, as in . . ."

"As in the daughter of the mogul and the model, Helena Shea, who was recently detained by the LAPD for the murder of the girl's step-mother. This one's gonna be sticky. I've arranged for a plane to get you up there. How soon can you be at LAX?"

"One hour."

"Listen, Ty, the police will be hounding those folks, and with the media hoopla already in full swing, you'll have to tread softly."

"Why me?"

"'Cause, honey, you're the best."

"I'll do what I can."

"Know you will. Good luck. Keep me posted."

Tyler hung up the phone and tried to pull his thoughts together. He went into the kitchen, turning on the coffeemaker. Quickly showered and dressed. He poured his bitter brew, and started to head for the door, when he felt a strange need to call Claire Travers. He tried hard to shake it but couldn't. He had no reason to call her, did he? For God's sake, she was a tabloid reporter, and the fact that the press hadn't yet heard about the girl's disappearance gave him a leg up, at least for a few hours. Claire was only supplying him with whatever information she had on the porn star Bridgett Core. But the feeling wouldn't dissipate, and Tyler had learned not to ignore his feelings.

"Okay, okay," he said aloud. He flipped open his cell, pulled the number she'd given him up, and dialed her.

"Crazy," he muttered. *I could lose my job for this.*

"Hello?" came her soft, muffled voice after the fourth ring.

"Claire, it's me, Tyler Savoy."

"Tyler? What . . .?"

"Don't ask. I'm not certain why I'm doing this, but something tells me that you can help me."

"What is it?"

"Can you meet me in Santa Barbara in the morning?"

"Sure, I'm due up there anyhow to follow up on the Helena Shea story. But why are you going? Is it about the case?"

Tyler took a deep breath before confiding in this virtual stranger. "*Please* keep this confidential until it breaks in the morning, Claire, but Frances Kiley has gone missing."

CHAPTER THIRTY-SEVEN

POLICE TROMPED IN and out of Patrick's house; search crews with dogs combed the perimeters; friends, neighbors, and family phoned once more; and a rescue helicopter circled the surrounding area, illuminating the cliff-side. It had started raining in the middle of the night, making the search more difficult. Worst of all, the media masses were back for more blood, speculating about all the activity.

A lanky police detective with beady eyes stood in the family room with Helena and Patrick. "We've got an agent coming in from the FBI. He's with the division we call CASKU."

"CASKU?" Helena asked.

"The Child Abduction and Serial Killer Unit."

"What?" Patrick said in amazement. "What do we need him for? She hasn't been . . . I mean she isn't dead," he insisted.

"Mr. Kiley, your child has been missing for more than two hours. Since we haven't turned up anything on the cliffs or in the sea, foul play could very well be involved. Finding her backpack also indicates something is probably amiss. We're required, at this point, to ask these investigators to assist us. I don't want to add to your alarm, but we do also have search parties looking for her body out at sea."

The detective quickly apologized and left. Another officer showed up—this one older, shorter, and barrel-chested, and not any more sensitive than the others. He asked the same questions they'd already answered a dozen times. Helena felt ready to collapse, swimming in a surreal nightmare, which suddenly became much worse when she heard Detective David Collier's voice.

"Okay, people, what have we got here?" he bellowed. The officers from SBPD all looked at him as if he were some bizarre apparition.

Helena's lawyer, James verbalized all of their thoughts. "What are you doing here, Collier? This is way out of your jurisdiction."

"I think this disappearance is some type of ploy, and it's all tied into my murder investigation. Special circumstances are indicated, prompting me to be here, and a judge has granted me permission." Collier handed James a subpoena, cleared first by a Los Angeles judge and another in Santa Barbara.

"This is bogus," said James. "There is no way in hell you got this signed by two judges in the middle of the night. I'll tell you something else, Detective, when I find out how you pulled this little stunt, and when I find that this piece of paper is bullshit, I'll have your badge! You'll never work on another police force in this country. Hell, you won't be able to get a job doing mall security."

Helena watched James's face turn purple.

"Be my guest," Collier chortled. "Now I need to speak with Ms. Shea then Mr. Kiley."

"No, you don't," James shot back.

"It's all right. We have nothing to hide," Helena said, thinking that maybe this hothead detective could help. All she cared about at present was getting Frankie back.

"Great. Is there somewhere we could go?" Collier asked.

Patrick pointed to the library, the one room in his home not filled with police. "You don't have to do this, Helena," James told her.

"I know."

"In fact, I don't believe he has a legal right to be here."

"I haven't—we haven't done anything wrong." She glanced at Patrick. "Maybe if he realizes this by questioning us, he can turn things around and help find Frankie and whoever really did kill Leeza."

"Don't count on it, sweetheart. This guy is after your blood. I'm going in there with you."

"Fine."

Patrick watched as the three entered the library, closing the doors behind them. As Helena and James sat down, Detective Collier paced back and forth.

"Come on, Collier, quit the dog-and-pony show. What the hell do you want?" James asked.

"I'll tell you what I want, Counselor. I want to see justice served. I've got a dead woman, a burn victim, and now a missing child. What's the link in all three cases? Your client and her lover."

"We are *not* lovers."

"Whatever."

"Collier, can't you see you're digging yourself into a hole that you'll never get out of?" James said.

"No, Counselor, what I see are some similarities to another case, where a child wound up dead but the small-town police force did such a shoddy job pursuing it that an arrest won't ever be made. That's not going to happen here. I guarantee foul play is involved, and your client is in on it. After all, Ms. Shea, what did your daughter know about Ms. Kiley's murder? Maybe she overheard you talking with your lover, her father. Maybe she knew what you two did. I'll bet she even knows who you hired to do this! Or did she know that you started the fire that nearly killed your so-called friend? Why don't you come clean, make it easy on yourself. I can almost guarantee we can make a deal with the district attorney."

"I did not kill Leeza Kiley!" Helena screamed. "And I would never harm my daughter or anyone for that matter! Get the hell out of here!"

"Your client seems to have an anger-management problem, Counselor. I've taken note of that before. A jury won't think too much of her with that temper. I'll bet a couple of dozen people outside this room heard that little outburst."

James rose abruptly from his chair, "You're harassing my client, Detective!"

At that moment, the library doors opened abruptly. A tall man with dark hair and chiseled facial features walked in and said, "Jesus Christ, I might've known." The man confronted the detective. "Collier, you're way out of line."

"Well, well, look what the cat dragged in. I don't have to go anywhere, Savoy. I'm conducting an investigation here, and you're interrupting an interview."

"More like an interrogation. I'm FBI, Collier. I outrank you. I'm going to have to ask you to head on back down the coast to your own jurisdiction. CASKU is working this case. Your case is about one hundred fifty miles south."

"Screw you, Savoy!" Collier stormed out of the room.

The agent turned to face James and Helena. "Talk about temper. As you witnessed, Detective Collier and I are not exactly close. He usually sends his goodbyes to me in the impolite form of a profane action with his middle finger. At least he was a little more creative this time."

Helena smiled for the first time in days. Whoever this man was, she immediately liked him. She stood as he stuck out his hand.

"Hello, I'm Tyler Savoy. I'm the agent they sent up from CASKU. I'm sure that the officers already explained who I am and what I do."

"Somewhat." Helena nodded. Patrick came into the library and put an arm around her shoulders.

"Part of my job is to profile what we call UNSUBS, meaning unknown subjects, or, in layman's terms, the criminal." He paused and the sound of his voice took on a more compassionate tone. "In this case, I will be profiling the type of person who might have taken your daughter. I need to go over a few details with the officer in charge, then I'll get back with you folks. Why don't you try to relax for a moment? I know how disconcerting Detective Collier can be."

"Thank you," Helena said, watching as the agent left them in the library.

"I'll get you some coffee," James said.

Helena turned to face Patrick. "Is Frankie coming back? Please tell me she is."

"Yes," Patrick whispered. "We have to believe that. There's no other alternative."

Helena collapsed into his arms and cried. All barriers were down between them now, no room anymore for old hostilities and resentments. They were two parents who loved their daughter, and wanted only to see her again—alive.

CHAPTER THIRTY-EIGHT

THROUGHOUT THE MORNING, several people at the magazine came up congratulating Claire for a story well written. Though she smiled and thanked them, she wasn't proud of her work. The story somehow left a void deep in her stomach. Even getting the front page gave her no sense of joy. When she'd found out the Kiley kid had disappeared, she'd tried to stop the presses. She knew how her work would impact the girl's family and felt like she was rubbing salt in their wounds. How miserable for her parents.

She looked at her watch. Damn, she was running behind. She had to get up north. She'd been trying to gather her information on Bridget Core and finally had everything, including the interview with the mother, which had been dictated onto an old steno pad.

It was a quarter past nine. She should've left by now, but she had to talk to Paul, her editor, about the Kiley story. She wanted off of it. Her conscience was bothering her.

"What the hell are you doing here, Travers? You're supposed to be up in Santa Barbara with the rest of the buzz. Get on out that door. I'm not paying you to dick around," said Paul Vernezza, her very Italian, very arrogant boss.

"I've got a problem with this story."

"Problem?"

"Haven't we attacked these people enough? We've already convicted and tried them. Let's get all the facts before we hang them!"

"What you've got, Claire, is a problem with me—and it's a problem that'll only get bigger the longer you sit around here. You're supposed to get anything that sounds good, and if they're facts—wonderful! We're not destroying lives; we report on the scandals of people destroying their own lives. They're public figures, and as such aren't entitled to their privacy. Privacy, schmivacy. They do dirt; we dig it up. Now go, dig!"

"Take me off of it."

"What the hell are you talking about?" He stroked his long black mustache, a nervous tic. Claire knew that his tough guy act was simply that, an act.

"It's personal. I really need to be off of this story."

"Hell, no! Chop, chop, Travers. I've had enough of your crap. Let's go!"

Claire slammed down her fists on top of her desk. "Look! I told you I can't write this story!"

"Ha, ha! Very funny. Now, get me the dirt on that Shea woman and her ex and their kid. Get it *today*!"

Before she had time to think about the consequences, Claire walked around to the front of her cubicle where Paul Vernezza stood. She stabbed the eraser end of her pencil into his chest and yelled, "You know what, Paul? Get your own dirt! I've got better things to do." She grabbed her purse off the back of her chair and stormed down the hall.

"Travers, get your ass back here! I'm your *boss*! I said . . ."

Over her shoulder, she replied, "I heard what you said. But guess what? I quit! I'll be back for my things later." She smiled, elated and really proud of herself. Claire marched from the building where she'd worked for nearly eight years. Now it was over, just like that. No worries. Something else was around the corner, she was sure—something a great deal bigger and better. She got behind the wheel of her Camry, and before long, she was driving north on the Ventura Freeway, headed straight for Tyler Savoy.

CHAPTER THIRTY-NINE

"I'M GLAD YOU like the old movies. I love them. They have a quality about them that filmmakers can't churn out today." He turned to look back at her as he popped *The Raven* into the VCR.

Frankie hadn't picked out the movie, although he was trying to make it sound like she had. She definitely didn't want to watch an old horror flick with him.

She could tell by looking outside that it was early in the morning, maybe six or seven. Condensation sat on the windows. She'd actually spent an entire night in this pit of hell.

He came over and sat back down on the sofa, right next to her. Fortunately, he didn't sit too close. She shrunk back a bit. He smelled strongly of expensive cologne, like the kind her father wore.

"By the way, since we haven't exactly had a formal introduction, you can call me *Poe*. I know I told you my name last night, but I wasn't sure if you remembered it. I know your family and friends call you Frankie, but I prefer Francesca. It's such an elegant name, so classic and beautiful, like the young Francesca da Rimini in Dante's *Inferno*. It's much nicer than Frankie, which sounds to me like a little boy's name. And you are definitely *not* a little boy." He looked her up and down.

She shuddered. *Stay calm and collected.* What was with his weird obsession with Edgar Allan Poe? If she ever got out of here, she'd remember that detail about him. Freak.

Frankie had studied Poe in her English class the previous semester. As haunting as his work had been, she was sure he'd never kidnapped anyone, and she knew he'd never killed anybody, at least not in the real world.

"Nicholson is great, isn't he? But that ridiculous haircut, my God—it's ghastly. Don't you think? He looks like a homosexual or something."

"Uh-huh."

"Brianne wouldn't watch this with me. She was too fragile, and, well, this kind of stuff would've been too much for her. You're a lot stronger than she ever was."

Afraid to ask exactly what he meant, Frankie wondered who Brianne was, and *where* she was. Brianne was probably the woman in the photographs. He was obsessed with the pictures and referred constantly to this Brianne person. And then there were the creepy masks hanging all over the place. She tried not to think about the one that looked so much like Leeza.

"Would you like a coke? Some popcorn?" Frankie shook her head. "Now, come on, Francesca. I want your stay here to be as pleasant as possible, considering all you've been through in your life. You deserve a treat. It's a movie. We've got to have a snack. I know it's the breakfast hour, but I want to spend as much fun time with you as I can. I've got to go to work, so I thought we could be together early this morning. I'll make some anyway. You might change your mind."

He went into the kitchen to fix the popcorn, and Frankie decided to appease him by eating some, even though she felt like barfing it up directly on him. That would be perfect. Then he'd have to undo her handcuffs.

"I did change my mind," she said in a barely audible whisper.

She hoped it wasn't poisoned.

"Good girl. I thought you might." He set down two bowls of popcorn on the coffee table along with sodas.

"Could you undo my handcuffs?"

He stared at her for a long moment. "I see your point." He went back into the kitchen, but she didn't turn around—too obvious. She heard him close a drawer. He came back over and undid the handcuffs, but left her feet shackled.

"Thank you." She mustered a thin smile.

"You're welcome. See? I'm not such a bad guy."

The movie seemed to last for hours. Frankie laughed whenever he did. She didn't want him to think that she was frightened.

He ejected the movie and turned off the VCR. "I'd love for us to watch another, but it's getting late. I've made you a sandwich. I set it on the nightstand in your room. That way, you can eat when you get hungry. Okay?"

Frankie nodded, wondering where he worked. Did he have a wife and child? Was he one of those sickos that seems ordinary to his neighbors and lives a double life? He reminded her of the kind of people she saw regularly on the news, the ones the neighbors always thought were such nice guys before they murdered their entire family out of the blue and then committed suicide.

He unshackled her feet and held onto her tightly as he escorted her back to her quarters. "Okay, Francesca, I'll be nice and leave your hands unrestrained for now, so that you can eat. But I have to shackle your feet again. There *are* rules around here. If you abide by them, you'll be fine and we'll have a lot of fun. First, don't try to escape or yell out. No one lives nearby, so no one can hear or help you, anyway. I'd hate to see you waste your energy. If you ever try to leave me, Francesca, then I'll regretfully have to kill you.

"Finally, it is imperative that you be grateful for everything I do for you. Therefore, when I offer you something, I want you to take it, indulge yourself, and learn to love it. I trust you won't disappoint me. I have a feeling you are of a different caliber than your mother, and will be grateful for all I have done and am doing for you. Please do not disappoint me. *Do you understand?*" He got right in her face so she could smell his foul breath.

Frankie wanted to cry, but instead responded with a meek, "Yes." She wanted to ask him why he'd mentioned her mother. It startled her. Was Helena also in danger from this man?

"Good. Oh, and there's also a bucket for you next to the bed. I'm sure you can figure out what that's for. I'd prefer you to hold it though." He left the room.

Frankie heard a sound of several locks being turned outside the door. She didn't let her guard down until she heard the gravel crunching under his car tires as he drove away. She stared at the tuna sandwich he'd made her. She wanted to hurl it against the wall.

The comment he'd made about her mother terrified her. She had to escape this dungeon and get to Helena before he did. Tears rolled down her cheeks. She wiped them away, enraged at this psycho who got off on calling himself Poe. She missed her mom and dad who must be worried sick about her by now. More than anything, she longed to be with them. She had to get out of here and back to her parents—to her family.

CHAPTER FORTY

HELENA COULDN'T SLEEP, eat, or even cry any longer. Tyler Savoy was at least of some comfort. He'd assured both her and Patrick that he believed in their innocence. He'd gotten Collier off their backs, but Helena was certain she hadn't seen the last of the sneering detective. Tyler had also been sensitive and seemingly understanding when she'd told him about the incidents leading up to all this. Though he didn't accuse her of hiding anything, he also didn't indicate whether or not he thought the man's phone calls and the fire had anything to do with Frankie's disappearance. He did promise to speak with the inspector in charge of the arson team leading the investigation into the fire at Shea House. She was grateful to him for that.

In her mind she kept re-playing the events of the last two weeks, wondering where she could've done something differently.

Her head ached so badly that she really wanted something much stronger than an aspirin to relieve it. Her despair was immeasurable. Her child was missing, possibly hurt, or worse—although she refused to accept that; her dear friend was lying in a hospital bed fighting for her life; the recovery center she'd invested her heart and soul into had literally gone up in smoke just when it was ready to open; she was suspected of murder; and the public had already tried and convicted her, making her a complete outcast.

She silently repeated the Serenity Prayer over and over again to no avail. She walked back into Patrick's bathroom to clean up. Looking for his toothpaste, she found a bottle of Valium inside the medicine cabinet. Her hands shook as she held it, staring at it. It was half-empty. She set it back inside the cabinet and quickly shut the door. But her demons kept saying, *Go ahead, it's all right. Just take one. Maybe you can relax, feel better, and focus on finding Frankie. It's just* one. *You'll be fine. Go on, take it.*" She really did need some sleep, so she could think more clearly. But if she took one, what would it mean? She was so tired, and her head hurt so badly, and damn the world for turning its back—and now Frankie was gone. Without trying to justify it any further, Helena took out the pills and poured a few into her hand.

"What are you doing?"

She abruptly turned around to see Patrick.

He took the pills out of her palm. "This won't help. Dammit, how could you think *this* would help us right now? Will a pill bring her home? My God, Helena, have you lost your mind?"

"I, oh, I . . ."

"Don't try to give me an excuse. I won't have you here if you can't be sober. I'll send you back home, and you can face the wolves on your own. You can't weaken, not now. If you fall now, you'll be hurting her even more."

"You bastard! Just when I thought you'd changed, that you even cared!" She heard how shallow and selfish her own voice sounded.

"That's why I can't let you do this. Our daughter is missing. I can't have you clouding everything up by using drugs."

The hurt overwhelmed her. He was right, she had weakened and that was no way to bring Frankie back. "I was scared. I'm not coping well."

"And you thought these would help?" He held up the bottle.

"No," she whispered, sinking to the floor, her back against the wall. He sat down next to her. Her body shook as she sobbed for all the loss and helplessness she felt.

Patrick's voice softened, "I do care," he said. "Very much. I've never stopped caring. I may have made some serious mistakes in the past, but I've always cared, Helena. So please don't do this. You've got to pull yourself together. Our little girl needs both of us." He looked kindly into her eyes and gave her a warm, supportive smile. "Savoy wants to see us. Come on."

She took his hand as he helped her to her feet and followed him like a small child, ashamed of what she'd almost done.

Patrick's home was like a police headquarters—all manner of equipment was set up everywhere, and the media had been warned not to call the house. That, however, did not keep them from gathering outside the gates; at least Savoy had cordoned them off.

Savoy took the two of them into the library. "Listen, I think Detective Collier is right about one thing."

Oh, no. Helena thought. *Here it comes. He's ready to level the boom on me.*

"I think foul play was involved in Frankie's disappearance. I believe someone took her, and that whoever did it is connected to the Leeza Kiley murder and may have started the fire at your recovery house. I think we're looking for this man who's been making the phone calls, taunting you. I don't think Rachel Winters was his intended victim at Shea House. I think he wants to hurt you, Helena. First he burned your work. Then murdered someone you have reason to hate and set you up as the primary suspect. Now he's made his ultimate move. He's taken your child."

"So this is about some kind of revenge?" Patrick asked.

"Possibly," Tyler said. "I'm inclined to lean that way, only because he doesn't follow the typical MO of a serial killer. They usually choose victims by type. For the most part, the victims are people the perpetrator doesn't know. They often choose upper-middle-class victims, to achieve some celebrity status. In many cases, they envision themselves in a kind of avenging angel role, purging the world of evil. I can go on, but you don't need a textbook definition of a serial killer. Although I don't feel this kidnapper falls into that category, he does have some of these traits. Nothing seems to fit quite yet, but this looks like a vendetta. As I said, I do believe this man is a killer—and that he killed your ex-wife—but I don't think he's killed Frankie. He wants to punish you, Helena, for some reason. He's taunted you, framed you, and now taken away what you hold most dear. He is systematically trying to destroy you."

"This is insane," Helena replied.

"I know, but please trust me. I don't think your daughter is a runaway or that she fell off the cliffs. I believe she's been abducted. Somehow, someone got to her, which means, given both the security precautions at this ranch and your recent arrival here, that they've been following you and planning this for some time. What I need from you is a list of possibilities—people who might have a personal vendetta against you."

"I've made a few enemies, I suppose," said Helena. "But I never thought any were psychopaths."

"I want to look around again, go back through Frankie's room, just to see if we've missed anything. While I do that, I'd like you to think about people, even people from years ago—go back to your childhood and think about who might feel the need to get even with you, for any reason. I don't care how farfetched it may seem. Psychopaths carry grudges for a long time, for the most ludicrous reasons. I'll be back after I go through her room again." Tyler left the room as Patrick and Helena tried to digest what he'd told them.

"I've never been so scared," said Helena. "We may have messed up in our pasts, but does it warrant this? I can't imagine that either of us ever made anyone this angry."

"It does sound bizarre. I just have to believe that Frankie's still alive."

"Me too. But how long before this bastard hurts her?" Helena asked.

"I don't know. I really don't know."

CHAPTER FORTY-ONE

THE PSYCHO WAS back again. Frankie closed her eyes, trying to shut out the footsteps approaching her. Painful stomach cramps combined with a major headache made her ache all over. He tapped on her door. Frankie didn't reply. She shut her eyes tighter, still hoping she would wake up from a bad dream. No such luck.

"Lovely child," he cooed, "it's me, your knight in shining armor."

"Go away, please?" she begged, thinking maybe he'd have the decency to leave her alone.

"What? What is this?" He came to the side of her bed and stroked her hair. "Are you asking your great friend Poe to leave? Never!" He smelled of musk and something she didn't recognize—like cinnamon, but not. "Don't you want, more than anything, to see your dear friend, my angel? Open your eyes when I favor you with my presence."

She reluctantly did as she was told, as the fear of death overtook her once more. "I'm sorry," she felt compelled to say, understanding that he was growing angry. "I don't feel very well."

"Such a shame. And I've planned quite a lovely evening, one

in which we'll really get to know one another."

Frankie didn't like the sound of this. Maybe if she told him she was starting her period it might turn him off. But then again, it might turn him off completely, and then he'd hurt her, or worse. She decided to keep her feminine problem to herself. With her manipulative guile, she tried to sound interested in his offer. "I'd like very much to know you better."

"Good," he cut her off. "However, since you're feeling under the weather, maybe you should go a few days without food or water. I'll bet your bladder would hurt if I left you here for a few days all by your lonesome without a pail even to dispose of your waste in. Wouldn't it? You know, I really have gone out of my way to make sure you're comfortable here. And this is the gratitude I get? I thought I talked to you about appreciation, and what might happen if you failed to show it. You're no different than your selfish bitch of a mother!" he yelled. "I think you need a lesson in gratitude."

"I'm sorry. I'm really sorry. It's just a little stomachache. I'm fine really. I'd love to have dinner with you. Please don't be angry."

He abruptly sat down next to her, and stroked her hair again. "So silky," he murmured. "So beautiful." He pulled her hair tight, locking it around his thick fist, then pulling tighter. It felt like he might rip it out. "Please, don't be angry with me," he mocked her. "It's my itty-bitty tummy. Don't be angry?" He let go of her hair, ripping some out of her scalp as he did. He stood and began pacing. Frankie tried to pull her bound feet underneath her.

"Don't be angry with you?" He slapped her across the face, and she winced. He unlocked her handcuffs from the bed, then dragged her by her hair to the bathroom where he shoved her head into the toilet.

This was it, the end. Let it be over quick, please, God. She prayed for her mother, her father, her sins, anything and everything she could think of. Just do it. Just do it. Get it over with.

He pulled her head up yelling, "You don't understand, do you?! You have a chance to be my Princess, yet you *refuse* to cherish my gift. Well, you'll learn appreciation here, Francesca. I'm beginning to see that manners are not your strong point, but that's your mother's fault. Don't worry though, I'll teach you all you need to know."

Then he shoved her head back into the toilet where she gagged on the water, choking and struggling to get her face back up.

Suddenly, he pulled her head back up again. "All right, now, take a shower for God's sake! That toilet is filthy! I hope you've learned something here, Francesca. Have you learned something?" His face was as red as a hot ember.

"Yesss," she stammered.

He locked the door to the bathroom while she took her shower. The water actually felt good, something normal in a house of horrors. He ordered her to get out and get dressed, then locked her to the bed with the handcuffs once more.

"You know, I'm not so hungry, either. Suddenly I'm feeling like a night out on the town without you! Maybe the next time I come back, whenever that might be, you'll be a little more gracious. I think by then you'll have completely understood today's lesson. Goodbye, Francesca." He walked out the door, bolting it as he left.

Frankie lay there in the darkness, not knowing whether to feel relieved or not. She cried softly until she heard his car drive away, then she started to sob. He was so awful, and she was so scared and alone. For all Frankie knew, she might be left for days or weeks, to die in this hell. Now she wished he had drowned her, because in her heart, she was sure she wasn't leaving this place alive.

CHAPTER FORTY-TWO

THE LONG DAY turned into evening with no news about Frankie. At least James had contacted the DA and arrangements had been made for Helena's arraignment. James said that he thought the DA was softening and wising up, considering the events of the past twenty-four hours. The reporters and television crews, however, hadn't let up at all. All sorts of speculation and accusations were being reported—hurtful, derogatory untruths. Although this hell had only begun a few days before Leeza's murder, it felt like an eternity had passed.

Helena's main concern was her child. She was also very worried about Rachel. She picked up the phone on her bedside table and called Tim, thinking that a connection to the outside world would help. She called him at home, letting it ring several times until she heard his voicemail. She decided not to leave a message. It was nearly eight, so she called him on his cell phone, and he picked up on the third ring.

"Hi, it's me." Helena could hear commotion in the background, as if he were at a restaurant. She felt guilty for disturbing him, especially since he was holding down the fort, making sure her business didn't fall apart.

"Oh, sweetie, I was hoping you'd call. I didn't want to call you at the ranch, so I decided to wait to hear from you. How are you?"

"Honestly? Terrible."

"Have the police heard anything? Have they found her?"

"No, nothing—not a trace."

"I'm so sorry. If there's anything that I can do, I will."

"You're already doing plenty. Everything okay at work?"

"Sure. A little slow, but good. Clients are calling worried about you. All this business about you murdering Leeza is so ridiculous! I tell you, the corruption in the DA's office, not to mention the LAPD, is hideous!"

"They've questioned you?"

"Oh yes, that bastard detective, what's his name?"

"Collier?"

"Right. He's been by twice, snooping around. I finally told him that without a search warrant, he had no business being there."

"I'm sorry. I sure didn't want you dragged into this. You've been so good to me."

"Please, don't worry about a thing. We'll all get through this, rest assured."

"Thank you." She heard a male voice call for Tim, so she said goodbye and hung up. She didn't want to intrude any more than she already had. He was such a wonderful friend. He was even staying at her place, attempting to keep the media away.

She closed her eyes, trying to use the meditation techniques she'd been taught in recovery, but they were no help now. A knock at her door brought her quickly back to reality. She motioned Patrick in. He sat on the end of the bed and took her hands in his. They sat quietly for a long time.

Patrick finally broke the silence, "I love your hair," and Helena understood his need to escape their current troubles.

She too, wanted to forget that a dozen men were in the other room concerned with getting Frankie back. "You always did."

"Do you know that I've missed you?"

Helena didn't know how to respond. Her emotions in part were numb. All she could say was, "Me too."

He touched her cheek. She closed her eyes and let him trace the outline of her cheekbones with his fingers. He placed his hands on either side of her face, and she opened her eyes. They communicated an entire conversation in that silence. Each could read the affection, hurt, and loneliness in the other's face.

Helena wanted him to hold her, hoping it would ease her pain, and his. Her heart beat rapidly, as their lips joined. The warmth that came from Patrick's mouth felt sweet. She knew then that he really did still care. As their kiss turned from gentle tenderness to raw passion, Patrick pulled Helena on top of him.

Something clicked inside her. She knew that if this went any further it could be very damaging for both of them. As suddenly as it had begun, she stopped. She rolled over, lying next to him, straightening her blouse. Patrick sat up looking dazed. Tears clouded her vision. "I can't. I'm sorry. It's all wrong," she whispered.

"Its not. We love each other. I know that. We always have. Nothing wrong is going on here. We need each other now, Lena. I know I need you, and I can see the same written all over your face."

Helena stood up. "We can't force this, especially not right now. We did that once, and we hurt each other and our daughter. We owe it to her not to get our emotions all mixed up. You're wrong, Patrick, it's not right. It's never been right between you and me."

CHAPTER FORTY-THREE

TYLER DIDN'T LIKE any of it. Collier was on a rampage to find anything he could to bring down Helena Shea and Patrick Kiley, not only for arson and Leeza's murder, but also for their daughter's abduction. He insisted that they'd hired a professional to do the dirty deeds, even though he had little evidence to back his theory.

Collier believed that they couldn't handle the kid and had decided to get rid of her. Tyler called Loretta down in Los Angeles, and she'd brought him up to speed on Collier's shenanigans. Tyler pleaded with his boss to do something about the numbskull, saying that he was only making things worse for him and his team. He reminded her that Collier's theories were fueling the damn media blaze, making Tyler's relations with the reporters difficult and unnecessarily time-consuming.

"I'll see what I can do," Loretta told him. "But you know how these police departments are when they think we're treading on one of their cases. Looks like I might have to pull rank. As I've said a dozen times if I've said it once, I really hate getting into a turf war with the local PD. I don't think it's ultimately productive for either of us, but for you . . ."

"Thank you. I knew I could count on you to put the hammer down. One other thing I'd like to ask you to do for me down there. Would you pay a visit to Ms. Shea's friend Rachel Winters over at the UCLA burn center? I know that Helena's been very concerned about her. She'd feel relieved if I could tell her that we have someone looking in on her. And I'd like someone to question Rachel, ask her about the night of the fire. Who knows, maybe she saw someone. She might have a missing piece we're unaware of."

"You think it's possible our man is also an arsonist?"

"Not by trade. I think he's got a vendetta, and he's determined to destroy anything having to do with Helena Shea. I have a strong feeling that the same individual is responsible for all three incidents: the arson, the murder, and the kidnapping. He's trying to destroy her by taking everything she values away from her."

"Sure I can do that for you. I'll interview her myself, but I'm pretty certain Collier's already spoken with Rachel already."

"Oh, I'm sure he has. But Collier's almost certainly trying to dig up anything he can that could be twisted into implicating Helena. However, we might see things differently, if you get my meaning."

"I do, Ty."

"I don't understand why he's pressing so hard to convict this lady. If I didn't know better, I'd say he's the one with the vendetta."

"No. He's just a washed-up cop who knows that frying someone like Ms. Shea will score him points."

"If you want to know my opinion, Loretta, I think he needs to retire."

They both laughed, and Tyler thanked her once more before hanging up. Then, he picked up the phone again and tried to get a hold of Claire, knowing that she'd arrived in Santa Barbara around noon. She didn't answer, and he figured her cell was out of range or turned off. When they'd spoken earlier she'd suggested they get together for dinner. After a little prodding on her part, he'd agreed.

"Everyone has to eat, don't they? Even FBI agents," she'd goaded.

"I'd like to, it sounds really nice, but I'm very busy with this case," he protested.

"Look, why don't you come over to my hotel? I'll order up some room service. We'll have a quick dinner, then I'll release you back to your work. Besides I have that info you wanted on Bridgett Core."

"Boy, you sure know how to get to a man, don't you? Since you put it that way, I'd be delighted to join you for dinner."

They'd made plans to touch base this afternoon and then signed off. Remembering the conversation now, he realized he was looking forward to seeing her. He was brought back to the present seeing a picture of Frankie on the shelf above her desk. What kind of hell was that poor kid going through right now? He thought she was still alive, but if so, was she injured? What was this sicko subjecting her to? She was so pretty with her dark hair and light eyes and a big smile on her face. She looked a lot like her mom.

He got up from the chair and found Helena and Patrick in the kitchen where they were making sandwiches for his team. "Hey, I need to leave for an appointment, but if you need to reach me, I'll be at my hotel. Don't hesitate to call," he told them. They both looked at him, worried expressions on their faces.

"Would you like a sandwich first?" Helena said, obviously not wanting him to leave.

"I really appreciate that, and thanks for taking such good care of my men. Unfortunately, I need to get going."

Patrick nodded, but he could tell neither wanted him to go. "Will you be back tonight?" he asked.

"Probably later. In the meantime, three of my men will be on duty here at all times. They know exactly how to get in touch with me. I'm no further than ten minutes away."

"You could stay here tonight, if you'd like," Patrick suggested.

Tyler realized that his presence had a soothing effect on their frayed nerves. "Thank you, but a little distance might honestly give me some perspective. It's happened more than once, believe me." Tyler thought of Claire and knew he wasn't getting out of the house simply to gain a new perspective.

****

As Tyler stood outside the door of room 237, he felt a little nervous. Was this a date? Though Claire Travers wasn't a colleague, he did think she could offer some insight into the case. But if anyone found out that they'd so much as spoken . . .

He hadn't dated anyone since Susie's death except for one girl his sister insisted he go out with. *That* was a fiasco. But something intrigued him about the tabloid journalist, so he rapped on her door. He heard movement on the other side.

She opened the door, smelling like evening jasmine, and looking fantastic in a tight, gray turtleneck and blue jeans. She took his jacket and hung it in the closet. She was already chilling a nice Chardonnay, and had set out some fruit, cheese, and crackers.

"I took the liberty of ordering dinner. Hope you're a surf-and-turf kind of guy."

"Sounds great." She handed him a glass of wine. "I like your choice in wine."

"I hope you're not on duty. I know that old line: 'I can't, I'm on duty.'" She laughed, and he liked the sound of it—full yet feminine.

He laughed too, releasing the tension in his neck and shoulders. "Technically, until this case is solved, I *am* on duty, but I don't think a glass of wine will hurt."

They sat outside on the balcony overlooking the Pacific, making small talk while they waited patiently for their dinners to arrive. Tyler let down his guard, pouring himself a little more wine. They enjoyed each other's company, and their conversation steered clear of business. But after dinner, Tyler said, "So, you have some info on Bridgett Core?"

"Nothing really jumped out at me, but I made a few phone calls for you."

"You didn't need to do that."

"I thought maybe something would come of it."

"And?"

"Some women who knew Bridgett back in early '95 said she dated a lot and liked to party pretty hard. I got a few names of some of the guys she hung out with. I figured you could look into them."

"Of course."

"I also got a hold of a gal who was on Bridgett's last set. She said their makeup artist had gotten friendly with Bridgett even though he creeped everyone else out. They were all pretty sure he was gay."

"That doesn't fit the MO. Did she tell any of the cops this?"

"No. These women don't like talking with cops, so she stayed out of it, said she knew nothing."

"What's this guy's name?"

Claire looked through the file for a minute, "Here it is— Richard Shelton."

Tyler took the file from Claire and scanned it. "I'll call this down to my boss to see what she can find out. I'm too wrapped up in the Kiley case right now. I'll have to let my Jane Doe rest until I get back."

"Hope it helps."

"Me too."

She smiled again, and Tyler felt his gut sink. What a pretty lady Claire Travers was. For the moment, the case was forgotten.

"Heard anything about the Kiley girl?" Claire asked.

"I'm thinking someone out there really wants to get even with Helena Shea, destroy her. Bet we hear from him soon."

"For ransom?"

"I think so, hope so. What I really hope is that he hasn't hurt the kid, because I do think he murdered Leeza. He's sick. They're all sick. You have no idea how many children turn up missing each year. Often it's a family member, but in as high as forty percent of the cases, it's a psychopathic stranger. They molest, kill, or sell for profit. They could be anyone, even a neighbor from a few doors down whom you'd never suspect, just like that case in San Diego where the guy lived across the street from the little girl. He just walked in and took her from her room. That poor child had sold the asshole a box of Girl Scout cookies a week before. Sometimes, you just never know.

"And you wouldn't believe the pornography rings out there that involve young children. The Internet has made it really difficult to get these creeps. If you want to make a difference in the world, Claire, use your journalistic skills to educate people about these kinds of problems."

"Interesting you should say that, because I quit my job today. I couldn't take being a journalistic pariah any longer. I need to do something more meaningful. Your suggestion is a good one; I like it.

"I'm proud of you. Now you can use your talent for something positive, and I can be seen in public with you." They both laughed, delighted to be together. He wanted to kiss her. The thought of this surprised him. For once, Susan's memory didn't blur his emotions. Just then his cell phone rang.

Tyler groaned. "Sorry."

"Answer it."

He clicked on his phone and said, "Tyler Savoy here."

It was one of the men from his team who he had out combing the woods for Frankie. "We got a body—in the woods just south of Oxnard."

"ID?"

"Nope. Mutilated. Female though, about the size of our vic."

"I'll be right there." Tyler hung up the phone as soon as he got an exact location and turned to Claire.

"Bad?" she asked.

He nodded, hoping he wouldn't have to tell Patrick and Helena that they'd found Frankie.

CHAPTER FORTY-FOUR

AS A NEW day dawned, Tyler was just returning to Patrick's ranch from the crime scene. Some monster had tortured and bludgeoned a teenage girl to death, but it wasn't Frankie. Tyler wondered if it wasn't the same UNSUB.

Pulling into the ranch, he saw Claire's car, but even more surprising he found Claire and Helena drinking coffee in the kitchen. "Helena?" he said, noticing the shock in his own voice, while glancing over at Claire.

"Good morning, Agent Savoy. This is Claire Tra . . ."

"Travers. We've met. I thought we'd agreed not to invite the media into your home. I thought you wanted that as much as the Bureau." He eyed Claire suspiciously.

"Believe me, I agree, especially where Ms. Travers is concerned," Patrick said walking into the kitchen.

"Please call me Claire."

"Somehow she got through the phone system early this morning and said that she thought she could help with the case. She doesn't work for *The Scene* any longer and claims to want to make some amends by helping out if she can, perhaps write some responsible journalism. We could certainly use somebody in the media in our corner, couldn't we?

"I told Helena I want to make amends, do something to help. Maybe I can lend a hand or at least give some support," Claire said.

Patrick stood in the doorway, shaking his head. "This woman has done nothing but harm us. Now she waltzes in wanting to help? If I had answered the security gate's phone, she wouldn't have gotten in."

"Patrick," Helena pleaded, "she's *already* helped by distributing Frankie's photo. She's also trying to get the press off our backs, trying to convince them that I had nothing to do with the fire or Leeza's murder. And as far as I'm concerned, even if she *is* here for the inside scoop, which I really wouldn't doubt, I'd rather she get it from our perspective. And, I have to say I'm to a point where I'll take all the help I can get in getting our daughter back. I actually think it's time we talk to the press."

"I know you doubt me, and with good reason, but I'm telling the truth. I'm not here to bring you down. That's not what I want to be about any longer. I really do want to help you locate your daughter. I might be able to do that with my connections," Claire said.

"Folks, may I have a word with Ms. Travers?" Tyler cut in. "Maybe we can sort this out."

Helena glanced at Patrick, who nodded.

Claire took her coffee mug and left the room following Tyler. He crossed his arms over his chest, staring at her. "What are you doing?"

"It's not what you think, I swear. It's not about the story. After talking about these people with you, I feel terribly guilty for the things that I've written about them over the years. You made me see how decent they are, and how wrong and judgmental I've been."

"Really? Well, you might be able to convince a distraught mother who's so exhausted and obviously out of her mind she can't think straight, but you haven't fooled me. I know reporters really well, and I think your reporter's nose smells something juicy and worth some dollars. By the way, how *did* you finagle your way through the front door?"

"I used your name, showed them your card, cell number, and pager."

"Jesus Christ, Claire! You're using me, too? Did you really quit *The Scene*, or was that just a con job to get inside to wreck these peoples' lives some more? I believed you wanted to do something worthwhile."

"I do," she said, hands on hips. "Whether you believe me or not."

"I'll let you stay, but only at Helena's behest. If they want you out, you're out!"

"Fine."

The ringing of the phone stopped them both. Tyler charged out of the kitchen and into the family room where the wiretap was set up.

"This might be our man," Tyler shouted. "Helena, come around here and get this phone. Now wait until I give you the signal to pick up." He looked around at all the monitors and men giving him the thumbs up. He nodded, and Helena picked up the phone.

"Hello?"

Tyler could tell immediately that the person on the other end had said something upsetting to Helena when her face turned pale as a newly laundered sheet.

****

Helena had followed Tyler's instructions to pick up the phone on the fourth ring. Her palms were clammy, and her stomach sank when she heard that same weird male voice on the other end.

"Ms. Shea? This is you, isn't it?"

"Who is this?" Patrick's hand rested on her shoulder, as if willing strength into her.

"Who is this? Who is this? No quicker than our last conversation, but what can I expect from a former model? Not too bright, are you?"

"Please tell me where my daughter is. Please, I'll do anything. Pay anything, whatever you want," Helena cried out hoping this madman would release Frankie.

"I'll pay anything," he whined, mocking her.

Helena held the receiver tighter. This wasn't a prank. This was the maniac who'd stolen their child.

"I don't want your fucking money. I have what I want and it's beautiful, she's beautiful, and the things I'm going to do to her will be beautiful too. You will never see your child alive again. Do you hear me, you fucking whore? Never! I've taken away everything from you now, haven't I? How does it feel? But you did this to me! I could've been good and whole, but you made me evil again! Now you'll pay with everything you thought you possessed—freedom, friends, and family."

"Oh, God," cried Helena. "Where is she? Don't hurt my daughter, please! I'm sorry for the things you say I did to you. Please don't hurt my baby. I'll do anything, please."

"Good," he laughed. "You're right where I want you, in your own hell, where you'll have plenty of time to think about what you've done."

As the line went dead, Helena fell back into Patrick's arms. It had been *him*. Her fear and hatred grew along with the pain in her chest, as if someone was slowly, relentlessly squeezing the life out of her.

She searched Tyler's face, but did not see what she hoped. He, too, looked desperate for answers. What could she have done to make someone commit such a vicious act against Frankie? But it wasn't about Frankie—he was challenging her to come find her daughter. She could hear it in his voice. That was exactly what he wanted.

CHAPTER FORTY-FIVE

RICHARD SAT WATCHING Francesca sleep. He felt bad for how he'd treated her earlier, but she really needed to obey him. Once he woke her, she would receive her next lesson. He believed that she had "appreciation" down. Her next lesson would be about bravery. Richard's goal was to create the perfect companion. These lessons would benefit them both. If Francesca became what he wanted her to be, well, the possibilities were endless.

He had returned to the cabin shortly after phoning Helena. He wondered how she was doing. Certainly his call would've sent any parent into a cardiac arrest. Good. The thought of her suffering was delightful. Suffer, suffer, suffer. He had suffered for many years at the hands of others.

His cabin out in the backwoods had been made into a magician's dream world by the use of electronics and hydraulics. Richard had installed walls in his victim's room on levelers. Thus, he could turn twenty feet into ten or two. It was a great head game to play with the women he brought there. He had yet to play this game with Francesca. He looked forward to her reaction to small spaces. Would she react the way he had every time that hypocritical bitch he'd had to call *aunt* would throw him into the basement for hours at a time? Richard remembered the humiliation of urinating all over himself, terrified of the shadows on the walls which looked like monsters coming to get him. Would Francesca feel panicky, not being able to move? He'd soon find out.

"Francesca?" He shook her lightly. The analgesics he'd been dicing up in her food obviously worked, because she slept most of the time—exactly as he'd expected. There was no room for error in his plan, and leaving her with any energy could be dangerous. She began to move, and he repeated her name. Her eyes fluttered, as if trying to focus. "Hello, sleepy girl." She didn't reply. "I've planned a great day for us. First we're going to try a little experiment. Do you need to go to the bathroom?"

"No."

"Good, then all you have to do is stay right here." He patted her leg. "Sure you don't have to go to the bathroom?"

"Do you want me to?"

After the previous night, the girl's fight had seemingly died. "Not unless you need to."

"I don't."

"Then let the games begin." He left her room, since he'd already rearranged everything while she was sleeping. He typed in the codes on his computer that would make the walls do as he commanded. It took only minutes before he heard the levelers shifting.

"What are you doing?" she screamed. "Please stop!"

He enjoyed hearing her scream louder and louder as the walls closed in on her. It took him back to when he'd screamed for his aunt to let him out.

Richard stopped the walls when they were exactly where he wanted them. Francesca now only had space for her bed. Ah, wonderful! Nothing could make a person nuttier faster than taking away their space.

"Please don't do this," she cried.

"Quit your sniveling." He looked up at the television monitor to see her huddled up, shackled, handcuffed, and scared to death. He took a still photo of the image to send to Helena. He planned to send Helena an entire album of Francesca's "last days."

He could hear the girl sobbing and remembered another girl he'd made cry like this—his beautiful Brianne.

As he listened to Francesca, he decided he couldn't take it anymore. She had to stop that racket she was making. It was time to teach her a lesson. Once he did that, she would never complain again.

CHAPTER FORTY-SIX

FRANKIE'S TEARS DRIED on her cheeks, and she stopped trembling, her will to live fading. What was the psycho doing now? With the walls closed in on her, she now knew what it was to be in a straight jacket with nowhere to go and forced to listen to the ravings of a lunatic. In her private prison, he would read to her. If she heard anything more about ghouls or death, she would make him pay attention to her wails, or at least drown out his horrid voice.

Why didn't he just kill her? This must be part of his sadistic fun—drive her batty and *then* take her life. At least if she were driven mad, maybe death would go unnoticed. But she doubted that. She stared at the walls he'd closed in on her, wondering when all this would end—because she already knew how it would. This fucking Poe dude would never let her out of his insane hell.

A thought scarier than death confronted her, and she shivered from the fear of it. What if killing her wasn't his goal at all? What if she really were an experiment for him, like some bizarre Nazi science project? She'd read about the Holocaust and knew something about what Dr. Mengele had done to the Jews. Frankie couldn't get a read on this psycho, but he was as sadistic as any crazy Nazi.

For now, Frankie felt numb, as though she were dulled somehow, which of course, she was. If she had a razor right now, she could slit her wrists without too much trouble—except that Frankie wanted to live. She'd been through hell, much more than most teenagers. So far she'd soaked up all the crap, knowing that it had to get better. Her dad had taught her that. But fretting over this psycho's plans drained her of any hope of a real life again.

The walls began moving once more. *Here we go, maybe this time he'll just finish this game.* But if Frankie had learned anything from this creep, it was that he never did what she expected, like when he'd shoved her into the toilet. She'd figured he'd drown her then. It was apparent, torture was his thing. He wanted to torment her, make her keep guessing at when and how she would die.

Instead of closing the walls in on her completely, he opened them all the way out, opening up the room again. Moments later, the lock turned and he came in.

"Was that fun, Francesca? Interesting, huh?"

"A blast."

"Do I detect sarcasm?" He stood at the end of her cot, hands on hips, waiting for an answer.

"Of course not." She was tired of fearing him, tired of it all, and yes, she'd decided to be a smart ass. Maybe he'd get mad enough at her to finally put her out of her misery.

"I've got to say that I wasn't thrilled by your weakness. But seeing who your mother is, I should expect that. Anyway, I've prepared another section to this particular lesson, only this time I get to have all the fun, and it's to teach you how to be courageous, because you need it."

"Oh, goody fucking gumdrops. Do I get a purple heart when you're finished?"

He took a step back, glaring at her. But she didn't care if she'd pissed him off. She was going down with a fight, even if it was only through a verbal assault.

"I see you're a comic. I'm impressed. But I don't care too much for comedy. I like horror much better."

"No joke. You're a real Stephen King, aren't you? Well, get used to it cause I'm freaking Jennifer Aniston, only you aren't my friend."

"Okay, Francesca," his face turned a raging purple color. "Time for your lesson. You're boring me with your dribble." He pulled out a large plastic bag and threw her flat onto the bed. Everything happened so fast. He covered her face with the plastic bag over her head and held it tightly around her neck.

She panicked, growing dizzy. She started to fade and knew this was finally the way she was to die—thankfully, because she couldn't go on this way. As the darkness overtook her and she relaxed, allowing a warm, peaceful wave to pass through her, the bag was removed. She gasped for air, coughing violently, tears rolling down her face.

He stood. "Now, I think you learned something here. Why don't you think about it, while I go shopping? And you're wrong about us not being friends. We're best friends. In fact, I'm your only friend."

He locked the door behind him, while Frankie begged God to either save her or take her life.

CHAPTER FORTY-SEVEN

TYLER WATCHED PATRICK pace the floor. Everyone was frustrated as they had failed to trace the call from Frankie's kidnapper. Helena and Claire had gone outside for some air to brainstorm about who might want to get even with her. Perhaps not surprisingly, Claire was turning out to be an asset. He knew that as a reporter she would know the right questions to ask Helena about her past, maybe even get better results than the police; and because she could empathize as a woman, she might have the right touch to help jostle Helena's memory.

This case still had Tyler baffled. This perp sounded absolutely *possessed*, and Tyler was convinced that this case was linked to Leeza's murder and the fire at Shea House. After the phone call, Tyler had been forced to correct his initial assumptions that the MO was about money as well as revenge. It still was clearly about revenge, but the kidnapper didn't want or *need* money. And that scared Tyler.

Helena furnished the FBI team with the names of people she thought might have a serious beef with her. Agents were busy checking out a handful of possibilities. So far, nothing had come of it.

When the phone rang again, Patrick raced for it. An agent held up his hand. "Hang on a sec, Mr. Kiley. We've got to get the trace going." Patrick held off until given the signal to answer. After saying hello, he handed the phone off to Tyler.

"Savoy here."

"Ty, it's Loretta. Couple of things. I've got an I.D. on your Jane Doe down here. Nick Yamimoto says you promised him a pay raise if he worked around the clock on this. Guess you forgot to tell him you had another case going, because he did it. We can discuss that later," she said. "Anyway, the girl's name was Brianne Jacobs. Reported missing a year ago. The boyfriend called it in at the time, a Rick Shelton."

Tyler jotted down the name, then paused. "Did you say Shelton?"

"Yeah, when she turned up missing, he called and some uniforms were sent over to his place on Wilshire to talk to him. Apparently, he told them that she just didn't come home one night and he was worried. Police cleared him, figured it was a romance gone bad and she'd split. It happens all the time."

"Obviously they were wrong." Tyler told Loretta about Claire's findings with Bridget Core and Richard Shelton.

"Wow, well if Rick and Richard are one and the same we may have our man. I'll check out a few more things concerning Brianne Jacobs and call you back. I'll also get some uniforms to head over to this man's apartment. I also wanted to let you know that I visited Helena's friend Rachel at the hospital. Collier was by, but she's got a nurse who's as protective as an attack dog. He only let me in because of my credentials. The good thing is that she's getting better, but she's severely scarred. The nurse told me that they'll have to do quite a bit of plastic surgery, but Rachel's spirits were high, considering. The interesting thing is that on the night she went to the center to look around, she did see a man there. She hid though, because she knew that she wasn't supposed to be inside. She figured that he was an inspector because he was a 'real preppy looking guy.' That's how she described him. She didn't want Helena, or herself for that matter, to get into trouble."

"Did she describe this guy any further?"

"She says she didn't see him all that closely, but yes." Loretta read the description. "Sound like anyone you know?"

"Sounds like a lot of people I know. I may have to drive down and visit with her myself. Can you have someone draw a composite of the description?"

"Already being done. I'll be in touch shortly to let you know what I find out about the Jacobs girl and this Shelton character, and I'll fax you the composite when it's finished."

Tyler hung up the phone, finally feeling hopeful, but it was Loretta's second phone call that really got his juices pumping.

"Guess where Brianne Jacobs worked?"

"Where?" Tyler asked.

"Shea Models."

Tyler's mouth dropped open with the realization that the Jane Doe case he'd been working on for months was connected to the Shea case. Stunned, he hung up the phone as his mind put pieces of the puzzle together. He walked over to Patrick. "Come outside with me for a minute?"

"What is it? Have they found her?"

"Not yet." Tyler headed out to the pool area where Helena and Claire were talking. Patrick followed. When they reached the women, Tyler asked, "Do either of you know a Brianne Jacobs? Or a Rick or Richard Shelton?"

Helena spoke up. "Brianne was my assistant right before I checked into Betty Ford. In fact, she drove me out there."

"Do you know what happened to her?" Tyler asked.

"When I got out, I'd learned that she'd left the company. I

was confused about it, because we'd gotten pretty close. Then I found out that the police had talked to my employees because her boyfriend had reported her missing."

"Did you find that odd?"

"Sort of. Yet, it made sense to me at the time, because he frightened her a bit. He was pretty controlling and very strange. I had suggested that she leave him. Brianne was a little flighty, so I figured when she left, she'd disappeared to get away from him. By not telling anyone where she went, I thought that she'd taken my suggestion quite literally and had left the area. Why?"

"I have an open Jane Doe case—a body actually—down in LA, and she's just been identified as Brianne Jacobs."

Helena's eyes grew wide, her face ashen.

"What does this mean?" Claire asked.

"Brianne's boyfriend, this Shelton character, may be the kidnapper who has Frankie."

"But why?" Patrick asked.

Helena's face flushed. "Like I said, I told her to leave him. She was young. She said that they had no 'real' sex life, even though he was always talking about necrophilia and bizarre stuff like that. I'd never met him, but from everything that she told me about him, he sounded like a creep. She was very pretty and sweet, and he was something like fifteen years older than she was. She didn't have a family and had a difficult life growing up, having been thrown around the foster-care system. She was good at her job, and even did some modeling for the agency. I wanted to take her in, but then everything turned sour and I went into treatment. I thought at some point she'd contact me, but I was not the most pleasant person to be around in those days, and I thought maybe I'd burned my bridges with her."

"You didn't give the police this information?"

"Well, no. When I heard that the boyfriend reported her

missing, I knew that she wanted to get away from him. Why would he report her missing if he'd harmed her?"

"You'd be surprised what these guys will do."

"Was he investigated in relation to Brianne's disappearance?" Patrick asked.

"Apparently he checked out okay. My boss has a team headed to his place now. All we can do is wait for a call from her and go from there."

They headed back into the house, where the wait for the phone to ring felt like an eternity. When it did, Tyler answered.

"I've got something here," the agent on the line said. "He owns a cabin near Oxnard. There's a wooded patch out there." The agent gave him the address.

Tyler hung up the phone, ran out the door, and hopped into his car. "I'll call as soon as I know anything!" he yelled out his window as he sped toward the main gate, heading south of Santa Barbara. He wasn't sure if he'd find Frankie dead or alive, but now he was certain he would find her.

CHAPTER FORTY-EIGHT

FRANKIE WAS ALWAYS tired. It had been over a week since he'd taken her. Thank God he'd leave for hours at a time, so she got a break from enduring his endless reading of favorite passages from Edgar Allan Poe. They only further depressed her.

Frankie prayed during the hours that he was gone that he'd have a car wreck and die a painful death. But then she would die in this hell, never to be found. Now he was back. She would try hard not to upset him again. She didn't even have the strength to be a smart ass.

"Wake up, my lovely." He shook her. She shrank from him. "Look what I have for you."

Frankie squinted at him. He must've been drugging her. That would explain her nausea and exhaustion. He held up several brightly colored boxes, smiling like a freaking circus clown.

"It's a special night, darling. You need to focus. Now get up and open your presents. Christmas has come early this year."

She stretched out her arms so that he could undo the handcuffs, knowing that it would be easier on her if she went along with his twisted charade. She unwrapped each present—makeup, hair clip, long black satin gown, and a sheer white negligee. She closed her eyes. What did he want from her?

"Perfect for you, aren't they?"

"Perfect."

He grabbed her wrist hard, pulling her so close he spit on her face. "Listen here, I've spent a lot of money on you. Most women would be more grateful. Brianne was, until your mother got a hold of her. Brianne paid for that, and so will you and Helena if you don't start acting right. Now I'm going to undo your shackles. You get your clothes off, while I start your bath. *Understand?*"

Frankie nodded.

"Good girl." He dropped her wrist and bolted the door behind him.

Frankie wiped the tears off her face. There was no way she'd let him rape her. She wouldn't allow him to strip her of her dignity. When he returned, Frankie was wrapped in the robe he'd given her.

"I see you're cooperating. Good." He took her by the hand and led her to the bathroom. As he stood in the doorway, Frankie froze. "Go ahead. I'm going to bathe you. It's the beginning of our first really special night together."

"Please, no, I can't."

"Take off the robe and get into that fucking tub. I'm the one giving the orders around here."

Frankie did what he told her to do as tears filled her eyes.

"No more crying. I'm not going to hurt you. Mother likes you, and so do I. She liked Brianne, too, but *your* mother ruined that. You're sweet and innocent, like my Brianne was. Did you know that while we were together, I didn't need to harm anyone? She had saved me from doing that. Now you'll save me, without your meddling mother. Go on, get in the tub."

Frankie stepped in. "God, you are beautiful," he sighed.

Frankie slumped over. "Sit up straight." He poured liquid soap onto a sponge and began washing her back, her face, arms, fingers, neck, and breasts.

It was now or never as a plan of action began to take place inside Frankie's head. "Ooh, that feels good," she said. If only she really had the courage to go through with it.

"I told you it would," he said.

As he moved the sponge down her waist, she grabbed his hand. "Why not come in with me? I'll wash you." Though she inwardly shivered in disgust, she knew she had to do this to save her life.

He smiled his sickly smile. She watched him weigh her words. She tossed back her hair and arched her back, like the girls she'd seen in those tacky commercials on late-night TV.

"All right, if that's what you want." He stripped down and faced her. Disgusting. Frankie had never seen a naked man before, and she was repulsed. He sat behind her and asked to wash her hair. She let him, nearly passing out from it, but knowing that if she'd come this far, she'd have to follow through in order to get out alive.

"Let me wash your hair, now." Frankie shifted around behind him, trying hard not to vomit. She felt him relax. He trusted her. This was right where she wanted him. There was no time to linger. It had to be done quickly. She poured a large handful of soap into her palms and before she could back out she smeared it into his eyes.

"Fuck! What the hell? You little bitch!" he screamed. He rubbed his eyes and reached for a towel. Then Frankie kicked his exposed genitals as hard as she could.

Howling in pain, he slumped over, screaming more obscenities. She ran naked for the door. He'd locked all the bolts. No time to look for the keys. He scrambled around in the bathroom, screaming at her. She grabbed the hammer he'd been using to mount photos of her and Helena. After ripping open the curtains, she shattered the large window with the hammer, then kicked out the rest of the glass with her bare feet, and climbed through. Slivers of the glass cut into her, but she didn't even feel the pain.

It was difficult to see with pine trees looming over her, creating shadows in the twilight of dusk. Fresh air filled her lungs, bringing her fully back to life. She ran frantically through the woods, searching for a road or some sign of civilization. She sensed he wasn't far behind, but she didn't look back.

When she thought she couldn't run any longer, she heard a car and half-laughed, half-cried out. There was a clearing through the brush where she saw a car pulled over. And there he was, as if waiting for her. Their eyes locked. Frankie collapsed to the ground.

****

Tyler had been driving up the winding road that led to Shelton's cabin. He whipped around the curves faster than he knew he should. The sun was setting, making it difficult to see. Bright patches of sunlight blinded him when he came around the turns.

He tried to radio in for back up but had no luck getting reception with the mountains blocking transmission. He hadn't been thinking rationally when he'd run out of Patrick's home. With all the twists and turns in the road, Tyler was afraid that he'd gotten lost. He pulled over to check the map, sensing that he was near the cabin.

He started to crank back onto the road and looked to his left, where he thought he saw a figure emerging from the trees. It was Frankie—naked, hurt, seeming more animal than human as she screamed something primal into the early evening. But she was alive.

****

Gone! She'd escaped. Richard was dazed by what had taken place. He threw some clothes into a duffel bag and left the cabin, determined not to be caught, knowing the authorities would be coming through the door momentarily.

He'd watched Francesca climb into a car with some man. If he'd had a gun, he would've blasted them both. He couldn't believe he'd spared her life for so long.

Richard was angry for being naïve and so easily manipulated. He'd thought he had found someone to replace Brianne. How stupid and foolish to believe in that little bitch. When she'd lured him into the bathtub, he'd thought she'd seen the light. Perhaps they *could* be lovers, and she'd never want to go back home. But no, just like Brianne, she'd betrayed him.

Brianne would have never turned on him if not for Helena. It still hurt to remember the night she'd died. As he'd sped down the coast highway, he could see her beautiful eyes staring up at him as he drove out to the desert. What had he done? Oh, God. Brianne wasn't breathing. It wasn't supposed to be like this.

He shook her over and over, screaming her name. "Brianne, Brianne! Wake up! I'm sorry!" He pulled her slender body close to him, rocking her in his arms. Her torn blouse fell from her back. "I didn't mean to. I never meant to hurt you." He'd choked her during a fit of rage over what he'd read in her journal.

Before making the decision to bury her body in the desert, he'd carried her downstairs to the embalming station, but halfway through the procedure of preserving her, he'd stopped. Unlike the others, he couldn't *collect* Brianne. He wouldn't be able to stand to see her this way, because unlike the others, he'd loved her.

When he'd been with Brianne, he hadn't needed to kill, hadn't even thought about it. She'd replaced his rage with love; he thought he'd never have to feel that kind of hatred again.

His emotions swung from sadness to extreme anger, making him hungry for more violence. "I didn't do this, Brianne. Helena did this. Thank God you wrote it all down in your journal so I'd know who to blame. She's nothing but a lying, conniving drunk. But don't worry, baby. I'll make sure she pays." On that trip to Brianne's grave in the Mojave Desert, he devised his plan.

It would've worked, too, if he had killed Francesca. "Another time, another place," he said aloud as he sped away.

CHAPTER FORTY-NINE

NO ONE KNEW where Tyler had gone when he ran out in such a hurry. Helena and Patrick were upset by his absence and the way he'd left. His failure to communicate could only mean something bad had happened.

Claire brought in coffee for them. Helena leaned her head on Patrick's shoulder. By now the house, pretty much emptied, had grown ominously quiet, everyone lost in their own thoughts. The phone rang again. Each time it did was extremely disconcerting.

Patrick picked it up. "Hello."

"It's me, Patrick—Tyler."

"Where the hell have you been?"

"I found her. I found Frankie."

Patrick cried out, "Is she . . .?" His hands shook. "Thank God. All right, we'll meet you there!" Patrick's eyes filled with tears as he turned to face Helena. "It's Frankie. She's alive. Tyler found her." He wrapped his arms around Helena, and they held each other tight for a moment before leaving for the hospital to see their daughter.

****

Richard had to think fast. It wouldn't be long until the cops figured out his identity. He had to get out of the country, lie low for a while. He called someone he used to know, when he'd first moved to LA. A dude big into drugs and porn, he knew his way around a prison cell. He also knew how to get anyone pretty much anything they needed, including false identification. He'd done it for Richard before, and Richard had made sure to nurture that contact with respect and generosity. It was good to know people in low places whom he'd always be able to count on in a pinch.

He checked into a cheap motel, dyed his hair black and placed graying highlights around the sideburns, put in blue contacts, and with his expert skills in cosmetics, added quite a few years to his age. He donned glasses and a mustache and put on a pair of navy slacks and a tan cashmere sweater he'd picked up at a quaint shop on Rodeo Drive. He picked up his new ID, then went to the Santa Monica pier where he ditched his car and called a cab to take him to LAX.

He caught his first flight to New York, figuring he'd go somewhere in Europe, maybe Spain or France for awhile, someplace he could go and play the dapper gentleman tourist. He took out his new ID and decided he liked his new name. He was James Hilyard now.

CHAPTER FIFTY

WITH SEVERAL STITCHES and a bandaged arm, Frankie was almost ready to leave the hospital. Collier had shown up to question her, but Tyler muscled him away. The detective still had no intention of giving up his relentless campaign.

"Go home, Collier. It's over. This psycho is strictly an FBI collar now. It's obvious these folks had nothing to do with everything that's happened. So head south, get a good night's sleep, and let it go."

Collier walked away, giving him his usual gesture. Tyler hollered after him, "Hey Collier, what's your bone with these people anyway?"

Collier stopped, but didn't turn around. "Read *The Times* obits for February 13, 1996. Maybe then you'll understand."

Tyler shrugged and headed down the passageway to Frankie's room. He'd learned a lot about Richard Shelton in a short amount of time, including the fact that Richard's aunt and uncle had raised him after his mother was murdered. He also discovered that the aunt had died in a suspicious farmyard accident, and that Richard had inherited everything after his uncle died. Tyler was sure there was a lot more to the story than what he'd turned up so far. He hadn't been able to get a recent employer's name but he was sure that, too, would surface.

Tyler greeted anxious but relieved parents. He knew they'd want more answers than he had at present. Frankie smiled at him, even though her face was bruised and swollen. "How did you know where to find me, Mr. Savoy?" she asked.

"Just doing my job—with a lot of help. I'll fill you in when you're up to it. Now please, call me Tyler."

"I think they'll release her soon," Helena said, her hand on Frankie's shoulder.

"Good. Hey, can we talk? I need to show you something," he said to Helena. She followed him out of the hospital room. "She seems pretty stable, considering what he did to her. She's one tough kid. You should be proud."

"I am—very. It makes me absolutely sick to think of what he did to her and what he could've done."

"I think she'll be fine, if she's anything like her mom." He smiled and Helena smiled back. "Hey listen, my boss faxed over a composite here to the hospital and a photo of Richard Shelton, while I was waiting for you and Patrick to arrive. The composite drawing is from a description Rachel gave to Loretta of a man she saw inside Shea House while she was there. The composite pretty much matches the photo, so it's pretty obvious to us now that Richard Shelton most likely did not only kidnap Frankie, but also started the fire at Shea House. And I'm certain we'll be able to tie him to Leeza's murder. Do you want to take a look? I still need a positive I.D. from Frankie to confirm that this is our man, but everything points in that direction."

Helena nodded, but when he showed her the fax, he had to catch her as her knees buckled in. "What is it, Helena? Do you know him?"

"He's my assistant, Tim Girard."

CHAPTER FIFTY-ONE

RICHARD SHELTON, a.k.a. Tim Girard, was a killer with a knack for becoming who he needed to be to accomplish the task at hand. The fact that he seemed to be a master of disguise would make tracking and catching him far more difficult.

There was still a lot of missing information about Shelton. Evidently, he could easily change his name, face, and voice, even his perceived sexual identity.

Helena couldn't believe how cleverly he'd wormed his way into her life, and that she'd considered him one of her best friends. How could he have fooled her so easily? How could she have not seen that he was evil and sick? She'd completely trusted him.

Tyler had explained to Helena that whenever she'd called what she thought was Shelton's home number, the call was automatically forwarded to a cell phone, making it appear as if Tim were always available to her. And he'd played the role of the gay assistant to a tee, even occasionally frequenting gay clubs and bars, so that he'd be known in the community. Similarly, he'd joined AA, and become Tim G., recovering alcoholic and the anchor of Helena's sober support group. He'd had the whole thing mastered. His acting as though he were homosexual in recovery had thrown everyone off his path. He seemed so sincere and loving.

Helena vividly remembered the day she'd met him at an AA meeting soon after she'd gotten out of Betty Ford. She'd been on a break out on the sidewalk drinking coffee and smoking. He, too, was drinking coffee and smoking a clove cigarette. He struck up a conversation with her about the program, claiming that he'd been sober for three years. "I see you got your sixty days," he observed.

"I never thought anything would be so hard," she'd told him.

"I know, sweetie, believe me. I started pounding back the booze when I found out my partner had AIDS. I didn't know how to deal with the loss, so I drowned my sorrows."

She understood that kind of loss. His story seemed so completely genuine that they spent hours talking about their lives and quickly became friends. She loved "Tim's" sense of humor and style, and soon she'd hired him as her assistant at Shea Models. He'd proven himself dependable, and she'd given him the flexibility to come and go as he pleased. With that kind of leeway, he was free to stalk and plan her demise.

Helena couldn't help feeling confused and betrayed. On the one hand, it was as if she'd lost this great friend that she'd cared so deeply for. But then, when she thought about what he'd done to Frankie and Rachel, and even Leeza, that phony friendship melted away to reveal a monster underneath toward whom she could only feel nausea, hate, and anger.

Frankie walked into the family room where Helena sat on the sofa, lost in her thoughts. She sat down next to her mom. She'd just come out of the shower and smelled like almond shampoo. Helena stroked Frankie's wet hair.

"I thought he was going to kill me," Frankie said weakly.

"You must've been so frightened. They'll get him, honey. Tyler promised."

"The worst part was thinking about how angry I've been lately, and that if I could only see you and Dad one more time I'd tell you that I love you and forgive you for everything, and hope you forgive me for being such a jerk. I now know that I really need you. And I understand why you gave me up. All I want is to have you as my mom."

"I'm all yours, Sweetheart, and nothing will ever change that. We're going to make it through this."

Frankie hugged her. "Do you think you could sleep here in my room tonight? I know that sounds like a baby thing. But, well . . ."

"No it doesn't. Of course, I'll sleep in your room with you. I think we'll have to make room for Ella, though." They looked down at the dog at Helena's feet, wagging her tail.

Patrick came into the room. "What's this? A group hug and you left me out?"

Laughing together, they included him. Frankie pulled away first. "I'm going to get something to eat. I'm still hungry."

"Dad or I can make you something."

"Nah, you don't need to. I think I can manage."

"You sure?" Patrick asked.

"Yes, I'll be all right. It's not like this place isn't barricaded. I see all those FBI guys out there."

They watched her head for the kitchen, then Helena said, "I'm worried. She's acting too normal, considering what's happened."

"She's probably still in shock. I'm worried, too. That's why I've come up with an idea. I think the two of you should take the jet to the islands tomorrow. Stay at my place in Maui."

"I don't know." She raised her eyebrows, giving him the skeptic's look. "Don't you think a vacation is a bit premature?"

"No. I think it's exactly what we all need. I've already spoken with Tyler, and he'll be sending some of his men with you. It'll give you both a chance to recuperate."

"You said it's what we all need. What about you?" Helena asked, still not exactly sold on the idea.

"I'll be there in time for Frankie's birthday. Tyler thinks he has a lead on Shelton, and I'd like to be involved. We're heading up to a small town near Redding where Shelton was from. Then, on to New York where they think he might have gone."

"Let the police do their job, please. Last time I checked you weren't a cop. Going to Hawaii feels wrong right now. I'm not sure that Frankie is up to it. For that matter, I'm not certain that I'm up to it or that I'd feel safe without you there. And what about the media? The last thing we need is for them to follow us."

"I understand that you would feel that way, but getting away from the spotlight will allow Frankie and you to begin getting back to basics. Shelton hurt our daughter, and I'm determined to go after him with Tyler. Don't you worry about the reporters. Tyler says he's got that one covered, too."

"It's dangerous. You heard what they've said about him—a very clever criminal mind. He's a damn psychopath and serial killer. Look at how he weaseled his way into my life without giving me an inkling of his true identity. He's that good."

"Lena, I'm going after him. We're bringing him down."

"Bull-headed as ever, I see. I can't talk you out of this, can I?"

He shook his head. "I'm going with Tyler on this hunch he has. If it doesn't work out, I'll fly out to be with you and Frankie."

"Okay, but what if he finds out where we are?"

"With this manhunt, he won't have a prayer of getting to you. Besides, Maui is magical. Remember?" He cocked his head, a grin spread across his face.

She did remember the fortress he owned there, hidden behind foliage on top of a cliff overlooking the ocean. They'd spent a couple of days there when they were together. *Magic* did describe it. She smiled back at him. Maybe it would be a good thing, as long as they could ditch the media and Richard Shelton couldn't find them.

"Fine. We'll go. But on one condition." She held up a finger. "That is, if this hunch of Tyler's doesn't pan out, you'll quit playing the cop and come be with us."

Patrick stood. "I told you that I would." He clapped his hands. "Good. It's all settled. I'll tell Frankie. She loves it over there. After Leeza and I split up, I had the place redone. Think you'll be pleasantly surprised."

"Patrick, about Leeza?"

"Yes?"

"Was there a service? I mean did you take care of it?"

He let out a long sigh. "I obviously couldn't attend, but yes I arranged a small service for her."

"That's good. When we return, I need to go to her grave. There're some things I need to tell her." Patrick looked at her quizzically. "Basically, I need to make some amends to her, tell her that I'm sorry. We may not have been friends, but she didn't deserve to be murdered by that beast. And I'm also sorry that I ever caused her any despair. The affair we had was wrong. Our love may not have been wrong, but you were married and I can understand how hateful she must've felt. I don't agree with the way she took out her anger on Frankie. But I have to face facts, and that is, I had a part in it all, and now I wish I could've said those things to her while she was alive."

"I think she'll hear you. I've felt the same way myself. I know that I caused her a lot of pain, and truthfully Leeza was simply a vulnerable little girl deep down who struck out when hurt. It's crazy how we always think we have the time to tell people we know just how we feel, and then they can be gone in a heartbeat and we missed our chance."

"I don't ever want to miss any more chances again," Helena replied.

CHAPTER FIFTY-TWO

THE NEXT MORNING, Helena, Frankie, and Claire took off on the Gulfstream. Helena had invited Claire along. The world wanted their story, and Helena had given the exclusive to Claire.

Tyler delivered as promised by giving the media the slip. They'd pulled an FBI van into the garage, and the women had ducked down under blankets in the back. Two agents sat up front, with Tyler between them. As they pulled out of the gate in the wee hours of the morning, only a couple of reporters were hanging around. It was fairly simple to get them to the airport unnoticed.

Knowing she had the inside track, Claire's former boss begged her to return to work. He'd offered her carte blanche—but she wanted to write an exposé about the scandal-peddling media and how it had impacted one particular family. Claire really wanted to write a full length book about the story, but she'd had difficulty convincing Helena.

"It'll sell like hotcakes. It's not like your life is some big secret," she told her, as they flew west over the bright blue Pacific.

"I know, Claire. Do an article, but a book? I'm tired of being exploited. And, I don't want Frankie involved."

"It wouldn't be like that, I promise. It's not about the money.

I'll write what actually happened in a way that the world will finally understand the real Helena Shea and Patrick Kiley."

Helena stared at her, obviously weighing the proposition. "I'll let you do it on one condition. Since you say it's not about the money, then half the proceeds go into rebuilding Shea House and to charities that help find missing children."

"It's a deal."

"Story is yours, my friend, but I get final okay on everything."

"Not a problem."

Helena looked over at Frankie, whose hand was entwined with Helena's. She'd been holding it since the plane had taken off. The poor kid had already slept halfway through the flight, obviously exhausted.

"She's amazing," Claire said.

"That she is. I wish I'd known her as a child. It's difficult to comprehend that she's almost a woman now."

"I bet."

They sat in silence for a while. Eventually, Helena drifted off to sleep. Claire watched mother and daughter, recognizing her own longing for that connection with a child. She was surprised to realize that a part of her strongly wanted that to happen with Tyler. She looked forward to seeing him again. She would spend a few days on the island getting her story, then fly home. Hopefully, when all of this was behind them, she and Tyler could get to know each other better.

Just thinking about him made her giddy. Was this what it was like to fall in love? She was pretty sure she was falling for Tyler Savoy, but could he ever fall in love with her?

CHAPTER FIFTY-THREE

THE FOLKS IN Dobson, the town outside of Redding where Richard had lived with his aunt and uncle, remembered Richard for a variety of reasons. Tyler spoke to the man who'd owned the town's bakery. Like many bakers, he carried a few extra pounds around the belly.

"An odd one, that boy." The man made a face, wrinkling up his large nose, his salt and pepper eyebrows furrowing together.

"Why was that?" Tyler asked.

"Well, it's not like you could blame him—not after what happened to him."

"You mean with his mother?" The divine smell of baking cinnamon rolls made Tyler's stomach growl. "Hey, by the way, can I buy one of those rolls off you?"

"Sure. They get to everyone." The baker laughed, handing him the sticky treat. "I was pretty good friends with his Uncle James, and he told me that the boy was crushed when he found his mama shot to death. James was pretty well devastated by her death, too. He really loved that sister of his. But, Valerie, oh boy, no way she wanted any part of them."

"The aunt? Know what that was about?"

"Well, I can't say for sure." The baker crossed his arms in front of his large belly. Tyler took some money out of his wallet to pay for the roll. "No, no it's on me. There's been a story or two going around, especially after they found poor old James—well, you know."

"Tell me." Tyler took a bite out of the roll.

"James was found, well, having sex with dead-as-a-doornail Mary Neils. He had a heart attack right there on top of her." The man leaned in to whisper, "Heard Mary could do that to you." He winked at Tyler.

Tyler realized that perhaps Richard wasn't the only offshoot of his family's dysfunction.

"It's been speculated amongst some around here that the boy was actually James' son. Some folks knew Elizabeth and James as kids, and they say they both had a real tight relationship with each other, know what I mean?"

That would account for a lot. Combine genetic inbreeding with an abusive childhood and you couldn't have a better scenario in which to mold a psychopath.

"My missus—she's no longer with us—used to say that Valerie would carry on about that boy and what a freak of nature he was. Val liked to tipple at times and it loosened up her lips. She told my missus that Richard thought his father was Mills Florence."

"As in the makeup all the stars used way back when?"

"Yep. But Val said no way that the sister had ever been to Hollywood. She nearly came right out and said that Richard was James's son."

"What do you think?"

"Don't know what to think."

Tyler would be sure to check out Richard's birth certificate. He asked the man a few more questions and headed back to the motel where he met up with Patrick. A beer in his hand, he tossed one to Tyler.

"Needed a cold one, huh?"

"It's been interesting," Patrick said. "I feel like I stepped into Mayberry, but with a demented edge to it."

"I hear you, pal. You know, if my higher-ups find out you're with me, I could get canned."

"I'll take the heat as a concerned father seeking revenge. There's no law saying a man can't ask questions or be in the same town as you."

"No, there isn't. But we didn't stay at the same place together." Tyler took a swig of his beer.

"Gotcha."

"I spoke with one of the cops who'd gone out to the farm the day the aunt died. He's always doubted the story that James told, but he was a rookie, and the police chief bought it and advised him to leave it alone. Seems James was well liked around here. Anyway, this cop was a few years older, but he went to school with Richard and remembers that the kid was weird. After the aunt died, Richard moved away. No one has seen him since. Not even at his uncle's funeral."

"Uncle, ha. Have I got news for you." Tyler told Patrick everything that he'd learned from the baker.

"Yeah, well here's another doozy the cop told me. He said that there was a little girl who went missing way back. The dad later killed his wife and himself, and everyone thought that it was all connected. This cop, who is now the chief of police himself, said that he wouldn't be surprised if Richard Shelton hadn't done it; said he had a hunch."

"Like I suspected, Shelton has been at this for years. We've got to nail him, Pat."

"I hope we can."

"We will," Tyler replied, but he wondered, as he knew Patrick did, if they would ever find Richard Shelton.

****

"I think this asshole has us on a wild goose chase," Tyler said as they sat in the Plaza bar in New York City.

Patrick was enraged that they hadn't found Richard. They'd left Dobson a couple of days ago and had been all over the LaGuardia and Kennedy airports interviewing people on a shaky tip that he might have flown out of one of them. It came from a low life who had crawled out of the woodwork upon hearing there was a decent sized reward out for Richard's capture. The man had apparently supplied Shelton with new I.D. under the alias James Hilyard. But Richard had probably wised up by now and changed his identity once again.

"Let's just head out to the islands," Patrick said. "I don't like my girls being there without me any longer. This jaunt has gone on way too long. I get the feeling Shelton is laughing at us from wherever he is, like we're some big joke to him."

Maybe a few days in Maui would shed some new light on the case. And if Tyler was honest with himself, he found that he was missing Claire. "Let's go then."

"Okay, when?" Patrick said.

"Now." They both tossed back their drinks and then booked the next flight out.

CHAPTER FIFTY-FOUR

HELENA WAS THRILLED to see Patrick, though she tried not to show it. She still wasn't sure what she wanted from him. To try again? To become a family and have a committed relationship? She didn't know, but thought maybe that might be exactly what she wanted.

Even though security guards had surrounded them for the past week, she felt safer with him on the island. Going to Maui had been good for them, as Patrick said it would be.

Frankie had really been able to open up to both Helena and Claire and tell them details of all of the demented games Shelton had played. "The only way I think I can get on with my life is when they catch him. I don't think there's any other way. I'm afraid of him and where he might be." Frankie shuddered as she told them this.

It saddened Helena to hear the fear in Frankie's voice, but she understood it. She felt the same. Now, with Patrick here with them, maybe Frankie could rest easier. Helena remembered how comforting her own father's presence had been during times when she needed to feel secure.

She and Patrick sat out on the verandah, watching another amazing Hawaiian sunset as Frankie swam in the pool below them. Claire had gone over to meet Tyler at The Grand Wailea

Hotel. Everything was so tranquil that Helena hated to bring up the subject, but felt compelled. "Did you turn up anything on him?" she asked.

"He's got quite a history. It turns out that the uncle he was raised by was actually his father. Seems his mother and father were also brother and sister. He found his mother murdered when he was only eleven."

"Ooh, how horrible."

"He comes from a long line of extreme dysfunction."

"How did I let him into my life? I trusted him. Tim was the first person I'd call if I needed anything."

"He earned your trust to discover who you were and what you were about. He focused on your vulnerabilities. Then, he struck."

"But why? Is this just about my advising Brianne to leave him? We only had maybe a couple of conversations about it. It would never have crossed my mind that my advice would cause her to be murdered and bring about all this chaos. It's so, I don't know, inconceivable, I guess. And to think he's killed, what did you say, twenty women or so?"

"Probably more. Right now the FBI is working on identifying each one of the death masks he made."

"My God, when I think about what he could've done to Frankie. But why didn't he kill her? What made him change from the deranged serial killer to whatever he was trying to be with Frankie?"

"In his twisted brain, he'd conjured up a fantasy of being a regular guy with a wife, picket fence, a dog and maybe a couple of kids. For some reason he saw all of that with Brianne, and it was, to him, as if he'd been released from killing. He stopped for a while when she was with him. But Tyler says he's certain that, no matter what, he would've started up again eventually, even if his relationship with Brianne had worked out. Tyler found a journal of Brianne's in a safe Shelton kept at the cabin. She wrote in it about your suggestion to leave him. Tyler figures that when he found that, he killed her for betraying him, but he had to blame you for her death because he still loved her. So, he decided to get even with you."

"So, did he really love Brianne?"

"Not in the terms you and I think in, but in his head he'd convinced himself that it was love. There actually are some of these lunatics with wives, families, and friends—like Ted Bundy—really bizarre. Apparently Shelton tried to have romantic relationships throughout the years without any obvious success. Maybe it was because of her youth or naiveté, but according to her journal, Brianne seemed to genuinely care for him. But there was always a clear undercurrent of fear in their relationship. Tyler believes that one of the reasons Shelton's need to kill subsided during his stint with Brianne was because he thought he'd found a replacement mother figure. His intimacy needs were being met, even though they weren't sexual with each other. Although a grown man, and a very calculatingly intelligent one, Richard Shelton is still emotionally that eleven-year-old boy who found his mother murdered."

"My God. Do you think he'll come after us? If he's that insane, and he blames me for all of this, I have to think that he'll come back," Helena said. "I don't want the three of us always looking over our shoulders."

"We'll be fine. We've got plenty of protection, and they'll find him. Trust me and the police, okay?"

Helena nodded, but was not convinced at all.

"By the way, I've also got some news on Collier."

"I don't like the sound of that." As Helena reached across Patrick for a pitcher of iced tea, she felt a buzz being so close to him.

"Don't worry, they've dropped all of the charges against you.

Tyler says that Collier is being investigated by Internal Affairs for the way he conducted this investigation. Looks like the detective had his own vendetta with you."

"What?" Helena set her glass down on a rattan and glass side table.

"He had a daughter who'd sent some pictures to your modeling agency some years back. In fact, it must've been right after you first set up shop. She received a standard rejection letter in return. She was an unstable kid, dabbled in drugs, didn't get along with her folks all that well, and had delusions of becoming a superstar. She'd sent her photo to all the local agencies as well as a few in New York. Yours just happened to be the last one to come back to her, and she couldn't take it. She overdosed on pills with all of the rejection letters next to her, yours on top."

"He blamed me for her suicide?"

"The industry, probably, but meeting you put a face on it for him, and since you were in so much trouble, he couldn't help himself. I think in his mind he'd convinced himself you really were a monster who'd done all of those things. It probably relieved him of some of his own guilt."

"I had no idea. I feel sorry for him. I didn't think I'd ever be the one to say something like that about Collier, but I really do—losing a child, well—we *know*, because we almost lost one ourselves. There were moments when I thought we had." She sighed, then took a long sip of her mango iced tea. Grasping the cold glass tightly in her hands she said, "You know I'm ready to get out of this business completely. It's so harsh. I can't even tell you how many of those letters go out, and yes, you become a bit jaded, so many young girls out there want to be models. I'm truly tired of leveling the gavel on them. Besides, the longevity of the career is so short, and if you don't know how to invest or budget your money, you can't win. When we get home, I want to sell the agency, put all my focus into rebuilding Shea House, and help women get their lives back instead of helping to break them down."

"It's a business, Lena. Like anything, it's cutthroat."

"Let's say I'm tired of cutthroat."

"Can't blame you. And I'd also like to help you rebuild the center."

"I think I'd like that." She held her glass to his. "Cheers." They clinked their glasses in a toast to these new possibilities.

That night they all watched a movie together, but Frankie fell asleep on the couch before it was over. Helena covered her up, not wanting to disturb her.

Patrick took Helena's hand. "Let's go for a swim."

"What about Frankie?" She looked down at her sleeping daughter.

"She's fine. We're safe here."

"Well, all right. Let me get my suit."

"You don't need one." His smile was inviting as she reached for his hand.

"The hell I don't. This place is surrounded by security guards. I don't want to be their evening's entertainment."

"They can't see through the bushes. Besides, they're mostly down at the gate and on the perimeters."

She gave him a dirty look and went into her room, coming out quickly, wearing a black bikini. She found him by the pool already wading in the velvety warm water.

"Come on, the water's perfect."

She dove into the swimming pool with its cascading waterfalls and rock formations built around it. He swam up to her and put a knee between her legs, lifting her up onto it. He kissed her on the neck. That unmistakable flutter of butterfly wings could be felt dead in the center of her stomach.

She kissed him back as the worries about men in dark suits patrolling the house disappeared. It had been years since they'd been in each other's arms like this, and she was truly spellbound by him as they slowly found each other and made the present moment completely their own, in which anything was possible.

Their lovemaking continued outside the pool, into their bedroom, throughout the night becoming feverish and passionate, and then turning into something loving and sweet, as everyone and everything faded from their minds and they made up for all the years they'd lost. When they finally fell asleep, they were exhausted and oblivious to anything in the outside world.

CHAPTER FIFTY-FIVE

IT HAD ALL worked so well, except that "Daddy" was back in town. Richard hadn't even had to get rid of the journalist broad, because that jerk-off FBI agent was shacking up with her at the Grand Wailea. Oh yeah, Richard had gotten the low down on the entire crew and knew exactly what that Claire Travers and Tyler Savoy were up to, though they had no clue he was right under their noses.

He'd read every American newspaper he could get his hands on while abroad, and was delighted to see that he'd become one famous son of a bitch. A smart one too, because Richard knew he was still outsmarting them at every step. They hadn't caught him, had they?

Maybe he'd pay Ms. Travers and the Savoy freebie a visit, once he was done here. Get a room over at that Grand Wailea after he changed his identity once more. It was a real snazzy place. Mother would've liked it.

Richard took all of his equipment down to the docks where he loaded it onto a little speedboat. A few years back he'd taken scuba lessons, deciding that he really liked the ocean. He'd spent quite a lot of spare time in the water.

He blackened his face, strapped on scuba equipment and weapons, and climbed into the boat. Two hundred yards out, he jumped in and swam to shore. The house stood on the cliffs right above him. He looked at his watch—four a.m.

The place was dark, but he didn't need to see; he'd studied this place for the past week, once he'd figured out where they'd gone. He'd known about the house in Maui because of Helena herself. She'd confided in him about the time she'd spent with Patrick there. Richard had taken the chance that Patrick still owned the place and had gone there. If he'd been wrong, it wouldn't have been a loss really, considering he'd been having a lot of fun in the sun. Eventually he'd get to them. But as luck would have it, his genius of a mind had been correct. He could play these people like chess pieces.

Richard knew exactly where each of the guards was located and when they changed shifts. As he climbed the cliff face, he reached the ledge nearest the pool. Lucky for him, there was no fence on this part of the property. The ledge ended above a steep cliff and the water below.

He'd been waiting for this. He'd made his way from LA to New York, then Paris, and finally to Hawaii. He'd landed on the big island, then chartered a boat to bring him here to Maui. He'd bought a gun from a low-life haole up country. The man didn't ask questions, and Richard certainly didn't offer any information.

He didn't want to go through the smaller airport, even though he looked completely different than he had in LA. Security was so tight these days that he was afraid that somehow he'd be spotted.

Richard crept around to the front gates. It would be necessary to be fast and sure. There would be no room for mistakes if he was to get this done and get away cleanly.

He spied one of the guards reading the paper. Too perfect. He approached his unsuspecting victim with the stealth of a cat; sneaking up behind him, he wrapped his large hands around the neck and squeezed it like a vice. His black belt in jiu jitsu definitely paid off. To feel the energy of life as it escaped the man's body was rejuvenating. He'd never killed a man before. It was different than with women, good. In a way, it provided him with a more immediate rush, without the exhausting labor it took to go through his necessary rituals with the ladies. This was easy, fast, no challenge to it at all really.

Strangling the man, he couldn't help envisioning his father, the man he'd thought to be his loving uncle. The man he'd loved and needed, but who'd in the end betrayed him. If he could've, Richard would've tortured *Uncle* James. He would've made him suffer terribly for all the pain he'd caused!

No time now to think of that. His prize was sleeping inside the house. Richard moved just as silently to the next guard's location, covered the man's mouth, and silenced him with a knife through the heart, twisted just so, to rupture an artery and allow his victim to bleed to death. Ah, the sounds a dying man makes—so satisfying.

Killing was pure ecstasy, and he enjoyed using a variety of methods. He went quickly to his next victim. The element of surprise was still on his side.

The last man, like the others, didn't know what hit him, as Richard simply removed a small pistol from the waterproof fanny pack around his waist and, with perfect aim, shot the man in the back of the head. The silencer made a slight thud, as if someone had dropped a book on the ground.

Now it was time to get inside and really have some fun. He found and shut down the breakers for the electricity and cut the phone lines. Stupid not to have those dogs here in Maui. For Christ's sakes, did they actually believe they were safe with a few bozos watching the place? Dogs would've been more trouble than the frigging FBI and their puppets. Idiots! Assholes! All of them, simply incompetent!

He opened the bamboo doors that led to the kitchen, and just like that, he was in! He heard a noise from the family room and stopped. Had he missed one of the security men?

As he peered into the family room, he was thrilled to see that the noise was coming from Francesca, waking up on the couch. Absolutely beautiful!

She stood and dragged herself towards the back of the house. He followed. She stopped halfway down the hall—she'd heard him. He had gotten too close to the wall and scraped against it. That was okay. He could actually hear her breathing become more rapid and smell the fear emanating from her. Glorious.

"Mom? Dad? Is that you?"

He grabbed her from behind, covering her mouth. "No, sweetie. It's me. I've returned for you."

She tried to wriggle out of his grasp, but he was far too strong. Her movement only aroused him. How funny that he'd convincingly pulled off being gay for so long and done such a wonderful a job at it, when what really turned him on was the feel—and the smell—of a terrified female.

"Now, stop that! You know, this was how I did your step-mommy. I hated killing her. I kinda liked her. We had a lot in common. Such a shame."

"Frankie? Honey?"

Not yet! It was the daddy man. Damn! He needed more time! Richard let her go. He would have to deal with the big guy first, and then he could do whatever he pleased with the women.

"Dad, it's him! He's in the house!" Frankie screamed as she ran into her father's arms.

"Go get your mother! Get out of here!"

"No, Dad!"

"Go!"

Richard heard him try to switch on the lights. It was obvious Patrick couldn't see him. "You fucking bastard, I'm gonna kill you!"

"Really? I think it's the other way around." Richard saw Patrick lunge for him, as his eyes had already adjusted to the dark. They both tumbled to the ground, but it was too late for Daddy Boy. Richard fired his gun when he saw him jump. Patrick struggled with him, fighting to save his family and himself, but it was to no avail, as Richard had wounded the man.

Patrick Kiley weakened, calling out for Frankie and Helena to get away before he collapsed. Richard knew Patrick wouldn't be a problem anymore.

"Come out, come out, wherever you are," he taunted, heading for where he figured the bedrooms were. As he turned the corner of the hall, he heard something in the front of the house. He headed back that way, seeing both mother and daughter in the dawn's light coming through the patio doors. Helena grabbed Frankie by the hand as they ran for the doors.

He sprinted towards them, firing his gun. "Uh, uh, uh, no, no ladies!"

He'd nearly clipped Helena in the shoulder. She tripped, but managed not to fall. Frankie kept running. Richard caught up with the weakened Helena and grabbed her around the neck. She was kicking and fighting as hard as she could.

"Never knew you were so feisty. All those mornings drinking lattes with you whining over this and that and having to listen to your dribble and pretend we were friends. No. More than that, I had to feign being your best friend. Fooled you, huh? Well the charade is over, Lovey. No more lattes for you, I'm afraid. It's time to get serious. I want the two of you in here. Front and center, Francesca! Come join the party! Come out, come out, wherever you are, or I'll have to blast one right between Mommy Dearest's pretty eyes. Daddy can't help you anymore, and we all know how helpful mommy has been in the past. So, please stop being stupid. Let's make this easy for all of us."

"Leave her alone," Helena screamed.

"Shut up, bitch. I'm telling you, Francesca, if you don't listen to me, I'll hurt mommy real bad. I can hear you crying, Francesca. Don't cry, Princess. She isn't worth it. She's mean, and she ruins lives. Look how she ruined Leeza's, Brianne's, yours, and most of all mine. Come out here. We can be so good together. We'll get rid of Mommy Dearest, and you and I can live happily ever after. You'll be the princess, and I'll be your prince. Remember the story about Ligeia, Poe's true love? You can be my Ligeia. It'll be wonderful."

"You sick fuck!" Helena howled.

"Now, I've had about enough of you. It's time to send you on your merry way. See you in hell." Richard smacked her across the face with his free hand. Helena winced. He hit her again, harder this time, with the back of his gun, knocking her back onto the large glass coffee table, shattering it. Shards of glass spread everywhere.

It was a lovely watching her crash hard against the floor. "Ouch, that must've hurt," Richard said. No response from Helena, no cry, no movement, nothing. Richard turned his eyes to the kitchen where his Francesca could be heard screaming.

CHAPTER FIFTY-SIX

FRANKIE WATCHED IN horror from the kitchen as her mother smashed right through the coffee table. She sobbed, thinking both her parents were dead.

"No more games, Francesca. Come on out here now, so we can talk. I love you, I really do. But we need to get straight on a couple of issues. Come out on your own, I don't want to be forceful. I'll give you a minute to compose yourself.

"You, know, I'm not thrilled about the way you left the cabin. I don't take lightly to being teased. I'll have to punish you for that. It really hurt me when you did that. I thought we were friends. After all, it was you who said that we were going to have a special night together. I even told my mother about you! Why did you leave me? I know it's because of your mother here. Mothers can be so opinionated. My mother didn't like a lot of the women I brought home over the years. I know how it feels to make a parent proud, how important it is. But Francesca, she doesn't deserve your love. She abandoned you."

Frankie saw him pace around her mom. She inched her way into the family room as quietly as possible by going around the other side of the kitchen, through the dining room. Thankfully, he was busy with his tirade. She made it to the fireplace that opened up into the family room and grabbed a poker propped next to it.

"What are you doing, Francesca?" He looked up at her from

her mother's body. "You wouldn't want to do anything stupid, now, would you?"

"I wouldn't?" She charged him as he raised his gun to shoot her. She concentrated forcing the sharp end of the poker straight through his stomach, knowing he could fire and kill her at any second. Richard screamed as the point went through him, dropping the gun as it fired into the air.

He fell to the floor, screaming. He grabbed Frankie's ankle, and even though he'd been grievously wounded, his strength was unworldly. With the stake sticking out of the side of his body, he pulled her down to the ground. She struggled, while he grappled to put his hands around her neck. She kicked him in the stomach and was able to push him off. He tried to lunge for her again as a loud pop sounded from the floor near the coffee table.

Richard fell on top of her legs, dead. Frankie screamed and squirmed out from underneath him. She saw her mom sitting up, the silenced gun shaking in both hands.

"It's over, Mom." She went to her and put her arms around her. "It's finally over," Frankie sobbed.

The gun slipped from Helena's hand as she stroked her daughter's silken hair. "Yes it is, baby. It really is."

CHAPTER FIFTY-SEVEN

Eighteen months later . . .

HELENA TRIED TO hold onto a wiggling twenty-month old Jeremy Winters as his mother Rachel cut the white satin ribbon strung across the front porch of the newly rebuilt Shea House. The baby had grown into a toddler and desperately wanted down.

The crowd that was gathered all cheered. Rachel walked over to Helena, taking Jeremy from her arms. They embraced. Tears of joy blurred Helena's vision as she walked up the stairs to the top of the porch. She saw Tyler and Claire, now newlyweds, up front holding hands. Claire's slight bulge in the tummy showed off her early pregnancy. Her book about their ordeal had sold as she'd predicted, and because of the profits, Shea House had been rebuilt faster than expected.

"I want to thank everyone for coming. This truly is a dream come true. Shea House will be able to provide housing for thirty women and their infant children. The goal is to help these women to not only find shelter but to also regain a sense of self-esteem, to become educated, and to help them become self-sufficient. When the women do find work, Shea House will provide childcare until they can afford housing and care on their own. What we're doing here is very exciting. And we appreciate all of your support.

"Now, I'd like to introduce a few of my favorite supporters—not that all of you aren't wonderful—but these people in particular have really helped to get this project off the ground. Please welcome Tyler and Claire Savoy, major contributors to seeing Shea House rebuilt. And Claire, who is the new pregnancy columnist over at *Parenting Magazine,* will be by the House twice a week to provide advice and support to our pregnant ladies.

"I'd also like to welcome Rachel Winters. Rachel will be working in the daycare center. As many of you know, Rachel survived the fire here a year and a half ago, and she's come so far since that time. I can't tell you how pleased I am that she's decided to take a position with us, and we gratefully welcome her and her wonderful little boy, Jeremy."

The crowd cheered for Rachel and her son. Rachel *had* come a long way from that day when Shea House burned down with her trapped inside. She'd undergone several surgeries and extensive therapy, and was progressing rapidly. Upon her return from Maui, Helena researched and found the best plastic surgeon in the country who'd done a wonderful job with the skin grafts Rachel needed done. It was an excruciating ordeal, but Rachel proved yet again what a brave young woman she was.

"Last but not least, I'd like to welcome my daughter Frankie and my fiancée Patrick Kiley. They, along with many others, have actually come out here on weekends and put their own blood and sweat into building Shea House. They will also be here on a volunteer basis on the weekends, as they're moving back to Los Angeles soon. I love you both very much." Loud applause erupted through the crowd. "Now, everyone please come inside, enjoy the tour and lunch."

Helena stepped down off the porch, allowing the guests to come through the front door. Patrick and Frankie and Frankie's boyfriend Chris Highland approached her. The kids were holding hands. Helena couldn't help wishing her daughter wasn't almost grown up. She was getting ready to graduate from high school and would be attending USC in the fall, with plans to study, of all things, forensic science!

Frankie had finally gotten that kiss from Chris Highland. The one she'd thought about way back on the night Richard had abducted her while she was on her way down to the beach to be with her friends.

Patrick limped slightly from the gunshot he'd taken in the leg eighteen months earlier, but other than that things had gone very well. He, too, had gotten back all that he'd ever wanted.

"Thanks for embarrassing me, Mom." Frankie laughed and threw her arms around Helena.

"Any time."

"I'm starving. We're going to head inside for some lunch, okay?"

"Great speech, Ms. Shea," Chris said.

"Thanks, Chris. You can call me Helena."

The young man nodded and led Frankie into the house. Helena and Patrick watched the two of them together, knowing that before long Frankie would be out on her own.

Patrick put an arm around Helena's waist and pulled her close. "Ever thought this day would come?" he asked.

"Not in a million years, but I'm ecstatic it did."

"Me, too. We're finally a family, Lena."

"Yes we are. We really are."